STAR-CROSSED
WITH SCARLETT

SHELLEY MUNRO

MUNRO PRESS

DEDICATION

For Paul, my husband, partner in crime, and fellow adventurer.
Every day is a good day.

INTRODUCTION

A dragon shifter determined to save his people...

...must sacrifice his potential mate.

The moment the *resonance* traps Ransom, he's tossed into a living hell. Everything meaningful to him is in danger unless he follows the orders of a prince lying in stasis.

But that's not the royal's only demand.

Prince Kalim expects Ransom to deliver Scarlett—the woman Ransom's dragon desires.

Captured by a dragon. Scarlett Mitchell can't believe this twist of fate and, once she learns of the dragon-man's quest, she struggles with the blast of excitement and yearning that seize her imagination. She's the queen of lists and measures the pros against the cons in every decision—a lesson taught by experience. Life works better when she reins in her spontaneity.

She should turn her back on this dangerous journey, but she can't.

Romantic sparks fly between Ransom and Scarlett as they travel to the final showdown with the prince. Painful secrets from the past poke at weak spots and emotions run high while a volcanic eruption threatens to annihilate everyone and everything in its path.

Two star-crossed lovers...

Courage, determination, and pure grit are required to save the day before this ill-fated quest turns into another impulse gone wrong, or worse—a death trap.

You'll love this shapeshifter romance because it contains a fiery dragon, a sassy feline shifter, and a villain who wants it all. Failure is not an option.

1. A Growly Alpha Makes His Move

Reception Area, Middlemarch Resort, Tiraq

S carlett Mitchell scowled at the compuscreen and figured Mungo wouldn't reappear to relieve her anytime soon.

Joe had sported the *look*. She'd witnessed the same determination and lust, the excitement, the pure love on the faces of her other brothers as they'd captured, courted, and claimed their mates. Yep, Joe had been a male shifter on a mission, and she figured once Mungo returned to reception, she and Joe would be official mates.

Which made her the last Mitchell standing.

In this branch of the Mitchell family, at least. Ma would happily scribble in her genealogy books and add Mungo to the family tree.

Grandchildren were the next logical step, and that might take the pressure off her. Scarlett dissected that thought for a beat and grimaced.

Gah! Who was she kidding?

It'd place her front and center, a target for her family-minded mother. After all, she'd married their father at age eighteen, and Scarlett had turned twenty-three last birthday.

She muttered alien curses under her breath—ones she'd learned during her trips to the marketplace in Dalcon.

The pressure weighing down her mind remained.

Heavy.

Worrying.

The truth—Scarlett's battle to remain single wasn't the only thing bothering her. Ever since she was a kid, she'd had *feelings*. A sense of what was to come. Most came true, and right now, she was experiencing the tingling prediction of something. Of what, she had no idea, but the details would become clearer until *poof!* Every vague perception exploded into reality and rained down on her head.

Unfortunately, the knowledge she received never helped much.

Perhaps it was favorable news regarding her bid for the premises on the planet Dalcon. So far, she hadn't mentioned her plans to her family. They'd fight her decision, which was why she intended to forge ahead and present them with solid facts. A business strategy. Budgets. Profit forecasts. Her design portfolio. Show them her samples. Play to her strengths and shower them with information. Give them reasons to agree to her proposal rather than present arguments. At the least, she'd have proof she'd considered her future for a long time and was not jumping from her safe existence into a risky proposition.

Impulsive wasn't *her* any longer. Yay! Look at her adulting.

She tapped her finger on the compuscreen, a smile playing on her lips. Satisfaction. Soon she'd move to Dalcon, open a shop, and offer her jewelry design services to those who required exquisite and original pieces.

Independence. Freedom.

While she loved and adored her family, their dreams weren't hers, and besides, the resort catered to women. The pool of men on the island wasn't an enticement to stay.

These days, instead of dating, she spent her free time gathering raw materials for her jewelry creations. A pros and cons list had helped her to this decision. She'd fought and persisted until her brothers now only grumbled when she told them she was off to Dalcon to buy precious stones. A white lie since she foraged for materials on neighboring planets.

A chuckle escaped as she recalled a recent gathering trip and the man who'd grabbed her, accusing her of theft. When she'd kept fleeing, he'd chained her before he'd taken a snooze. For a cute man, he'd sure slept a lot and hard-out. He'd never heard her shift to feline and slide free of the binding chains. Never heard her collect her bag of clinking tools. Never heard her reclaim her precious stones.

But she'd escaped more than an irate man.

On first seeing him, every single feline sense had gone gaga, for want of a better word. Yep, she'd grabbed her spoils and beat a speedy retreat before the situation worsened. Ever since the encounter, her nerves and senses had jangled, setting her on edge because her feline pined for the man.

A growly alpha. Sexy. *Tasty*.

Too bad he didn't fit with her life plans.

Now if he'd shown interest in a down-and-dirty fling...

She might've written a list for *that*. Memories of the trip led her mind back to her jewelry. Earlier this morning, she'd finalized the design for the ring Joe had commissioned her to create for Mungo. Her fingers itched to start work with the gorgeous purple stone she'd discovered while fossicking. She'd combine it with the golden metal she'd located in the Dalcon market.

Next up—earrings to sell in the resort store. Scarlett tapped the compuscreen. She required more stones, but the best ones came from...

A ferocious roar broadcast from outside. Every muscle in Scarlett stiffened as she turned to the doorway.

A huge naked man stomped into reception. Tattoos decorated one side of his torso and right arm, and his black hair grew long enough to strike his shoulders. A scowl dug into his face, pulling the faint scar that ran from the corner of his eye and bisected his cheek. But it was his gaze that drew her—his glitter of determination.

It was him.

For one traitorous moment, her pulse spiked with joy. Her feline perked right up with equal excitement until Scarlett seized her senses and reined them into submission.

Oh no! This was not happening. She refused to allow this man to do his caveman act again, even if his body was a muscular work of art.

A group of women passing through reception stopped to gape. Not that Scarlett blamed them. He'd gained weight since their last meeting, and his eyes—not green or brown but a shade in between—fired salvos of wrath.

He was...

Breathtaking.

Her feline issued an appreciative sigh, and it echoed, full of sexual heat and possibilities.

No. No. *No!*

She gave her head a hard shake and retreated half a step.

"You!" The man wore his arrogance like a cloak.

Every particle of self-preservation urged Scarlett to bolt. Instead, she lifted her chin and stared at him coolheaded. "This is a women-only resort. You need to leave."

The man stomped closer. "I intend to hie off, Thief, and you'll be coming with me." His rich voice held anger, implacability. A can-do attitude that didn't bode well for her.

Oh-oh. Along with anger, his features held resolve. Certainty coalesced in Scarlett's mind. This was what her subconscious had tried to tell her. The flimsy compudesk didn't provide enough protection. Maybe she could talk her way out of this situation.

"You're creating a disturbance and upsetting our guests. Why don't we discuss this in private?" She slid her hand beneath the desk and pressed the alarm to bring security and her brothers running. A quick glance told her the naked man had attracted more women, and rather than fear, his audience radiated interest.

She inhaled and scowled.

Arousal.

It polluted the air, and a growl escaped Scarlett.

His eyes widened, but her aggressive snarl didn't stop him from snatching her, trapping her against his hard chest.

"Oh!" a green-skinned woman said, her tone rampant with disappointment.

A Red Mumber female appeared equally despondent. "I wish he'd capture me." The woman's tentacle hair writhed and hissed and reached in the naked man's direction.

The man seized Scarlett's arms, holding them immobile. She fought, cursing her smart uniform skirt that restricted her legs and the pair of comfortable but impractical shoes.

"Let me go. You have no right to manhandle me."

The naked man dragged her to the door leading to the gardens, holding her with effortless strength. Seconds later, he tossed her over his shoulder. She pounded her fists on his back and grabbed handfuls of his black hair. The great big lug didn't stop but strode outdoors.

The interior door slid open, and Saber stepped through.

"Scarlett, what— Oh," he said in what Scarlett considered a

severe understatement of the situation.

An unwelcome thought slithered into her brain, drilling in like an unwanted pest. "Saber, so help me, if you arranged this, I will get payback."

"Not me," Saber said, his green gaze watchful.

"Then do something. Help!" Scarlett yelped.

Felix and Leo, two more of her brothers, skidded to a halt by Saber. Their shock told her that Saber spoke the truth. Nothing they'd done had contributed to her current predicament. Saber barked orders, and her brothers gave chase.

The man upped his pace, and Scarlett bounced on his shoulder. Not even the flex of his prime backside distracted her from her discomfort. Wow, the man bore a speedy capability. He sprinted through the garden, past startled guests.

"Help!" Scarlett hollered to her cousin Sam, who was working the poolside bar.

A large hand slapped her on the arse. "Quiet."

Enough. She kicked and pounded her fists before resorting to her teeth. They sank into the man's shoulder until she drew blood. The taste, the prickling of warning in her mind, had her teeth releasing their grip and her furiously spitting. Her feline gave a frustrated snarl because she'd enjoyed the coppery flavor.

Shouts rippled from behind them. The cavalry. *About time.*

"Release me, and no one will get hurt," she yelled.

The man slowed, and for one moment, she thought he'd heeded her. But no. The most godawful cracking noises rent the air. Startled, she took a beat to comprehend.

No. No. No!

Scarlett recognized this scenario. How had she missed this crucial piece of information?

He released her, but shock held her immobile, and she wasted precious seconds. She gaped at the man as his body expanded. Scales formed on his skin. *Scales.* Claws. Sharp white teeth. Flames roared from his great maw, and her brothers and their security team withdrew.

He was a freakin' big black dragon.

She stealthily retreated. With his attention divided, perhaps she could dart into the trees where his size would become a hindrance. He threw back his head and roared, flames shooting from him. He turned to her, his green-brown eyes full of intelligence, his wings extending from his body.

Before she took another step or sprinted for freedom, he seized her in his talons.

Frying fungus. If the dragon took to the air, she was toast.

Surprisingly, he bounded away, his feet striking the ground, instead of flying into the sky. The dragon grasped her in his claws, and his bouncy strides had her stomach writhing in distress.

He cleared the fence without breaking stride and headed for the open countryside. They passed the Scothage cattle chewing their cud and rows of grapes. The vegetable plots blurred as the dragon raced from the resort. Scarlett struggled, and a growl burst from him. She ceased her squirming to save energy. He wasn't flying, which meant a nearby destination.

She'd met him on Narenda and was at a loss as to how he'd discovered her whereabouts. When she lifted her head, she spotted trees. A furious caw blasted from overhead, and she raised her gaze skyward. *Holy frying fungus!* Fear rippled through her on seeing the gigantic bird that had them in its beady sights.

"Watch out for the eagle," she shrieked.

The dragon never slowed. If anything, he increased his pace. Horrified, she trained her gaze on the eagle approaching with talons extended. She'd heard Saber and Eva speak about the massive bird that'd carried them across Ione Island. The tale grew with each telling, or so she'd thought. This bird was as big as they'd claimed. Larger, in fact.

Why wasn't the dragon heading for the trees?

The eagle couldn't snatch them there.

She wrenched her gaze from impending doom to study their surroundings. Where was this dragon going? Where was he taking her?

They sprinted around a huge rock, and she gasped.

A spaceship.

Ah, that made sense. But they'd be no match for the eagle. The ship was of a size suitable for travel to Dalcon or a neighboring planet, but not for distance space travel.

They reached the spaceship with the eagle shrieking its anger from above. Lord, the bird was huge. Although he might quail at a dragon, he'd scoop her up in a comfortable beak full.

The dragon deposited her right next to the door and shunted her in encouragement when she hesitated. A tremble seized her hand as she reached for the door control.

The eagle screamed in frustration as a blast of heat prickled against her back. Finally, she coordinated her actions and struck the release. The door whizzed upward.

"Hurry, before the eagle attacks the ship."

Impatient hands seized her by the waist and thrust her inside. The dragon-man entered and shut the door in one swift action. He deposited her in a seat on the bridge of what amounted to a cargo ship. He took possession of the other seat and pushed buttons and controls with quick efficiency.

The ship roared and lifted off. The eagle rushed them, talons extended. A visible jolt struck the bird as if it was under fire.

Her brothers.

She spied them near the trees, focusing their attack on the bird. They shrank as did the trees and the hungry eagle. Their ship blasted through the atmosphere, a bump and jolt before the view turned black and the planet of Tiraq, a pale pink from this distance, grew smaller.

Scarlett wilted in her seat, adrenaline seeping from her to

leave anger and a flood of concern. Her feline liked this stupid dragon-man, although Scarlett couldn't fathom why. He might have a hard, muscular body, but his manners were lacking. She straightened and let her temper soar free.

"What the hell? You can't abduct me from my home. If you think I'll fall into your arms and accept this capture, you're deluded," she spat.

"Capture?"

Scarlett skewered him with her glare. "Isn't that what you're doing right now? Kidnapping me? You researched the family business and decided to punish me for stealing precious stones from your land. Do I have it right?"

He slid her a sideways glance, and that one trifling move grabbed her attention, made her recall he wore not a stitch of clothing. With a snarl, she averted her gaze from his sexy hide.

"It's not right, that's all." Instead of him, she focused on the pink planet as it diminished, and with it, her chance of rescue.

"What's your name?"

"Can't you cover up?" She gestured at his groin with a sniff. Unwillingly, a part of her noted the tiny scales on his cock. Her intrigued feline purred. "You go first. Your name?"

"Ransom Drake. I'm not kidnapping you."

"Let me see." She counted on her fingers. "You dragged me from hotel reception against my will. At our last meeting, you accused me of theft. How was I to know the stones belonged to you? You should have a sign informing visitors they're trespassing."

A fleeting smile curved his lips before he turned solemn and aggravating again. "I saved you from the big bird."

Scarlett snorted. "If you hadn't dragged me from the resort, I wouldn't have been in danger."

"Name?"

"Please." Scarlett folded her arms over her chest.

He sighed. "Please tell me your name."

"Scarlett Mitchell. If you're not abducting me, then why the frying fungus am I on this spaceship? My brothers will come for me. They'll hold you down while I kick your dragon butt."

"I need your help."

"Say what?" She gaped at him. "Ever consider advertising the position and picking from amenable candidates?"

He slapped the controls onto automatic pilot and stood. Once again, her gaze roamed his naked shoulders and tattoo. A dragon. Go figure. Given her shapeshifter status, unclothed males never fazed her, but this one pushed her discomfort button, and she wasn't sure where to aim her eyes.

Shoulders. No.

Face. Definitely not.

Lower. *Hell to the no!*

Scarlett jumped out of her seat and planted her hands on her hips. "Explain."

"If I blab to you, it will place people I care about in danger. I must find something, and once I do, my family and friends are assured of safety."

"A quest? You're on a quest? And you're dragging me along? Oh, good gravy," she muttered, aghast at his impudence. "What is wrong with the men in this sector? My brothers captured and wooed their mates. All I get is a stupid quest."

Ransom trembled with fatigue, and he fought to conceal this weakness. Scarlett Mitchell. Finally, he had a name for the infuriating woman who'd dared to steal precious stones from one of their collection fields. The woman who'd filled his mind way more than she should. Unfortunately, *he* had seen her in Ransom's dreams.

That was when his life had taken a different direction. Instead of the mental torture, so painful he'd slid into a coma, the prince of the Maphra race had upped the stakes. Ransom must find and capture Scarlett Mitchell and bring her to the prince's place of sleep.

Prince Kalim had declared it was time for the Maphra to rise and display their might. Centuries ago, they'd ruled. The prince intended to regather their splintered power and reclaim the position his forebears had vacated.

The Maphra ruler bore a bucketful of crazy, and Ransom feared he'd follow through on his threats to annihilate the dragons and the Incorporeal race who lived a peaceful existence alongside them.

He sighed. The one woman who'd impressed with her sassy attitude, her cheek, and effrontery at stealing from him. A woman who designed beautiful and distinctive jewelry to rival his own pieces. The woman his dragon claimed was their mate.

"Hey!"

While he'd been railing at his impossible situation, Scarlett had stood. She clicked her fingers, her green eyes flashing with impatience.

Ransom fought a smile. It was hard not to appreciate this mouthy woman who flaunted her capable ways. The dragon females of his acquaintance were so different. This woman reminded him of those who worked with Ry Coppersmith on the *Indefatigable*.

"Are you there?" Scarlett knocked her fist against his head. Not hard, but a request for his attention.

"I've put the ship on automatic pilot," he said. "I'll grab clothes before we land on Dalcon."

"Why are we going there?"

"To get supplies before we journey to Narenda."

She frowned. "Will you let me collect precious stones?"

"Yes." He forced the reply past the lump in his throat. A reward that meant nothing, considering he intended to hand her over to a despot.

"Yay! Narenda has gorgeous precious stones."

When he didn't reply—he couldn't, not with guilt beating him up—her frown deepened. Not that the scowl distracted from her beauty. With her golden skin and bright green eyes, her long black hair, and her height, she stole his breath. This day, she wore her long hair piled on top of her head in an odd round shape.

Curiosity nudged him. "What do you call that hairstyle? I've never seen it before."

"And he wants to discuss hair," she murmured, humor flickering in her eyes. "It's a variation of a donut-bun. Princess Layla set the fashion on Earth."

He must've appeared as blank as his mind.

"Princess Layla comes from a fictional world—a movie. Entertainment on Earth, my planet of origin. My family and friends left after a virus decimated our population. I don't suppose you'll return me to Tiraq?"

Regret filled him, but years of practice with his father kept his expression impassive. "I require your help."

"Why me?"

"You're brave. Courageous. You don't panic but use your brain instead. You have an adventurous streak, and you're independent. Those are skills I require to help me find the lost village of the Maphra race."

"I'm not adventurous." She straightened her shoulders. "I weigh the pros and cons before I act."

"From what I've seen, I beg to differ." A little part of him died. Lying to her hurt. This was betrayal. This quest, as she called it, would not end well for her. Him neither, since the guilt and fear would remain for life.

They stared at each other.

Scarlett broke first. "Do you have a map? X marks the spot."

"Your talk is peculiar."

She flapped her hand in dismissal. "Yeah. Yeah. I've heard that before. You're the one who's talking weird. I'm speaking the King's

New Zealand English. Never mind. A map. Do you have one?"

"You can study it while I dress." Ransom struggled with a yawn and failed.

"Why do you get so fatigued?"

"I've been sick," he said, striving for honesty in at least part of this partnership. Admiration for her intelligence filled him, propelling him to give her more. "A coma."

Perhaps if he confessed the truth, she might help him win against Prince Kalim. No, that'd place her in greater danger. His people too. It was best to keep the facts to himself.

"What happened to you?"

"A crash in the mountains. My pilot broke his leg. I injured my head and fell unconscious."

"And you're healthy now? Apart from your fatigue?"

"My mind functions as it used to," he stated. "I'll get the map. We can discuss our journey once I'm clothed."

"Your body is fine," she stated and accepted the map he'd drawn from the details relayed to him by Prince Kalim. "You look better since you've gained weight, but you're still too thin."

A spurt of pleasure shot through him. He turned away and found himself swaggering. *By the gods!* He schooled his thoughts to obedience since he never knew when Prince Kalim might make contact. The man loved to screw with him, keeping him off balance by pouncing into his mind. Lately, though, contact had occurred during the blacklight.

Ransom grabbed a pair of black trews and a tunic from his bag. He dressed rapidly, pulled on foot linings, and slid his feet into his boots.

"This map looks new. Where did you get it?" Scarlett asked.

"I drew it from memory."

"Memory?"

This was where his story turned sticky. "I was given an account of the old civilization. They were wealthy, but disease struck, and those remaining left the city."

"How do you know this information is correct?"

"I don't," he said, "but my sources are reliable."

"Will you share your sources?"

"No."

"I don't understand why you need me." Scarlett's penetrating gaze skewered him and swamped him with another wave of guilt.

"From my observations, you're resourceful and interested in jewelry design. I learned this when I asked about you on Dalcon. When I was in the market, I spotted your jewelry, and the stall owner told me where to find you."

"Which still doesn't tell me why you've dragged me from my family to help you."

Perhaps a partial truth would ease her, lull her into a false sense of security. An invalid path to garner her cooperation.

"I wanted to speak to you again."

"Most men would ask for a date," she said, her tone dry. "Or buzz my com-circle."

"A date?" Some of her expressions confused him.

"They would court me," she stated, her big green eyes full of shrewdness.

He broke their visual connection, unable to lie to her face. In lieu, he scanned the controls and checked their course. He made a slight alteration—one they didn't require.

"Ransom?"

"I don't have time for courtship. I intend to join the warrior monks and must arrive before the sign-up window closes."

She frowned. "I've never heard of warrior monks."

Not surprising since he'd conjured them from his imagination. If he survived this quest, he'd hunt for a warrior faction. He'd heard of monks who gave their lives in service to right wrongs. It was a better life than he deserved, and with his brother Gryffnn at the helm, his clan would continue to prosper.

"I'll tell you about them later," he lied. "We'll make a list of the supplies and go from there."

"You're under the assumption I will follow your plan for me," she said in a sweet voice.

"Ah, didn't I tell you? Their kingdom was known for its wealth, and in particular, a unique, precious jewel that glowed with many colors. I'm hoping to locate these jewels because rumor says they possess stunning clarity. Not many jewelers have worked with these rare stones."

One quick scan of her visage told Ransom he'd hooked her with his promise of rare jewels. Her nod of acceptance was a brutal kick to the gut, and remorse almost took him out at the knees. He was leading her toward a life of imprisonment, a life of fear, a life where her beautiful spirit would get crushed.

He was driving her to a living death.

2. An Introduction to Mind Control

R ansom's fatigue clung once they'd landed on Dalcon. His shoulders slumped, and he shuffled with an old-person gait as they left their ship in a docking bay. Outside, Scarlett took control. With a shrill whistle, she summoned a flymo, one of the chubby utility vehicles used on most planets in the sector. Flymos were the donkeys of this region, with the locals using them as taxis or couriers to ship goods around the city.

A trio of Red Mumber males swaggered past her, their red skin and tentacle hair distinctive, their fit, bulky bodies, honesty, and no-nonsense attitude perfect for the security jobs most of them worked.

One, she blew a cheeky kiss. She'd sold Guam a necklace for his first wife the previous month. No doubt, he'd be back to purchase one for his second wife soon. The Red Mumber and their polygamy lifestyle were great for business.

Beside her, Ransom growled deep in his throat, and she turned to him in surprise. Jealousy. How cute.

"Guam is a friend. Where to first?"

Her mind continued to prickle. Ransom had told her only part of the story. She was of two minds whether to ditch him in the market—easy enough with so many friends amongst the hawkers—or tag along because she'd love to discover a precious stone to gain a competitive edge. With her upper-class contacts, she'd sell anything unusual fast. The highborn welcomed anything of beauty and uniqueness.

And did she admit this sudden change in routine was exhilarating? Even better, no one could accuse her of impulsiveness since Ransom had abducted her.

"Ransom," she prompted when it appeared he'd zoned out. "Where do we go first?"

"The market for supplies. Food and equipment." He wavered on his feet. His color had shifted from his normal golden tones to an ashen gray.

Scarlett dithered as she mentally listed pros and cons. Should she offer her strength to keep him upright, ditch him, or forge ahead? The prickles in her mind gave way to a shiny display case, spotlit to highlight the beautiful jewelry contained within.

Simple. Stunning. Gorgeous samples of her best work.

Scarlett hid her smile. No contest really since none of this was her fault. A quest lay in her future.

"I know a great place to eat." She'd get a message to Saber, and Ransom would never know. "There's a place here, and a decent hotel near the market we could stay tonight. You look as if you might collapse. I'd hate to waste my energy dragging you around. A full tummy always boosts my reserves."

His faint nod of compliance suggested he felt worse than he looked.

"Let's go, then."

They piled into the flymo and directed the pilot to the market. Ten minutes later, the flymo landed at the nearest drop-off point. Ransom paid the fare, and they walked up the street, Scarlett suiting her normal brisk I-know-where-I'm-going pace to Ransom's hobble. She led him past makeshift stalls and squeezed around pale blue beings and child-sized aliens with hard shells who scuttled rather than walked. Scarlett surveyed the dragon-man, and doubts surfaced. Was he strong enough to leave civilization for the backcountry area indicated on his map?

"Are you sure you're up to this quest?" Thank the stars Eva's restaurant wasn't far.

"Don't worry about me," he gritted out, his shoulders straightening a fraction.

Flymos darted overhead, avoiding the hordes of foot traffic but facing problems of their own as they jockeyed for airspace on their journey through the city. Market day was profitable for some, but it made for volatile crowds and short tempers.

Several Tigrus youths, recognizable by their striped skin, hooted with laughter as a robed nun tripped and fell. Dazzling pink fruits spilled from her shopping bag. They rolled along the rutted cobblestones, at least two cracking open to reveal the edible seeds inside.

Scarlett hurried to aid the woman. She collected the smooth-skinned pink fruit, returned them to the nun, and helped her stand to dust off her saffron robe. A growl had her head jerking up. The Tigrus youths retreated in a hurry, melting into the crowd and disappearing.

"Are you injured?" Ransom asked the woman.

"I be fine." The woman dipped her bald head, her expression serene as she righted the hood of her robe. "Blessings on ye both."

Scarlett fluttered her lashes at Ransom. "My hero."

"I loathe bullies." Ransom's voice held a harsh edge that

scratched Scarlett's curiosity. The dragon was a protective gentleman. Interesting.

"We will escort you to your destination," Scarlett said. "This area is rough."

"Thank ye. I'm heading to the convent." The nun gathered her bags.

"It's on our way," Scarlett said, recalling the sprawling complex from earlier visits. "Let me carry some of your bags. Really, it's no trouble."

"That be kind of ye."

Ransom took the more substantial bag, and Scarlett frowned, hoping the dragon didn't face-plant. His muscular carcass weighed a lot more than the pink fruit.

To her relief, they reached the carved gateway of the convent safely with all of them still upright despite the mass of people and the thieves who skulked amongst the crowds, alert for every opportunity.

"Are you remaining in the city this blacklight or do you intend to leave Dalcon?" the nun asked. "Because if you're staying, we have rooms to let." She turned her attention to Ransom. "You and your wife could sleep in the knowledge of your safety within our walls."

Ransom glanced at her, and Scarlett piped up before he rejected the offer. "It would allow us to take stock and check we have everything we require for our journey."

"Oh, are you traveling far?" the nun asked, showing the first sign of curiosity.

"To Narenda to visit friends," Ransom said. "Thank you. A room here for the evening suits us admirably." Some of the tension bracketing his mouth eased, almost as if he was glad of a reason to delay their departure.

Scarlett frowned. That couldn't be right. The dude was a dragon shifter. One of her premonitions prickled across her scalp, and she inhaled, scenting the air. Nothing in the vicinity, but something. Her skin bristled—a hand brushing her fur in the wrong direction sensation. She surreptitiously studied the nun.

The woman scrutinized the dragon shifter, her gaze sharp and dissecting for one so young. "Are ye not sleeping well?"

Ransom brushed off the concern. "I'm fine."

Scarlett didn't believe him. The nun doubted him, too, but neither contradicted the dragon.

"We lock the gates at dusk," the woman warned.

Scarlett inclined her head. "Thank you. We'll be back long before the gates close for the blacklight."

She placed her arm through Ransom's, her pulse skittering at the physical contact. Her feline sighed, and the contented purr echoing through Scarlett's mind raised a frisson of alarm. She flinched from the connection.

Ransom never reacted to her rapid withdrawal.

Frying fungus! This was not good. She could fight him and was confident of staying a skip or two ahead, but things might become dicey if her feline exerted a say. Perhaps she should take a pass on those stones he'd promised her.

If Scarlett's feline decided she wanted the dragon, this mission or quest or fake kidnapping might destroy her ambitions.

Ransom walked at her side, alert, scanning the surrounding beings despite his exhaustion.

Nothing wrong with his brain, then.

"What do you intend to purchase?" she asked.

"I have a list of requirements. We're traveling into a mountainous region. We'll land the ship and hike the rest of the way."

"How long will it take to find this lost world?"

"I'm unsure. My people live on the hot side where the weather remains at an even temperature. The region we're visiting is more seasonal and changeable."

"How cold will it get? Will we need warm clothes?"

"We must prepare for everything."

"Layers then," Scarlett murmured. "Will we carry food or hunt?"

"Both."

She nodded and slowed before Eva's restaurant. "This place serves delicious meals." On cue, her stomach rumbled. "Let's eat. I'm starving."

Scarlett jogged up the three steps leading to the entrance. The place didn't give off luxurious vibes. In fact, it possessed a ramshackle air but attracted trade from market visitors and entrepreneurs. They preferred surroundings that placed them at ease, and Eva's place did that.

Large flagstone squares lined the floor. Twelve square tables, big enough to seat four diners, filled the central part of the restaurant. Mismatched chairs added to the rundown ambiance, but the enticing kitchen scents and efficient service attracted repeat customers.

Scarlett headed toward a corner table with three spare seats. The diners mixed and mingled; an empty place considered an invitation for anyone to sit. A green-skinned man already at the table lifted his gaze from his half-eaten meal and nodded a greeting before returning to his food.

Ransom sank onto an empty chair with a groan.

"Food?" Scarlett asked. "We're required to order at the counter. The dish of the day is always an excellent choice."

"That's fine." Ransom fumbled with his electronic payment band.

"I'll pay. You can transfer your share to me later this blacklight," Scarlett said.

Robbie, Eva's second-in-command, stood at the counter taking orders.

"Hey, Robbie," Scarlett said before he could speak. "Is Eva still here or has she left for home? I left Ione Island before I grabbed my com-circle."

"Are you in trouble?" Robbie asked.

"I don't think so, but can you get a message to Saber? He'll be worried."

Robbie leaned closer and spoke in an undertone. His brown eyes were huge in his pale face. "Is the big dude you came in with holding you captive?"

"Not exactly. I've agreed to help him," Scarlett said. "He's not dangerous. I'll take two of the specials and two tankards of reeb." She waved her wrist, indicating he should ring up the order so she could make the payment.

"Eva never charges you," Robbie said.

"She does today," Scarlett countered. "Can I have those ales, and I'll tell him I'm going to the retiring room."

Robbie rang up the sale and held the electronic contact up for her to offer her wristband. Once they'd completed the transaction, Robbie poured her reeb.

Ransom's eyes had slid closed while she'd been speaking with Robbie. Scarlett settled the tankards in front of him, and Ransom started at the abrupt clink of metal against the tabletop.

"I've brought you a drink," she said. "Our meals won't take long. I'll be back in a sec."

His eyes narrowed on her. "Where are you going?"

"To the retiring room."

"Don't skip out on me," he warned. "I'll find you."

"Who me?" Scarlett forced astonishment into her expression and placed her fisted hand against her breasts. "I wouldn't dream of rabbiting." She winked at him. "You owe me currency."

She hustled toward the retiring room, taking a right-hand turn instead of a left.

"Scarlett!" Eva rushed to her side. A close-fitting white hat sat atop her honey-blonde hair while she wore a smart navy-blue tunic that clung to her petite frame. "I've just heard from Saber. How did you escape the dragon?" Her blue eyes scanned Scarlett from head to toe. "Did he hurt you?"

"I'm fine," Scarlett said. "I persuaded him to come here for a meal before we shop for supplies. He has a contact for some rare precious stones, and I agreed to go with him. Obtaining unusual stones is an item on my list. We're traveling to—"

"Why did he kidnap you?" Eva shuddered. "Saber said one of those eagles attacked you. I have nightmares about those birds."

"Ransom kept me safe," Scarlett said. "It helped that Saber and the others fired at the bird and kept its attention divided. Look, tell Saber we're traveling to the unexplored side of Narenda. The journey won't be speedy since the terrain is mountainous and we'll be on foot. Give me a month. He can send in the rescue troops if I'm not home by then."

Eva frowned. "But why did this dragon abduct you? Are you his mate?"

"No," Scarlett said, lying through her teeth. Perhaps if she repeated the fib enough, her feline would swing to her point of view. "I'm uncertain why he grabbed me, but it doesn't matter. I don't get a creepy vibe from him. He hasn't hurt me."

"But he's a freakin' dragon," Eva snapped. "I've heard rumors about the Narenda dragons. They're not domesticated, that's for sure."

"Eva, there is nothing romantic about my wish to accompany him. If I can get my hands on unique precious stones, it will boost my sales. It's part of my business plan. Please, don't fuss. I get enough of that from my brothers."

Eva wrapped her in a hug. "You're right. Sometimes, I want to bash Saber when he gets stubborn. Putting up with one bossy husband is bad enough, but you have him plus your other four brothers telling you what to do."

"You forgot my cousins," Scarlett said drily. "They enjoy

ordering me around too."

"All right. What should I tell Saber?" Eva's eyebrows drew together, and she pursed her lips. "Are you sure you need to achieve your goals this way? It's dangerous. He's a *dragon*."

"Don't fret. I'll be fine, but I don't have my com-circle and have no way of contacting the resort. Once we're done on Narenda, I'll ask Ransom to drop me on Dalcon. If not Dalcon, I guess I can get transport from the dragon's spaceport."

Eva's frown remained. "What are you doing for food during your journey?"

"We're buying stuff in the market."

"I've been trialing shrink-meals. I'm happy with the final product but haven't marketed them yet. Are you interested?"

Scarlett grinned. "Hell, yeah. There's a reason you're my favorite sister-in-law."

Eva snorted. "You used that same line on Casey when she gave you the pair of shoes you're wearing."

"I need boots," Scarlett said, observing her comfortable but impractical navy-and-gold shoes. Casey's aunt designed shoes that allowed the wearer to change the color on a whim.

"Lucky for you, I have a pair in my office. I'll pack them with the food supplies."

"Awesome. Make sure you send me an account for the food. I'll bill the dragon for his share."

"Are you sure about this?"

"My subconscious is telling me to go with the dragon. Don't know why." She shrugged, owning to excitement at a step out of the norm and the chance to add a tick to her to-do list. "Sometimes, you have to take a leap of faith."

"You have thirty cycles before I galvanize the troops," Eva said. "Thirty and no longer."

Scarlett made use of the facilities and returned to the table as a waitress delivered two steaming plates of food.

Ransom was alone. His eyes were closed again, and the tension in his facial muscles made her suspect he had a headache. His big hand curled around his tankard, pushing a shiver through her. She had a weakness for large men since she was tall herself.

"You took a long time," he said, his eyes popping open to glare at her.

"I did," she agreed. "I'd heard the restaurant owner has invented shrink-meals, and I talked her into selling us some. You add heat and water, and they pop into their original shape. They'll be ready for us when we leave."

He peered at her for a fraction longer before picking up his fork and spearing a morsel of meat. Scarlett wasn't sure what it was and never asked. She trusted Eva not to poison them.

Her stomach rumbled again, so she ate. The spicy sauce thrilled her taste buds while the mystery meat melted in her mouth.

"You're right about this place," Ransom said. "The food is tasty."

Scarlett nodded, her mind on their journey. "Why isn't one of your family or friends accompanying you? Why me?"

"You popped into my mind."

A strange expression marched across his face as if he regretted thinking about her or perhaps the admission. Scarlett held her breath, hoping he'd say more.

"I'd already learned you enjoy collecting precious stones. I figured I'd abduct you and give you a fright in punishment for stealing from the Drake clan."

A partial truth. Scarlett wasn't sure why she'd come to this conclusion, but her gut told her he was withholding information. Oh, well. Life at the resort had become tedious, and this little jaunt offered a change.

They caught a flymo to the convent, for which Ransom was grateful. He sank onto a seat, every muscle quivering with fatigue.

He had slept little recently—a conscious decision. Tonight, he feared his exhaustion would get the better of him.

The flymo pilot landed outside the convent gates, accepted the fare, and waited while they off-loaded their purchases.

"Are we sure we can carry all of this?" Scarlett asked.

"Once we repack it," Ransom said.

A young nun in a white robe opened the gate for them and showed them to their quarters.

Phrull, it was one bedroom. Plain and clean with a large bed. He started to protest, to set the nun right, to tell her they weren't husband and wife, but the nun spoke first.

"Ye were lucky to get the last room," she said. "Thank ye for coming to the aid of our sister. Those Tigrus lads enjoy their teasing."

"That's awful," Scarlet said. "I am friendly with several of the Red Mumber soldiers. I'll inform them of this bullying."

"Thank ye. There is no need," the sister said. "Ye are welcome to use our bathing house. We have separate ones for males and females. Ye will find the bathing house outside to the right. We break our fast at first whitelight."

"We'll be there," Scarlett said. "Thank you, sister."

Ransom remained silent, his mind stuck on sharing this room with the aggravating, enticing woman. Her honey scent filled each of his breaths and had his dragon quivering like a youngling ready to launch into his first flight. Grata, this would give his willpower a workout.

He placed his packages in the corner of the room and offered the nun a polite nod as she retreated. In the marketplace, they'd tossed their purchases into the packs he'd brought. He'd repack them now.

"You should rest," Scarlett said.

"I'd prefer to repack for our journey."

"I'll help."

By the time they'd packed to his satisfaction, exhaustion had him teetering.

"I'm going to the bathing house," Scarlett said. "You should grab some rest."

A few minutes later, he stood alone in the chamber. He wobbled two steps to the gel-bed and plopped on the corner. Maybe if he closed his eyes and slept, the prince would contact him straightaway. He'd be eager to learn of Ransom's progress.

Great gods, he hated this situation. Scarlett Mitchell was a stunning woman with talent and intelligence, and he was calmly delivering her to a despot. Fear bloomed inside Ransom, and he wasn't ashamed to admit his distress. Only a fool might approach the prince without caution.

Steeling himself, Ransom stretched out on the bed. He willed himself to relax, yet contrarily, his mind recoiled at letting go and sinking into slumber. Sleep would come without a doubt since his body kept trying to buckle, so fatigued were his muscles.

His heart raced as he created a corral in his mind for his dragon. Prince Kalim was unimpressed by Ransom's dragon status, and Ransom had learned it was best if his human side took the brunt of Prince Kalim's torture.

He forced the tension from his muscles and pictured the jewels in his hoard. One golden crown. Two sparkly tiaras, the perfect foil for Scarlett's glossy black hair. No. *No!* One uncomfortable crown. Two tiaras. Three. Four. Five ruby rings. Six. Seven. Eight. No, nine of the precious purple stones. All large enough to overflow his fist. He'd make at least one into a spectacular necklace, perfect for Scarlett's elegant neck. He'd design them at a length to sit above the curves of her breasts. A sizzle frisked his body, and blood flowed into his shaft.

Before he chastised himself and his dragon for placing these dangerous thoughts inside his mind, a fiery pain seared through his brain. A whimper burst free, and his brain crackled, energized and bright. Ripe for plucking.

The prince had arrived.

"Do you have the woman? How close are you?" The prince's imperious voice, higher than most males, whined to rival a jeweler's drill. *"Report. Give me news."*

Ransom waited for the prince to cease his questions before answering. He'd learned the hard way that the pain could get worse. The prince could crush his mind if he wished but had kept him alive because he needed Ransom's brain power. Somehow, the prince tapped the energy and used it to remain active. Those dragons who'd perished from resonance in the past had died in agony. There must be a solution, a way to cease this torture.

"Servant, report. Now."

"I have gathered supplies and fly to your region on the morn."

"Yes. Yes. Tell me about the woman. She is with you. She is biddable?"

Ransom almost snorted. Biddable, Scarlett Mitchell was not. He focused on the prince in case the alien grew impatient and stung Ransom's mind with more resonance. He'd done that before, rendering Ransom helpless for two cycles.

"Scarlett is with me."

"Excellent. I am unable to reach her mind. A strong mental barrier is a sterling quality for a queen."

"Yes, Prince Kalim," Ransom said.

"When will you arrive? My people grow weary of this solitude. Our food source is near depletion, and to survive, we must move."

"I have the map of your location. We will arrive soon."

"Remember the consequences if you fail me," the prince said.

"I will not fail," Ransom said.

A pregnant pause occurred, and it felt as if tiny needles were drilled deep within his brain. He forced himself to stillness, not to cry out or think, and to accept the alien presence drawing his energy.

A long moment later, the pressure eased but still, Ransom remained in place, his muscles locked while his body dealt with the tendrils of pain flickering along his spine and spreading across his torso. He wanted to wake, wanted to stagger from this chamber and from any temptation to sleep. Instead, he remained caught in this nightmare, a captive until the alien prince decided he'd fed enough for this blacklight.

Ransom was asleep when Scarlett returned from the bathing house. He'd removed his tunic and trews and wore a tight pair of black shorts. His bare chest gleamed in the lamp's light he'd left blazing for her, enticing her to study his tattoos. Hmm, a dragon. A muscular chest. A sexy chest. Scarlett hesitated. Getting close wasn't the brightest idea, especially with her feline urging her nearer.

The man moaned and tossed and turned on the gel-bed, obviously in the throes of a nightmare. She hesitated to wake him. Something ailed the dragon-man to make him tire so readily, and he needed to recharge for their journey.

Scarlett rechecked their bags and folded her resort attire and shoes. She'd leave them on the ship once they began the walking part of their journey. Ransom fell silent, although his breathing remained choppy. She'd considered shifting to feline and curling up on the floor but decided to keep her shifter status secret for now.

Warm after her bathing experience, she removed her outer tunic and lay on the bed, dressed in trews and a thin thermal shirt that hugged her upper body.

The dragon-man twisted and turned, encroaching on her space. His ice-cold hand landed on her arm, and a shudder ran through him.

Scarlett flinched at the slap of iciness. How could he be so cold? She reached out and placed her palm over his forehead. His entire body radiated this frigid winter-coolness. A virus or something

31

else?

He moaned again, the cry so full of anguish, her feline snarled. The harsh growl didn't awaken Ransom. He cried out, his limbs thrashing, his face contorted. Sympathy rushed through her, and she curled closer, fitting her warmer body to his chilled torso. She embraced him, and still, he didn't rouse.

Shifters typically possessed a higher body temperature than other species, and common sense told her Ransom should display the same tendency. She breathed slowly, her awareness of him heightening. His big body thrashed again, another pained moan escaping his clamped lips. She clung to him, instinct telling her he needed her warmth. Gradually, the dragon-man relaxed, the tension seeping from his limbs. His shudders stopped. His moans ceased.

Scarlett sensed the moment he slid into a proper sleep, the restful type that most beings required to recharge their bodies.

Her prickly, preternatural sense tiptoed through her mind again, and she wished she understood the invisible threat lurking in the darkness. Her gut screamed a warning, yet she'd remain clueless until she understood more. So she'd do what she always did. Ask questions. Persist and annoy until answers were forthcoming then make an informed decision. A pros and cons list.

A yawn escaped, and a second one. Maybe she should move to her side of the gel-bed, but she hated for Ransom to get cold again. If he resumed his twitchy tossing and turning, they'd both be exhausted come morning.

Still plastered against Ransom, she shifted her position again until she found a comfortable spot and closed her eyes. The last time she'd shared a bed with a sexy man, the experience was more aerobic, although ultimately relaxing.

She hoped Eva had calmed Saber and assured him Scarlett was fine with the status quo. If Ransom kept his word, she'd soon have more rare stones to coax and shape into gorgeous jewelry. Her own place—the fulfillment of a long-held dream. A life goal. What would these stones look like? What properties would they hold? As she added these questions to her list, another yawn burst free.

An adventure.

Yeah, after her hard work at the resort, she couldn't pretend she hated this escapade.

3. SEDUCTION OR BETRAYAL?

L ately, when he woke, he had to force himself from the bed and douse himself in hot water to get warm. Something about the prince and the energy he stole made Ransom's temperature drop as if ice ran through his veins.

This whitelight, shivers didn't rack his body. The torment in his head wasn't as wicked as usual, and the nausea that accompanied the attacks hadn't beset him. Not yet.

Ransom became aware of warmth searing his chest. Confused, he blinked and batted at the black hair obscuring his vision. He savored the honey-sweet fragrance filling his lungs.

Joy burst through him as his brain made an analysis. Scarlett. Heat radiated off her, warming him and driving away his usual chill.

While the prince had connected with his mind, he hadn't lingered as was his habit. He'd left. Ransom frowned, trying to recall what resembled dreams. Prince Kalim had arrived almost as soon as he'd fallen asleep. He'd demanded answers, then once he'd assured himself Ransom had Scarlett, he'd commenced the painful drawing of energy. The process typically left him achy, drained, and lethargic.

His head still ached, but the pain was bearable.

Somewhere outside, a bell clanged, and Ransom sensed the moment Scarlett awoke. Her green eyes were alert as she turned to face him.

"Are you okay?"

Ransom blinked before he could control his reaction. "That was the breakfast bell. We'd better move."

"Hmm, avoiding the question. Interesting."

She rolled off the gel-bed and picked up her tunic top, giving Ransom a glimpse of firm and slender muscles and full, high breasts. This time, he swallowed when she chuckled.

"Better pull those eyes back in your head."

Ransom started, this green-eyed woman shoving him even further off his game.

"And get dressed unless you want those sisters and the guests to swallow their tongues."

Frankly, he was more interested in Scarlett's opinion, but since she'd already turned away, he reached for his trews. Absently, he donned his tunic while he watched Scarlett run her fingers through her hair. The black locks were longer than he'd imagined, and his fingers itched to run through the silky length. Along with her honey fragrance, her hair gave off hints of flowers.

"Are you ready?"

Scarlett was dressed with her hair in the donut-bun thing. She appeared well-rested and prepared to attack any challenge tossed in her direction.

"I'll catch up," Ransom said, a part of him miffed because women frequently noticed him. They gawked. Flirted. They slipped him notes, offered their bodies. Other women wanted him, and the one green-eyed female who intrigued him, he couldn't touch. Instead, he intended to betray her to secure his family and friends.

She left without another word, the door clicking behind her.

If things were different, he'd pursue Scarlett Mitchell. He'd allow his dragon to take control, and they'd find an eyrie where they could seduce her to their way of thinking.

He heaved a harsh sigh. No, better to embrace his grouchy side, which wasn't difficult given the stress and pain that had become his norm. The prince had assured him the journey would take five cycles at most.

Then, all he had to do was awaken the prince and live with the guilt of having betrayed Scarlett Mitchell.

4. A Blunder Through Time

S carlett focused on the dragon-man's strong hands as he piloted his ship from Dalcon. Oh, she'd tried to pay attention to their surroundings—the other men in the spaceport, the view of Dalcon as they left the atmosphere and blasted into deep space, the planet's golden moons. But instead, her gaze crept to Ransom.

He puzzled her.

Intrigued her.

Raised her curiosity, which according to her brothers, never had a favorable outcome. They preferred her logical lists, which kept her on track. Yes, they teased her about her to-do lists, her planner with its colorful virtual stickers, but whenever she acted on impulse, disaster became her BFF.

She swallowed hard. *Not going there.*

Instead of staring at his hands and imagining his callused fingers trailing over her skin, she'd start her subtle interrogation. Back to the plan. Much safer for everyone.

"Do you have brothers or sisters?"

He finished inputting the course coordinates and set the ship to autopilot before he turned in her direction. She caught the flash of masculine interest before he tamped it down. The gleam of fiery gold in his eyes departed, leaving cool green-brown peepers.

"Are you going to sit there like a big ox and stare, or will we have a conversation?" Ah, yes. Her standard blunt, straightforward style. Her mother often told her she'd missed the tactful gene, this always uttered with grave parental concern.

His bright and unexpected grin made her girl-parts sit up and pay attention. "I have no idea what this ox thing is."

"An animal with four legs. Eats grass. An herbivore. Brothers? Sisters? Do you have any?"

"I have a younger brother and two younger sisters. One is a half-sister who was not raised with us. When my father died, I invited her to live with our clan. Gryffnn has a son and a stepdaughter. He recently mated with a woman from another planet."

"So you dragons don't keep to yourselves? You cross-pollinate." She winked.

"During my father's time, our planet was closed to visitors. After he died, I decided we needed contact with others. Now, those who wish to come to Narenda apply for visitor visas."

Scarlett stilled. *Oops.* "I didn't do that."

She received another of those charming smiles—a jolt to her system. "No, you thumbed your nose at procedure."

"In my defense, I knew nothing of the visa requirement. My visit was a spur-of-the-moment thing after I heard talk in the market. If you hope to enforce this visa thing, consider placing guards to stop unauthorized visitors. No one mentioned dragons, and until you, I never saw another being."

"I'll mention this to Gryffnn."

"Tell me about your sisters."

"Jacinta comes after Gryffnn, and Sable is the youngest. Jacinta is a typical dragon female. She's attractive with a trace of arrogance that keeps the males on their toes. Sable is my half-sister, the daughter of my sire's mistress who came from Blackon. Some look down on her since she is unable to shift. Due to a childhood accident, she lost an arm. We purchased a high-tech artificial one for her. Some consider her flawed."

"That must be difficult for her," Scarlett said.

"Sable runs our household. Over the last rotations, she has grown in confidence. I'm proud of her."

"What about your nephew and niece?" Scarlett's curiosity had turned to interest. "Are they dragons?"

"Hallum is a full dragon while Lys is not. I haven't met Lys yet, but I believe she resembles her mother." He hesitated as if measuring what to say. "Gryffnn's new family is complicated, but I've never seen my brother so happy. I respected Kaya before she paired with Gryffnn. Tell me about your family. You have brothers."

Scarlett pulled a face. "I have five, all older. They're bossy, they scare away potential boyfriends, and make my life difficult." She shrugged, then grinned since they'd say the same thing about her. "I love them. I also have lots of cousins, most of them male. There aren't many females in my generation, which is why the guys are ultra-protective. They're the perfect contraception."

Ransom's brows rose. "If they're so protective of you, why did I discover you alone on Narenda without a guard?"

"I didn't require one. I escaped you, didn't I?"

"How did you do that?"

She tapped her nose, indicating secrets. "I might require the same strategy a second time."

"Why were you alone?"

An uncomfortable question because she'd had to use sneakiness when she much preferred a direct approach. She dragged in a fortifying breath, prepared to dodge the question. "I told my brothers I was going to Dalcon to purchase jewelry-making supplies. To be fair, the first time I never lied, but I met other suppliers and heard about the neighboring planets suitable for fossicking."

"Not Narenda."

"Not Narenda," she agreed. "I didn't know I was on Narenda. When you nabbed me, I told you I thought the planet was unoccupied. That was the truth."

"We have friends who collect raw stones for us." He frowned. "Did you see any of the man-eating plants?"

"What? No. For real? There are carnivorous plants on that side of your planet?"

"Ry and his crew tried various ways of killing them and must've wiped them out. The plants aren't native to Narenda. We suspect pirates released them."

"Hmm, I didn't see pirates either. Why don't your people collect the raw stones?" Scarlett asked. "I find it's the best way to get what I want."

"Ah, you're not susceptible to the resonance."

"What's resonance?"

"The mountains emit a high-pitch frequency that destroys a dragon's mind after too much exposure. To keep safe, we contract the *Indy* crew to collect the stones for us. We build a small immunity by working with the stones, but exposure to large quantities is dangerous. It put me in a coma for almost half a rotation. I still have headaches."

"Then why are you risking your life traveling into the mountains? Didn't you say you were the leader of the dragon clan?" If the mountains gave her headaches, she'd stay far, far away. "Why are you going on this quest when you have others who could do it for you?"

His expression blanked, reminding her of Saber when something weighty tugged at his mind. This dragon-man was keeping secrets from her. One: he had bad dreams, and this resonance sickness was clearly still affecting him. Two: why did he need her presence? Three: something about this quest held a huge whiff of a dead rat. And, she was back to her lists.

Okaaay. So she'd lull him, let him think she'd accepted his avoidance, then when he least expected it, she'd pounce with perfect feline form.

"How much longer will it take to get to Narenda?"

"We should arrive in less than half a cycle."

Relief layered his voice. Silly dragon-man. He shouldn't get comfortable yet.

"Do you have a marriage contract arranged for you? I bet you have, right? An arrangement with another dragon clan to take one of their females as a mate."

"I will not take a mate."

Scarlett gaped. "It's a matter of genetics. Shifters get an urge to mate. It happens whether you like it or not!" Unfortunately for her, her stubborn feline was telling her she wanted this secretive dragon-man. Go figure. He might possess a pretty hide, but she was questioning his mental abilities.

He skewered her with his gaze. "What do you know about shifters? I wager your info came from the marketplace."

"I've met shifters." The truth. That they happened to be family, friends, and relations wasn't pertinent to the conversation.

"No mate," he reiterated, this time with gritted teeth.

"What happens if you die? Who will lead your people?"

"Gryffnn did an exceptional job while I was unavailable. He can lead the clan into the future."

"You don't seem happy about it."

"It is what it is," he snapped. "Do you always talk so much?"

"Yes." Scarlett offered him a sweet smile and tapped her chin.

"How about this? What is your favorite type of stone to work with? Your favorite item of jewelry to create?"

"I enjoy Narendanite. It's a purple stone and until recently, very rare. Ry and his crew found some and brought it back for us."

"Ah! I have some." She spoke rapidly before he accused her of stealing again. "I designed a ring for one of my twin brothers. I haven't crafted it yet, but I will once I return to the resort. My favorite piece is always the one I'm working on, although I prefer a variety. I hate making the same piece time after time."

Interest shone in him, and she congratulated herself on deflecting from the hot button she'd struck regarding the clan leadership.

"I find it rewarding to teach the younger dragons," Ransom said. "I design and make my own pieces when I have time. Recently..." He trailed off, the pleasure sliding off his face to leave his usual silent arrogance.

"Who taught you? Your father?"

Ransom barked out a laugh, and his disbelief was apparent to her. "It was beneath my father's dignity to teach anyone, including his sons. I learned jewelry basics from the master craftsmen in our clan, and I worked hard because I found it an escape from the other skills my father wished me to acquire."

"What skills?"

"Flying with precision. Spitting flames with accuracy. Wrestling. Swordplay. Clan history. Dragon etiquette. All talents desirable of a clan leader."

"That sounds like a lot of pressure."

Ransom shrugged. "I was the oldest son. It was my duty."

"What about fun? What did you do when you weren't studying?"

"My cycle was full of study."

"What about now? What do you do when you're relaxing?"

Ransom stared, and she could tell her questions perplexed him.

"My duties are to greet the guests when they arrive and issue them with room keys. I also research the guests, which is important, because we accept reservations from many races. It's imperative to learn about their customs and habits, the food they require, their courting and sexual rituals. We don't want surprises. If we have prior knowledge, we can handle most things our guests chuck at us. My oldest brother gets me to help where I'm needed but also ensures we have time off. We go swimming at our private beach. We eat family meals together and celebrate birthdays, and lately, my brothers are settling down with mates. I design my jewelry and take fossicking trips. Sometimes, I go to Dalcon with my brothers or their wives, and we'll head to the wealthy side of town to see a singing show or other entertainment. When we lived on Earth, I'd go out with my friends. We'd go to socials or dances, parties. That sort of thing."

"Why did you leave Earth?"

An icy-coldness swept down her spine, as it always did when she spoke of their reasons for departing Earth. This icy-coldness had a name.

Guilt.

Scarlett coughed to clear her throat. "A virus—an illness—swept through our country and killed many families and friends. My family was lucky since we didn't lose anyone, but we all had friends who died. My oldest brother suggested it was safer for us to leave, so we did."

Ransom nodded, but it was clear his thoughts were miles away. "We have parties and dinners, excursions, but they double as teaching experiences."

"But what about fun?"

"My father didn't favor frivolity."

"That's sad, but you're in charge now. You make the rules."

"Yes. I am tired. I'll rest and set the alarm to go off shortly before landing," Ransom said.

"Aren't you afraid I'll change the ship's course the moment you fall asleep?" She was half-tempted, but those rare stones he'd mentioned glittered like a prize. Something exceptional to start her fledgling business with a boom was precisely what she required. A point of difference. A tick on her to-do list.

"The controls are coded to me. You can't override them." Ransom unfastened his harness and stood. "I'll be in the chamber if you require me."

"Not that you sound smug or anything," Scarlett muttered.

She gritted her teeth on hearing his arrogant laughter. This dragon-man thought he was so funny, but she was no pussy. Well, she was, but not in the way he thought. If he was a shifter, shouldn't he sense her otherness? The logical conclusion was that whatever was making him tire easily—the virus or illness he harbored—had a blunting effect on his shifter senses.

While the man's highhandedness needled her, she hated him suffering. Her soft heart. Her mother complimented her on the characteristic. Scarlett found it a pain in her arse. She didn't want to sympathize with this bossy, alpha leader of a dragon clan. She'd prefer to hiss and spit and claw. Give him lip.

Purr, her feline side added helpfully.

Scarlett bit back a groan.

Not happening.

Tired of her thoughts, she unfastened her seat harness and tested the controls. Ransom hadn't lied. Nothing she did—not the single press of a button—yielded management of the ship to her.

Giving up on the fruitless task, she began a systematic search—any clue to help her decipher Ransom's unspoken plan. Frustration built when she discovered precisely nothing. She peeked in on Ransom. The man was asleep, doing his regular tossing and turning. The way he rested wasn't healthy. Most shapeshifters of her acquaintance were more self-aware. She strode to the narrow bunk bed and paused. Nope. He still didn't hear her.

Curious, she tested his temperature.

Icy cold again.

Scarlett pondered this as she returned to the bridge and plonked her butt on the nearest seat. Instead of the normal inky black of space, sparkly white wisps shot across the viewport.

She jumped as the ship's alarms rang.

"Ransom! A meteor shower." She skidded into the chamber where he was resting.

His eyes blinked open, and he stared, gaze bleary and unfocused.

"Ransom! I need you on the bridge." She grasped his shoulder and shook.

A bang resounded through the ship's interior. Then another, this one louder.

"The chunks of rock are big. Ransom. Hey. Dragon-man!"

He groaned.

An alarm sounded, the *beep, beep, beep* raising her hackles.

In desperation, Scarlett grasped his arm and yanked. She flinched at two deafening thumps against the ship's hull. Bang. Bang, in quick succession.

"If I die in this sardine can, I will haunt you," she threatened. She tugged his arm, and he fell off the bed.

"What the phrull?" he shouted.

She released him and backed up. "We've hit a meteor shower. The bridge. Now!"

"Why didn't you wake me?"

"Duh! Are you coming or not?"

A loud thud had Ransom scrambling to his feet. She wouldn't call his balance steady as he lurched from wall-to-wall and fell into the captain's chair.

"Grata. Grata. Grata!"

"Yeah. Yeah." Scarlett fastened her harness. "It's bad. Fix it and get us out of here."

A substantial, glowing chunk of rock whizzed past their ship, barely missing them.

Any average person finding themselves in a meteor storm would leap into action, survival instinct kicking in. While Ransom was present, his efforts were sluggish and much slower than they should be, given they might not survive a direct hit. The automatic pilot was propelling them into the field. *Frying fungus!* They were gonna die.

"Yield the controls," Scarlett ordered. "Otherwise we'll both die. Do it. Now."

Seconds later, the light on the dual control flashed. No time to panic. Scarlett seized the controls and pulled hard left to where the chunks of rock were smaller. Debris continued to pummel the outer metallic layer of the ship, the *ping, ping, thump* becoming a discordant musical score in her skull.

Incoming! She dodged most of a massive glowing rock that filled the viewport. It clipped the nose of their ship, spinning them deeper into chaos.

"Watch out," Ransom roared.

"Very helpful," she spat. "Shut up and let me concentrate."

Once again, she veered left, the ship's controls reacting with a sluggishness that concerned her. They'd already taken numerous hits. Had one of them damaged the propulsion unit?

Scarlet clutched the manual toggle and wove the ship between and around the larger chunks of rock. The dust from the storm obscured her vision, and Scarlett strained in her attempt to see. Another rock hit their ship with a clunk, sending them into a spin.

Scarlett gripped the toggle with sweaty palms and prayed. A second hard contact sent Ransom flying from his seat. His head collided with the wall, and he slumped to the floor.

"Idiot!" Scarlett shouted. "Why didn't you fasten your harness? Ransom?"

Ransom didn't answer.

Afraid to take her eyes off the viewport, since that was the sole way to see now, she guided the ship toward the less congested area. A spine-jerking shunt from the rear popped them to the right. Tinges of black space were visible beyond the dust and the mass of rocks.

"Woohoo!" Scarlett cried.

She guided their ship in that direction. Another collision had her head snapping back and the vessel bursting free of the meteor field.

In the distance, the pale planet of Narenda glowed a silent welcome. Scarlett unclenched her hands one at a time from the controls, letting the blood flow again without restriction. She increased their speed before glancing at Ransom. He lay still on the silvery floor. Blood trickled down his cheek. No puddle. Hopefully, his shifter genes would take care of his ouchies.

With the autopilot sending them into danger, she didn't want to risk her life that way again. Ransom would need to wait until she landed.

With their travel path input already, it was a simple matter of following the positioning system and guiding the vessel. They left the blackness of space and shot into the atmosphere of Narenda. As she took the ship lower toward their planned landing zone, she scowled. This was Narenda. She knew that for sure, but the landscape beneath them was full of verdant plants and...and...

She gasped as a big bird came into sight. It glided alongside the ship, its amber eyes sharp with intelligence.

With a flap of its giant wings, the bird soared past, outdistancing them in a few wing-strokes. Fast suckers.

Behind her, a groan came from Ransom.

"You're still alive," Scarlett said. "Can you consult your maps? We're on Narenda, but I thought this side was more barren after the volcanic eruption. There are trees everywhere."

Ransom groaned again, but he hauled himself to his feet. He staggered to the captain's chair and slouched, breathing hard for long seconds before straightening. "I wish people would stay out of my head," he muttered.

"What?"

"Nothing. I believe there is an open clearing in the trees two clicks to the west."

"Two-twelfths of a cycle?" Scarlett glanced at the chart she'd pulled up on the map screen. "Are you sure?"

"Two clicks," he confirmed.

Scarlett shrugged and set a course west. Soon, the trees became sparse.

"Over there," Ransom said.

"I see it." Scarlett guided the ship down. "Heck, the landing gear is damaged. Fasten your harness," she snapped. "How many knocks on the noggin will it take you to learn?"

Ransom fastened his harness with shaky hands. Scarlett sucked in a fortifying breath and tried the landing gear again. The struts groaned but slid into position.

"Might not be as bad as I thought," Scarlett said as they touched land and the struts took the ship's weight. "Yay! We're down."

She unfastened her harness and stood. Ransom did the same and rose, his face pale.

"How bad is your head?"

"Feels as if I ran into a meteor rock."

The ship tilted abruptly to the right, sending them flying off their feet. Loose objects sailed after them. A book struck her shoulder. Ransom hit the wall with an *oomph*, and Scarlett landed on top of him.

"Is it safe to move?" Ransom asked, a beat later.

"Think so."

"Good." Ransom curled his arms around her back and kissed her. The warm, physical contact of his lips on hers and the suddenness of his move startled her. She opened her mouth to protest, and the lout took this as an invitation to proceed. Her hands gripped his ears. She intended to yank them. She really did, but his lips softened, and he coaxed rather than demanded. He invited instead of presenting an alpha male challenge. Her feline voted *hell, yeah,* and before Scarlett recognized her surrender, she was participating. Exploring his luscious mouth. Tangling her tongue with his and gripping his shoulders, trying to climb into his body instead of assaulting him. His taste. A delicious honeyed sweetness. His scent of amber, warm and musky with a hint of burning earth. Addictive and enticing. His body—a hard stack of muscles that fit exactly against her curves.

Ransom pulled back, and Scarlett followed, pressing her lips to his again and nipping his lower lip. His dark groan thrilled her, and her feline purred, the sensuous sound echoing through Scarlett's mind.

She stirred restlessly, the drag of her nipples against his chest a silent demand for more, more, more.

Ransom separated their mouths again, his expression tender yet with a note of seriousness that told her this interlude was at an end.

For the best, she told her feline, and she scrambled off Ransom, taking care not to glance at the place that had been stabbing her. With the ship at an angle, the footing was treacherous.

"We'd better go. They'll be waiting for us," Ransom said.

Her eyes narrowed. "Who?"

"I'll explain later."

She grabbed his meaty biceps as he crab-walked toward the exit. "I don't enjoy surprises. Tell me now."

"They're listening," he said in a terse voice.

Scarlett did a slow blink and felt her frown etch into her forehead. What the hell? She released him and wordlessly followed his example of scuttling like a crab to reach the door.

"Our engineers have assembled a chute for your exit," a voice said in the universal language. "They will repair your ship while we speak."

Ransom disappeared from her sight, and when nothing startling occurred, Scarlett followed in his wake. She flung her legs over the edge of the ship exit and shot down a steep chute. Toward the bottom, the gradient eased, slowing her for the descent. Ransom caught her, holding her against his side as he turned to their waiting visitors.

Aw, a protective dragon-man. Cute, since his balance wavered like a human when they'd guzzled too much alcohol.

She slid her arm around his waist, silently offering him more stability as she observed their visitors. They were tall and slender with pale faces and long golden hair. Their locks were loose, apart from intricate braids at their temples that kept the rest of their hair from restricting their sight. Each had pointy ears that reminded her of characters from a fantasy novel. The group comprised male and female, and all possessed a military bearing. Soldiers with wary gazes, although their weapons remained holstered at their sides. Their bright clothing—tight leggings and fitted tops—matched the vibrant plants and flowers in the surrounding jungle.

Had that storm been an alien form of a tornado? Because they sure as hell weren't in Kansas anymore. Questions pinged around Scarlett's brain. Where the hell were they? Who were these people?

Okay, not Kansas. They'd landed on Narenda. Fact. She hadn't struck her head during their unfortunate run-in with the meteors and their hairy landing.

"Greetings." Ransom's attention centered on a female who stood to the forefront of the group. "You wish to speak with us?"

"Who are you?" Scarlett demanded, stepping up beside Ransom to present a united front. "And why should we trust you?"

"Shush," Ransom said. "Show some respect."

Scarlett gaped at him. Respect? These were trained soldiers. They carried weapons, and even if they weren't pointing at them yet, they could.

"We are Elevenoss people. If we intended to harm, we'd have

done it when you landed. Ransom assures us you will behave with decorum and are trustworthy. Come, we will eat while our engineers repair and strengthen your ship for the return journey." A thread of amusement wove through the woman's words, and her expression softened when she glanced at Ransom. "Let us go. We are close to our village."

Ransom limped, and a trickle of blood seeped from the wound on his head. Scarlett frowned at that because his shifter half should've repaired the injury or at least stopped the bleeding. She'd had the same thought earlier, but now anxiety struck her hard. Most shifter beasts, no matter the variety, were healthy specimens. Of course, Sly had been in a coma during his adventures in the fairy village. He'd lost weight, and his health had suffered because of the crazy princess who'd abducted him. Likewise, something was off with Ransom.

She did her best to help him remain upright, but the dragon-man was built, and his muscles weighed heavy. To compound the problem, the track narrowed and made walking abreast difficult.

"Please, let us help," an Elevenoss man said. He snapped his fingers, and a stretcher appeared out of thin air. Another snap of his fingers had Ransom in position, and two of the men picked up the litter and marched after the woman leader.

"Whoa," Scarlett muttered. "Magic."

The worry residing in her chest deepened. What if they refused to let them leave?

Scarlett trotted after the men, her mind busily working on a plan. Red parrotlike birds flitted amongst the treetops, their loud squawks deafening. She needed a series of steps to escape. A list. They rounded a bend in the track and entered a clearing. She took a beat longer to detect the dwellings since they were cunningly concealed within the trees and foliage. The aliens had used wood to construct their houses, and vines and other plants clung to the buildings.

The alien leading their group whistled. Three shrill notes, followed by one long beat. People emerged from their houses, and greetings flowed to their party. A woman bustled forward when she noticed the stretcher. Although she had the same build and pointy ears as the others, the same dress, her skin was a deep purple, and her hair a raven black.

"You have a patient for me?"

Her accent was thicker than the others, and it took Scarlett a second to decipher her meaning.

"We do, Mistress Aelene. Time is short." The woman Scarlett recognized as the group leader glanced at Ransom. "We will conduct our business while Mistress Aelene tends to your wounds." The woman caught Scarlett's gaze and held it.

A jolt ran through Scarlett as she experienced the hum of power the woman emitted.

"You will give us a chance to speak before you do anything stupid." The woman's voice held sternness and warning.

Scarlett scowled. "I abhor getting shanghaied by strangers. First Ransom and now you. I am irked." She folded her arms and didn't hold back on her glare. "You haven't even introduced yourselves."

The woman's lips quirked as if she was amused.

Scarlett failed to see the joke, and frankly, she was pissed. But before she could retort, the two males carrying the stretcher with Ransom headed toward a dwelling. Everyone else fell into step, and with a muttered grumble, Scarlett followed suit.

Mistress Aelene strode to a huge, towering tree. Up close, the wooden door was simple to discern, but from a distance, the textured bark, flowers, and foliage made the entrance seem part of the landscape.

Another surprise lay in store for Scarlett when she followed the group through the portal and into the vast room beyond. She blinked before pressing her lips together. Saber always said she spoke before thinking, and this was one of those times when it was better to watch and wait. These aliens sported weapons, and although they hadn't brandished them, their efficient demeanor told Scarlett they'd act decisively if necessary.

"Welcome Ransom Drake and Scarlett Mitchell." The woman gestured Scarlett to a seat. "As I mentioned, we must conduct our business with speed and get you to your ship. Ransom, we have told you of our plight. Are you willing to help us?"

How? When? What the hell? Scarlett pressed her lips together to trap her indignation.

"Daenys Gaylia, how do I know you speak the truth?" Ransom asked. "I've had a stomach full of lies recently."

"You don't know," Daenys said without hesitation. "But I have no need to make up this story. In your time, most of our people are gone. Check this for yourself. Only a few escaped the machinations of the Maphra and moved away from Narenda. The Maphra people have no soul."

"Most," Mistress Aelene interrupted, her tone tart.

"Of course," Daenys agreed. "I forget. You are different because you were raised in our ways."

Curiosity aroused, Scarlett opened her mouth to speak and stopped after thinking better of it. Best to remain silent and listen at present.

"You are traveling to the region where we used to live, which puts you in the position to offer aid."

"And if we don't wish to help you?" Scarlett asked. "From the little I understand, you want us to confront your enemies, and I presume, take them down. Two people against many." She shrugged. "I don't rate the odds."

Daenys turned her imperious brown gaze on Scarlett. "We are not monsters. We will not compel you to help, but we ask you to check on our allies, the Trolleris."

"And do what?" Scarlett demanded, equally cool.

A silence fell—a long one where Daenys stared at Ransom, and he returned her interest, his dark brows drawn together as if he found Daenys the most fascinating woman in the room.

"There," Mistress Aelene said. "I will give you a supply of painkillers to take with you. They should deal with your headaches."

"My headaches have gone." Ransom appeared surprised.

"They will resume once you leave." Mistress Aelene spoke with authority. "This is a brief respite, I'm afraid. Use the painkillers with caution because the Maphra will sense the interference and ask questions."

"I understand," Ransom said.

Scarlett scowled. She wished she understood because somehow, she'd missed most of the conversation. Mind-speaking. Yeah, telepathy made sense, but that raised even more questions.

Ransom could see Scarlett's mind spinning, and he understood. He'd be breathing fire by now if he'd been in her position.

"Rest here for the evening. Your injuries will heal by then, and Mistress Aelene can fix some of the pathways the Maphra prince has destroyed." Daenys's melodious voice soothed the nagging aches constant in his head since he'd fallen into a coma.

Ransom replied in a similar manner so Scarlett and the others couldn't eavesdrop. *"My mind is clear for the first time since the resonance downed me."*

"It's because we've intervened and dragged you into the past before the injuries occurred. Unfortunately, the pain will take you out at the knees once you return to the present time. Does she understand what the prince is, what he will do to her?"

"No." Ransom forgot to use his mind and spoke aloud.

"No, what?" Frustration sounded in Scarlett. Her eyes flashed with wrath and impatience, and her fisted hands showed her desire to flatten someone.

"No, we do not require supplies. Our ship is stocked for our journey," Ransom lied.

"Ransom requires rest to heal, but would you enjoy a tour of our village? Kane finishes his shift shortly." Daenys regarded Scarlett. "I believe he intends to go to the inn for a drink and a meal. I'm sure he won't mind the company."

Scarlett frowned while an objection formed in Ransom. The idea of a handsome Elevenoss male escorting Scarlett anywhere yanked at his temper.

Kane stepped forward, a male in his prime with a too pretty face that Ransom instantly wanted to dent with his fist. Jealousy. A new concept for him, and not one he celebrated. Women threw themselves at him—apart from Scarlett. A fact that galled. Instinct on her behalf, perhaps, because he intended to betray her. He swallowed hard and closed his eyes, not wishing to witness Scarlett's interaction with Kane.

A tap on his shoulder had his eyes opening again. Scarlett bent over him, and he breathed in her fragrance—a combination of the wild outdoors and flowers. An unusual scent for a humanoid alien, but it reminded him of one he'd sniffed before. The answer would come to his damaged mind one cycle. Not that it mattered.

"Are you comfortable here with Mistress Aelene? Is it all right for me to go on a tour?"

His dragon objected so loudly that Ransom winced.

Scarlett didn't react but regarded him with concern.

"Of course." He had difficulty shoving out the words, but he'd done the right thing. He should take comfort from that.

Daenys left with Scarlett and her people. Mistress Aelene remained.

"Try to sleep," Mistress Aelene said. "The prince cannot reach you here. You're exhausted, and you need to regain your strength. My potions can only do so much."

Ransom closed his eyes, experiencing exhaustion in every

muscle. Yet his mind refused to settle. Guilt plagued him because of his chosen course. He had no option. No choice. No alternatives. A big, fat no to every angle his mind conjured to fix this problem he'd landed in the middle of when he'd insisted on accompanying Nanu into the mountains. He twisted his body and groaned at the pull of fatigued and achy muscles.

"I can mix you a sleeping potion," Mistress Aelene suggested from her spot near the fire. She held two wooden tools and twisted and turned yarn to create a purple and white tail of color.

"Yes, please." He pushed himself to a sitting position.

"Does the prince come every blacklight?" Mistress Aelene asked.

"Most."

Mistress Aelene nodded. "Daenys said they've almost made the local Trolleris extinct. You are a mighty dragon. No doubt, he requires your energy to boost his own. He might siphon off some energy to keep the members of his court alive."

"He's threatening to latch on to my family and friends. He threatened to destroy them on a whim," Ransom said.

"Aye, 'tis something wrong with his line." Mistress Aelene tapped her temple to emphasize what she meant.

"I keep hoping I'll discover a way to defeat the prince. I only have contact with him. The rest of his people never touch my mind."

"There will be a pecking order with the prince at the top since he's their ruler. His sire had his people invent the resonance. He must've died in the epidemic that followed. We never understood why the Maphra people died off."

"It's not as if your remaining people could investigate." Ransom accepted the sleeping potion and drank it in two gulps.

As he welcomed the healing slumber, he fervently wished there was another way.

5. Secrets Upon Secrets

S carlett enjoyed her time with Kane. She'd thought he might resent spending his break acting as her tour guide, and she'd asked him point blank.

He'd grinned and winked at her, saying that spending time with a pretty female stranger might jolt the women of his race into seeing his worth.

The village was compact and functional, and the way they'd integrated their buildings with nature impressed her. Saber was talking about extending the resort to cope with demand. Maybe they could do something similar.

"And that's everything," Kane said, ushering her out of the communal lounge.

"Thanks for the tour," Scarlett said. "If you're ever on Tiraq or in the vicinity, let me know. I'd love to show you around our resort." She winked at him. "Our guests would adore you."

"I might take you up on that," Kane said. "Between assignments, we have a lot of waiting."

"What exactly do you do?"

"Guard our royal family."

"I'll let you get on with your free time," Scarlett said. "If you could point me to where we started, I'll get out of your hair."

His brow wrinkled, and he lifted his hand to pat his long blond locks. "I don't understand. No part of you is touching my hair."

Scarlett grinned. "An old Earth expression. It means I'll stop bothering you and let you enjoy your day."

Kane was silent for a moment. "Mistress Aelene says Ransom has fallen asleep and requires his rest. You are not a bother. My friends will want to hear more about the resort your family owns. I know I do."

"Are you certain?"

"We'll eat a meal and drink mead at the inn," Kane said. "You do not require rest."

This was what she'd wanted. Time away from her family to meet new people who weren't attempting to find mates. More ticks on her to-do list. Honestly, if she saw another moonstruck woman with sex on her mind, she might barf. So why was she hesitating?

Ransom...

No. The dragon-man was keeping secrets. It was plain he wasn't telling her everything about why they'd ended up here.

"I'd love to," Scarlett said. "As long as I won't be in the way."

"Don't worry. My friends are eager to meet you."

Kane led her along the winding passage that connected the buildings. As they neared the inn, the paths became busier with males and females, all dressed similarly to Kane. Greetings spread from person to person, and curiosity lit their handsome faces as they tried not to stare. She concluded the Elevenoss race didn't possess ugly people.

Kane ushered her into the Eagle Feather Inn. It was quieter and more orderly than a pub on Earth or in their resort bars. Why wasn't anyone talking? Laughing? The Elevenoss people drank from tankards and ornately carved horns. Some picked at plates of colorful food with their fingers while others sat at tables and ate with forks and spoons.

Kane guided her to a silent group with a proprietorial hand at the small of her back. As one, everyone turned to face them. It was plain creepy.

"Scarlett doesn't have telepathy," Kane said. "You'll need your oral skills to communicate with her."

Ah! No wonder the place was quiet. Everyone was mind-speaking.

"Scarlett is from Tiraq, and she and her family own a resort on the island of Ione."

"What sort of resort?" a man asked.

Scarlett hesitated, then went with the truth. "We run a resort for single females and specialize in captures."

Kane's friends stared.

"A capture is when a woman is seized by a man and taken away to a private place for seduction," Scarlett explained.

One woman frowned. "The women of your species enjoy this?"

"Yes, and not just my race but many of the local aliens. Our resort is fully booked until the end of this rotation," Scarlett said. "It's actually nice being away from the flurry of hormones and their desperation for a man. If you ever want a change in occupation, we require more male employees. If any of you are interested, contact the resort and ask to speak to my older brother Saber. He does all the hiring."

"What about women?" one female asked. "If we are interested in a sexual relationship with another female."

Scarlett blinked, considered Saber's reaction and bit back a grin. "Contact my brother and ask." She could imagine Saber handling that query. It wasn't something they'd considered, but they should, given the variety of aliens passing through their doors. Some appreciated more than one lover, and she was sure there would be races and people who preferred same-sex relationships.

"I'd be interested in working on another planet," Kane said. "We are many fighting for a few positions."

"When we first arrived on Ione Island, my brothers and most of my cousins, our friends were single. All of my brothers have mates now, as do many of my cousins."

"How many brothers do you have?" a woman asked.

"Five older brothers. Five bossy males who order me around."

Several women groaned in sympathy, and Scarlett grinned.

"My two brothers think I might hurt myself guarding the royal family," one said. "Father fears I might die during a sortie. Mother championed me and forced them to stand down."

"Scarlett, will you have ale or mead?" Kane asked. "And are you hungry? I am ordering snack food to have with my drink."

"Surprise me," Scarlett said. "Trying new things is fun. Can I give you credits to pay for my share?"

"Daenys told me to pay for you," Kane said.

"I can't accept your generosity."

"She will refund me," Kane said. "You and the dragon are helping us and are our guests."

Scarlett nodded but didn't ask questions. Instead, she soaked up information. One thing was becoming apparent—the meteor storm hadn't been an accident. Her gut told her the Elevenoss people had manufactured the tempest to meet her and Ransom.

Scarlett spent an enjoyable evening with Kane and his friends, and when the inn closed, Kane escorted her to the single women's quarters. He used a band on his wrist to open a wooden door bearing the number 143. Another flick of his wrist switched on the illumination.

"The lights and controls will respond to your voice when I program them for you. Speak into here. Say the words, 'I enjoy

Kane's company and want to see him again.'"

"Really?"

Kane grinned. "Central control must record your voice."

"Kane has a big ego," Scarlett said and tapped his nose.

Kane chuckled. "That should do it. All you need to do is say, 'lights off' or 'water on'. There is a list of instructions on the bedside cabinet. Or I can stay."

"Thanks for the offer," Scarlett said as she considered the implications. Her feline snarled, remonstrating and declaring her opposition to the idea. The truth—she'd liked Kane, but he didn't fare well against her attraction to Ransom. That kiss. Their kiss. It hovered in her thoughts, refusing to leave. "Maybe another time."

"Fair enough." Kane gave her a quick hug and stepped away. "I'll contact you on Ione Island once our next mission ends. You can show me around."

"That's a promise," Scarlett agreed. "I had fun. Thanks for welcoming me."

With a wave, Kane left, and Scarlett thought about going to bed. Her feline released a rumble of objection. "All right. We'll check on Ransom before we attempt to sleep."

By following the long connecting corridor, she found Mistress Aelene's house easily enough. She lifted her hand, ready to rap her knuckles for entry, when the door flew open.

Mistress Aelene held her finger to her lips.

"Is he asleep?" Scarlett whispered.

Mistress Aelene stood back in a silent invitation for Scarlett to enter. "I gave him a sleeping draft."

"How sick is he? Will he recover?"

Mistress Aelene's sharp gaze speared her. "He's a fighter, and I've treated him as best I can." She sighed. "Only time will tell."

"He should've stayed at home and recuperated," Scarlett said.

"No, he needs to follow this through for the benefit of everyone." The woman pressed her lips together.

Scarlett waited, but she uttered nothing further. Frustrating, but gradually, she was learning more, even if none of the pieces gave her a full picture. "Is there anything I can do to help him?"

Mistress Aelene hesitated. She frowned. "Watch him closely. Help where you can. That is the best any of us can do while the enemy is watching."

It was Scarlett's turn to frown. Nothing made sense. She should corner Ransom and demand that he share his plans and motives. For if there was one thing she understood, it was that collecting raw and precious stones was a convenient excuse. Ransom's part in this journey was far different and dangerous, given how the Elevenoss race tiptoed around giving her facts. Perhaps she should've let Kane seduce her. It wasn't too late. He'd pointed out his quarters during their tour.

"Thank you. I'll do that." Scarlett said.

"He's a brave man, and we owe him much," Mistress Aelene stated.

Scarlett wanted to ask questions. They tickled her brain, fired her synapses, and tripped on her tongue. Yet instinct and the weird knowledge of the future that came to her so mysteriously told her Mistress Aelene would refuse to quench her curiosity, even though Scarlett's gut insisted the answers were relevant.

Instead, Scarlett inclined her head. Her brothers would've teased her if they'd seen her reaction, her uncharacteristic control. They might've cracked a joke or two about the world ending while she imagined her mother smiling in approval at her maturity.

"You can sleep here if you wish," Mistress Aelene said. "I'm afraid it is a patient bed, but the covers are clean."

"Thank you. It's only for one night, I mean cycle. I'm sure it will be fine."

"If you or Ransom require anything, please ring the bell to summon me."

"Thanks." Scarlett kept her polite smile affixed until the woman left the room. Still wide awake, she checked on Ransom. The big guy needed his rest. If he'd been at full capacity, she doubted she would've escaped him during their last encounter. A flash of amusement filled her as she pictured his reaction on finding the chains empty but still locked. She looked forward to their next battle where they were both one hundred percent fit.

In his separate room, Ransom was asleep, but his body quivered, and he moaned as she approached his bed. What was wrong with him? No one had mentioned the cause of his illness.

She placed her hand on his forehead, and the cold clamminess of his skin had her jerking her fingers away. The room was freezing, too, and he didn't have a single blanket. Strange. Mistress Aelene seemed to know what she was doing and had the trust of Daenys, the group's leader.

"Scarlett," he whispered.

She peered closer, but his eyes weren't open. He rolled over onto his side and flopped back into his original position.

"Scarlett." Longing infused her name.

Oh! The dragon-man was asleep, but she was on his mind. She'd appreciated his kiss and relished the surge of happiness she experienced. He was a fine man, even if he had abducted her. Her brothers would like him. Her cousins too.

She drew a sharp breath. What the devil was she thinking? She had plans. Goals. Ambition. A list to conquer. A man—a dominant, bossy one with responsibilities—he'd attempt to mow over her objections. She snorted, easily imagining barefoot and pregnant as part of the scenario. That wasn't her.

Head straight, she retreated to grab some rest.

The next cycle, Ransom woke clear-headed and eager to continue.

He'd dreamed of Scarlett instead of the monster prince entering his mind. Daenys had explained that because they'd pulled them back in time, the Maphra prince would never find him.

Food scents wafted his way—something savory and meaty.

He sat up, testing his limbs before he stood. Better. Much better. He rose to his feet, stared down at his rumpled trews and tunic, and gave a shrug. Even though Daenys and Mistress Aelene had offered suggestions to fight the prince, chances were he'd die. He had to deliver Scarlett to Prince Kalim and risk everything to save his family, his friends. What did a few wrinkles matter in the scheme of things?

"You're awake."

Ransom lifted his gaze to meet Scarlett's enigmatic one. The woman never gave away much. He grinned. Once the prince set his sights on her, he'd attempted to use his growing powers to enmesh her too. He'd failed since the resonance didn't affect her.

"Cat got ya tongue?" She chuckled, her amusement vibrant and contagious, even though he didn't understand the source of her humor.

He sauntered toward her. "My tongue is fine. Is that food I smell? I'm starving."

She smiled, a pleasant picture with her black hair loose around her shoulders and her green eyes sparkling. The plain black trews and a matching tunic she'd purchased at the market on Dalcon enhanced her attributes rather than hiding them. "Mistress Aelene had her assistant deliver breakfast. Meat and eggs. Now that you're awake, you can eat with me, and I'll start my interrogation. You, Mr. Dragon Man, are withholding information. I want it."

Her words ran from his brain and stroked down his body when she spoke of want. His dick twitched with more vigor than he'd experienced during recent cycles. He had an intimate knowledge of desire when it came to Scarlett Mitchell—a need that had stayed with him since their first meeting.

Ransom didn't reply, but pushed past her and strode to a table holding two trays. He sat and waited for her to join him.

She sauntered closer, allowing him to appreciate her lithe, fit body. The silent sass that blazed from her face. Her intelligence.

"If you intend to question me, I require food."

Scarlett snorted and sat. "How did we get here? And don't tell me it was the meteor shower."

"As far as I understand, the Elevenoss race can bend time. They've yanked us back to give me information without their enemies' knowledge."

Scarlett picked up a tankard and sipped the hot beverage. She frowned over the top of the pewter vessel, her green eyes narrowed. "Your explanation raises more questions. They say curiosity killed the cat," she added in a mutter. "Obviously, there is sense behind the old saying."

Ransom didn't understand her oblique conversation. Nothing new there. Since their first meeting, she'd stymied him. He applied himself to the meat, which was bloody and hot, just as he preferred.

"Well, if they've pulled us back in time, how do we return? My brothers can't rescue me here. I was looking forward to seeing them kick your shapely butt."

"You look at my backside?"

Scarlett tilted her chin, giving him more sass. "And that's the part of the conversation he grasps. What part of mean, vengeful brothers did you miss?"

"I'm a dragon."

"Color me impressed." She had the cheek to yawn before she forked up a piece of meat, stuck it in her mouth, and chewed.

"I have fire." Ransom winced inwardly. Gryffnn would roar with laughter if he heard this discussion.

"You're ill," she countered, going for the jugular. "You're not at full capacity, and you need me along to help save your butt."

"You're a female."

65

Her green eyes narrowed, and her hair seemed to ruffle. An angry growl escaped her, and she reminded him of Camryn and Jannike, both feisty feline shapeshifters. He blinked and watched Scarlett calmly eat her meal.

"I might be female, but we have different strengths. We're mentally stronger than males. When are we leaving?"

The change of subject was welcome because she was right. Their situation would worsen if the prince entered Scarlett's mind. The Maphra race enjoyed tropical climates, according to Daenys. What if they attempted to force Scarlett to move them to the planet of Tiraq with its higher population and proximity to other planets?

"We depart once our ship is repaired," Ransom said. "Daenys promised her people would work late until we could fly again."

"You had long conversations without me," Scarlett accused.

"It's best if you don't have full information. The locals who live in the area we are traveling through are mind-delvers. Did you hear the stones and mountains sing when you visited Narenda?"

"No." Scarlett regarded him with a steady gaze, waiting.

"You're lucky. My people are susceptible, and even short exposure can kill us. I told you I was in a coma."

"Then why are you returning to the area? Why not stay in a safe place? Or, if you must travel there for your raw materials, send someone to do it for you as you've done in the past."

"I must stop the resonance."

"How?"

"The solution will come to me."

"Well, that's a plan." Scarlett sniffed, the tiny sound showing her disapproval.

Ransom drank, the herby scent and taste of his beverage telling him Mistress Aelene had added medicinal plants to aid his health. It wasn't disgusting, so he kept drinking. When Scarlett maintained her frown, he swallowed the dregs. "You think I'm crazy, but I have to do something. The Maphra rule their side of Narenda. They've murdered the Elevenoss with the resonance. They've almost annihilated another tribe of Elevenoss allies by feeding on them, and soon, they'll discover a way to feast on my clan. I can't allow that. Even if I die trying, at least I'm taking action to fix the problem my father ignored. Can't you be happy to receive the raw stones you wanted?"

And he'd given her a partial truth again.

"This resonance—can you describe it for me again? I mean specifically what happens when it traps you or one of the Elevenoss folk."

Ransom shuddered, his gaze turning glassy. "I mentioned singing, and that's what it's like at first. The song is sweet and bespells, but the tune morphs. It becomes higher and strident. Once the music gets to that stage, it's too late to pull away. When it happened to me, my body stopped functioning. The high-pitch sound still plucks at my brain. Eventually, it's too much, and the affected being blacks out. I lay in a coma for half a rotation." He didn't mention it was she who'd dragged him from his coma—or rather, the prince had decided he wanted this brilliant, striking woman who was stealing stones.

"You mentioned the Maphra race killed off most of the Elevenoss, and they did that with resonance," Scarlett said.

"Yes," Daenys said from the doorway. "The Maphra designed resonance with us in mind. With my people, the effect is different. We hear the noise—the song—and when we go closer to investigate, we hear a pop. That's the resonance digging into our minds, and once that happens, the Maphra can feed on our energy. They drain us dry until we are husks."

"What happens, then?" Scarlett asked.

"We disintegrate. It's a painful way to die. The Maphra show no mercy to their enemies," Daenys said. "They must be stopped."

Scarlett glanced at him. "Ransom is one man. The resonance is already sapping his strength. Oh, frying fungus! I'm so stupid.

The Maphra people are feeding on you. That's why you're sick and weak. I don't understand why you'd willingly place yourself in danger by confronting these people." She sounded worried on his behalf, and that caused his heart to leap with pleasure. "Or why you're dragging me along."

"My people are in danger, and the rocks no longer sing for me. The resonance has already trapped me, so I'm the perfect person to stop the Maphra. How can I not do my best to defeat this enemy?"

"But you are one dragon. How many Maphra are there?" Scarlett asked. "Why haven't you assembled a team to help? What about the people who collect your raw materials for you? Ask them for aid. And you're not telling me why I'm here."

"They have families. Children. I hate to place them in danger," Ransom said.

"What about me?" Scarlett spat. Her hair ruffled up again, and she reminded him of a spitting feline.

"The resonance doesn't affect you," Daenys said, thankfully answering for him when he wasn't sure how to make this right.

Scarlett had escaped him once with her resourcefulness. If she turned her back on him now, Prince Kalim—there was no predicting his reaction.

"We've given Ransom remedies to help him fight the prince. We're doing everything we can to aid from behind the scenes," Daenys promised.

"Why can't you bend time to before the resonance and take them out?" Scarlett asked.

A reasonable question and one he'd asked.

"We've tried that, and in each variation we produced, the Maphra race has placed a failsafe to stop us changing history. We have tried everything and continue to fight from a distance. Prince Kalim is ready to awaken. That is the reason for our urgency," Daenys explained.

"He's asleep?"

"In stasis," Ransom said. "It's my job—our job—to find him before he awakens fully and can move at will. Once he no longer sleeps, he can move around Narenda and travel to other nearby planets."

"I came to tell you your ship is ready," Daenys said. "We've strengthened the hull and ship's bodywork and added shields to increase protection. We've also added communication and a small room where it will be impossible for Prince Kalim to connect with you. This will give you a small respite, although you must use this sparingly if you wish to contact us. We don't want the prince to become suspicious. It is time for you to leave."

Ransom finished his plate of meat and drank the refilled tankard before standing.

"Won't this prince wonder why he hasn't been able to contact Ransom?" Scarlett asked.

"We've thought of that and factored it into your course back to your time. You will arrive before you left," Daenys said.

"As if that doesn't add to the confusion," Scarlett muttered. She rose and lifted her chin. "Why do you need me?"

Ransom shared a glance with Daenys.

"You're not answering me." Scarlett sounded frustrated, angry, and he didn't blame her. Guilt suffused him, yet changing course wasn't possible.

"You are making a great sacrifice. Our people will not forget," Daenys said.

Ransom shrugged, too weary to embrace the fear that had trailed him like a shadow ever since he'd first fallen into a coma. "I fight for my clan too."

He, Daenys, and Scarlett left the room and stepped into the forest. Daenys's people and bodyguards stood in a line, and as he passed, they saluted, their show of respect telling him how much was at stake.

He could not fail.

6. THE REAL ADVENTURE BEGINS

"I thought the return trip was meant to be easier." Scarlett's entire body vibrated, and her teeth clacked with each jolt and strike of a meteor.

The vista through the viewport didn't reassure her either. Huge chunks of rock colliding and pinging in all directions. The sole distraction was the multiple colors glinting off the surface of the red rocks. Some meteor chunks were studded with what resembled precious stones. A sizeable mass struck the ship, knocking them off their travel path. Scarlett gripped the armrests of her chair.

"This is not my idea of fun." She shot a glare at Ransom. His eyes were closed. *Closed.* "Who is driving the ship?" Her voice came close to a shriek. He didn't react but let out a baby snore instead.

"Ransom!"

"Do not fear, Miss Scarlett." Daenys's voice came from the instrument panel. "We control the ship. Let Ransom grab more rest before he faces the prince."

Daenys's order did *not* clear Scarlett's panic. "If I die, I will find you and make your life difficult. I hate secrets."

A sharp intake of breath sounded before Daenys's amusement rippled through the speakers.

"You talk a big game," Daenys said.

"I mean it. You and Ransom haven't told me everything."

"Noted. Prince Kalim saw you in Ransom's thoughts and decided he wanted you."

"Me?"

"He forced Ransom to find you. Make no mistake, if Prince Kalim gets control of you, you'll have a living death. Although I haven't met him in person, I had personal experience with his father before we escaped." Daenys's voice hardened. "The man tortured his lovers as foreplay. Male and female. No one was safe."

"And you're saying Prince Kalim takes after his father."

"Reputation suggests he does," Daenys said. "Look after Ransom, Scarlett. You and he together is our best chance of changing the future for the better."

"No pressure," Scarlett snapped.

Anger at Ransom for dragging her into this predicament blasted her as the truth of what Daenys was telling her sank in. *The prince wanted her.* Ransom had stolen her from her family. Resentment. Aggrievement. A touch of fear. She ground her teeth together. They couldn't have consulted with her? Asked for her help instead of abducting her?

"Dammit, I'm not anyone's gift. You have no right. All I wanted was a few unusual stones to make unique jewelry pieces."

"You think the prince offered Ransom an alternative?" Daenys scoffed. "Think again. We're all puppets in this mess. Even if you hate Ransom for embroiling you, do it for your people. If the prince succeeds, Tiraq is close enough to be next in his sights."

The harsh facts from Daenys pierced some of Scarlett's wrath, but she still wished they'd given her the truth.

A chunk of rock struck the hull of their ship and pushed them into a spin. Scarlett's fingers tightened on her armrests, and a harsh laugh escaped her. Death presented a way of avoiding the prince. It might happen because she couldn't see how remote pilots could get them through this field. Just as she was about to pray, another rock rotated them in a different direction.

"You're almost through the field. The jump through time might make you nauseous," Daenys warned.

Scarlett gritted her teeth. "You rub my skin the wrong way," she grumbled. "I might kick your arse on principle."

"I like you, Scarlett Mitchell. If your quest is successful, search me out. You and yours will be welcome in my court."

"Pardon? What c—?" Scarlett broke off as they catapulted free of the meteor shower. Her stomach swirled and bubbled, and for an instant, she thought she might vomit. She swallowed hard, the taste of bile strong in her mouth.

"This is a recording. Scarlett Mitchell, you must take the controls and land; otherwise, you will crash. You can kick my arse later. I look forward to it. Good luck. We depend on you. Signing off. Daenys."

The ship lurched, dropping fast before instinct kicked in, and Scarlett grasped the dual control. Heart pounding, she slapped the button transferring the captaincy to her. Her hands raced over the instruments, checking systems and navigation before their vessel slammed into Narenda's atmosphere.

"Come on!" She gripped the toggle and fought to level out the nose of their ship. "Come on."

Gradually, the fall slowed, and she flattened their trajectory. Scarlett heaved out a breath. *Phew!* She glanced at Ransom. The dragon-man was still asleep, still doing his cute baby snores.

"Maybe I'll kick your butt once we're on solid ground since yours is the only one available." Then, she sighed. If that man—the prince—was as evil as Daenys and her people indicated, and he was able to get into Ransom's head, the last thing Ransom needed was for her to cause difficulties. He couldn't fight this prince and her at the same time. Perhaps she could take the ship...

No, she couldn't leave him alone.

Ransom looked so peaceful. He was a striking man, even with the scar. Not a traditional handsome but harsh. Stern. A little arrogant. Ransom reminded Scarlett of her brother before he'd met Eva. Like Saber, Ransom was weighed down with responsibility, the burden of his people, and now he was fighting for their existence.

She and Ransom had talked about where they'd land, and he'd mapped out a course. Confident she'd manage until the dragon-man woke, she followed the plan. Narenda was a strange planet in that its position meant half was tropical while the other side experienced lower temperatures. Her research suggested that, along with its place in the solar system, the most recent volcanic eruption had affected weather patterns.

As they approached, the barrenness struck her. It was difficult to equate it with the tropical lushness of the past, where she and Ransom had spent the night. Her brothers would never believe her when she told them of her time-traveling adventures. Heck, she'd have to make it through this adventure in one piece first.

She landed their ship on a rocky plateau, much farther inland than she'd ever traveled on her fossicking trips. Below, a river of glacial water flowed into a turquoise-blue lake. Scarlett studied the high mountains where they were heading. A light frosting of snow and ice covered the highest peaks. The valleys held ribbons of pastel colors, the one below carrying pale blue and lilac streaks amongst the reddish rocks. It was stunningly beautiful, but now she'd learned of the hidden dangers, her appreciation diminished.

It was lucky she hadn't encountered the Maphra during her previous trips. Perhaps it was because she was a shifter. No, that couldn't be right since Ransom was also a shifter. It was strange he hadn't recognized this aspect of her when she'd sensed his otherness.

She hit her harness release and rose. Mindful of Daenys's words, she left Ransom sleeping and walked to the rear of the ship to check their packs. Everything was ready for them to begin their trek. She took a moment to study the map again, memorizing the landmarks Ransom had drawn and the route to where he thought the prince and his people lay in suspended animation.

"Scarlett."

Scarlett returned to the bridge. "Ah, you're awake. How are you?"

"Rested for a change. We've arrived." He didn't sound happy about the fact.

"Yes, I guess we'd better get moving. I've rechecked our packs and supplies. Everything is intact and ready for us to begin. I've decided you shouldn't go alone. I'm pissed with you for not telling me the truth, but I'll try to help fight this prince." She didn't mention that Daenys had told her everything. She knew the *full* truth about why she was here on Narenda.

"Thank you!" Ransom rose and stretched. "Thank you for agreeing to come with me. I'm sorry I lied to you."

Scarlett shrugged, admitting to herself if she'd known the truth, she might've still agreed to accompany Ransom. If the prince presented a danger to Tiraq and her family, she'd do anything to help keep them safe. Besides, the tedium of resort life was sending her crazy, although her mother *would* tsk-tsk at Scarlett's lapse in following an impulse.

The thought stole some of her excitement. "Jewels, remember. I don't suppose you've ever found jewels of that shade of blue. It's a stunning color and not something I've ever seen in jewelry."

"The pale blue?"

"Yes."

He shook his head. "Most of the raw materials we use are bright, clear colors. I've never seen that milky blue before."

"We should leave."

Ransom nodded. "We'll travel as far as we can until blacklight. I doubt my slumber will be restful this eve."

"You believe the prince will contact you."

He answered with a sigh. "Daenys says Prince Kalim has to limit his feeding on me because he needs my help. She suspects they've depleted their other food resources, so his power is not as great as it might be."

"That's scary."

"Yes, if we're not successful, he'll turn to my people to meet his needs."

Scarlett lifted her chin. "We won't let it get that far."

Ransom smiled, but it resembled a grimace. He didn't believe he'd make it out of this situation alive, and her conclusion was sobering.

What happened if they failed? What happened if she didn't make it back to Tiraq and her brothers came looking for her?

"Will anyone come looking for you?" she asked.

Ransom met her gaze. "Eventually. You?"

"My brothers." She imagined them suffering in the same way as Ransom. "They know where I am."

"How?"

The sharpness of his tone had Scarlett bristling. "Remember the restaurant in the marketplace where we ate?"

"Yes."

"My sister-in-law owns it. She made the shrink-meals. I told her our destination and for my brothers not to worry. But after thirty cycles, they'll come for me—if I don't return earlier."

Ransom scowled. "We'd better push hard while I'm able."

"Don't forget to pack the supplies the Elevenoss gave you," Scarlett said, spotting the pills and a single bottle. "What are they, anyway?"

"Some of them will help me block the prince, but I need a strategy. Daenys insisted I not raise his suspicions."

Scarlett strode to the outer chamber and picked up one pack. She slipped the straps over her shoulders, wincing at the weight.

Ransom followed suit, and they left the ship in silence. Outside, Ransom consulted the map. "This way."

They strode off the plateau and followed a faint trail that led through the pale blue and red valley. Scarlett almost wished she had her com-circle to record the stark beauty of the place. The cool, crisp air stole her breath. The sky was a brilliant blue, two or three shades darker and brighter than the blue in the rocks. She'd see animals and insects at home on Ione Island or even on Earth. Birds would wheel through the sky on the hunt for prey. She listened but heard nothing apart from their feet striking the ground.

"Are there no animals?"

"The prince and his people would've used the energy of the large animals to survive once whatever they used to run their survival system failed."

"So we might see smaller animals?"

"Possibly. Daenys told me they can't feed on the young. Feeding on the animals depleted the populations, which would create problems with the insects, birds, and perhaps some plants. Life is a delicate balance."

Scarlett winced at this reminder, and guilt slipped through her. Ransom spoke nothing less than the truth. On Earth, she'd visited her young friend who'd caught the feline virus. She'd sneaked out to see her against her mother's wishes. Unknowingly, when Scarlett hugged her friend, she'd become infected. Although Scarlett never sickened, Lori, Saber's fiancée, had succumbed. Lori's family had blamed Scarlett. They'd accused Saber. They'd all died except Lori's brother, and he now hated everyone who bore the Mitchell surname. Scarlett's fault and something she'd had to live with ever since.

She bit her bottom lip as another wave of remorse caught her, a wallop to her heart. Agreeing to accompany Ransom—she was allowing her impulsive side to rule her again. She needed her lists...a new list of pros and cons to marshal her thoughts and create a safe path. Allowing a bad impulse to rule her was ludicrous. Dangerous.

Scarlett clenched her fists and unclenched them before turning to Ransom. "Is the prince truly that treacherous? That capable?"

"Worse," Ransom said without elaborating.

"And he'll be even more threatening once he awakens?"

"Everyone who lives in this solar system will be at risk."

Nothing like a bit of pressure. Scarlett walked in silence, taking in her surroundings while picking out landmarks to memorize the return route to their ship.

They climbed a steep path, more suited to mountain goats. Scrubby plants and stunted trees clung to cracks in the rock face, while delicate, lacelike moss covered other rocks, turning them into displays of color and beauty amongst the red surface. Both breathed audibly by the time they reached the summit. Scarlett scanned the valley below. The splashes of moss-clad rocks reminded her of gardens, although the place was still barren compared to what it had been in the past.

"Rest or keep going?" Ransom asked.

"I'll travel at your pace." Scarlett pulled out a water bottle and slaked her thirst. "We should trek until it's dark. I mean, blacklight."

"I could do with a drink."

Scarlett nodded, and a thought occurred. "You're a dragon. Why aren't you flying directly to the place we need to find?"

"I can't fly. I haven't flown since before I fell into the coma."

"Bummer. Is it permanent?"

"Daenys and Mistress Aelene both thought I should fly again.

They think the prince has damaged my neural pathways, which is screwing with the part of my brain that helps me to fly."

"The more I hear about this quest of yours, the more I loathe it." *Should've made a proper list. Too late now.*

From the peak, they traveled downward, following a twisting trail through a forest of fossilized trees. A few were still standing, but most lay on the ground, the rings within the trunks mottled and striking cream and brown. Alive, the trees must've been impressive because the fossilized logs were gigantic.

When they rounded a corner, the volcano came into view. Despite past eruptions, the large cone remained intact.

"Is it extinct or dormant?"

"I'm not sure. No dragon has explored over here since the resonance. Ry never mentioned the volcano."

"We had volcanoes on Earth. The island country where we lived contained several active ones."

The path narrowed to single-file, and she let Ransom lead. An excellent opportunity to study him without censure or embarrassment. The full night's rest had helped, and he seemed more at ease in his skin. The faint lines at the corners of his eyes told her he sometimes laughed, although since he'd carried her off, his permanent expression was pained. The man bore muscles still, making a girl wonder...visualize his appearance at full fitness. His arse—a work of art.

In ordinary circumstances, she might let this dragon-man catch her.

Up ahead, Ransom halted, and she stopped beside him. The wind shifted, and she caught a whiff of sulfur blowing from the valley.

"Whoa!" She stared at the vast expanse of geysers and bubbling mud pools. "This isn't on your map."

"No."

"That answers our question about the volcano. It's more likely dormant."

"The diversion will take us an extra cycle."

Scarlett shrugged. "We need to make camp soon, anyway. At least the ground will be warm. This place can get cold at night. I've camped on this side of the planet."

"Yes," Ransom said, his voice grim.

Sympathy filled her on glimpsing his face. He looked resigned to his fate because they knew the prince would come to Ransom tonight. And if Ransom failed to appease the man, who knew what might happen next?

Ransom scanned the flat valley, and foreboding jumped in his gut. He'd hoped this trip might be a quick one. He should've known better.

"Which way do we walk?" Scarlett pointed at a trail branching off from the one on which they stood. "This goes in the right general direction."

"Let's go. We'll stop once we find a suitable place to camp for the blacklight."

Ransom forced his aching limbs into motion and prayed he remained upright. He'd lost fitness while he'd been in the coma, and it was taking time to recover. As for Scarlett, she seemed as fresh as when they'd left the ship.

A faint smile curved his lips when he thought of his sister Jacinta. Her idea of fun was relaxing in a resort with friends or attending parties at the luxurious homes of her Dalcon friends. Scarlett Mitchell was feminine, yet she bore an inner core of strength. She hadn't panicked when he'd grabbed her, and once he'd explained, she'd become more cooperative. The woman preferred to use her brain rather than her beauty to make her way through life, and he appreciated the quality. As much as he loved his sister, she did little to contribute to the family coffers.

A loud howl came from nearby, the shrill sound raising the hair at his nape.

"What the frying fungus was that?"

"Pass."

"What did Daenys say? Another tribe or animals?" Scarlett's frown dug deep as the howl repeated. "Something about that sound raises goosebumps on my arms. I don't want to meet whatever is making that noise."

"Me neither," Ransom agreed. "It sounds far away."

"I hear water," Scarlett said.

Ransom tilted his head. He didn't—wait, she was right. "You have excellent hearing."

The mystery creature's howl echoed through the surrounding mountains.

She grimaced, scanning their surroundings. "I wish I didn't. That is one freaky sound."

"We'd better keep moving," he said, leading the way. Much safer than following Scarlett. One: his dragon didn't have a chance to perv at her curvy form. And two: he could keep a better handle on his festering guilt. If the prince prevailed, Scarlett would never leave Narenda.

Ransom forced himself to drag one heavy foot after the other. He hauled his aching body up hills and skidded down slopes, his mind full of a monotonous chant. *One-two. One-two. One-two.* The red dust from the rocks irritated his scratchy eyes.

"Wait," Scarlett said. "I'm going to fill my water bottle."

"The water might contain diseases or impurities."

"We have no choice," she whispered. "Besides, I have a cast-iron stomach."

He stared at her, slow to understand her words.

"I've drunk the water before and have never been sick," she explained. "Give me your bottle. I'll fill yours too."

"Thanks."

Scarlett completed the task in half the time he would've, and shame filled him. He was a liability. A liar. They continued their trek in silence. Tired of his tortured thoughts and counting, Ransom was about to speak when Scarlett halted.

"How about camping in there? It's sheltered, and if those howling creatures check us out, we'll only need to defend one entrance."

Ransom forced his tired eyes to focus, his squint telling him Scarlett had picked an excellent site. "Blacklight will fall soon, anyway."

"You look as if you might vomit," Scarlett said.

He snorted. "The truth—I'm terrified at the thought of sleep."

"I'm sorry. This must be a living hell."

Her sympathy and caring almost did him in. An ache started behind his eyes, and his throat tightened. He couldn't recall the last time he'd cried. His father had knocked the tendency out of him early, but Scarlett made him want to weep.

The guilt cut him deep, and he fervently wished there was another way. Daenys had told him he had to follow Prince Kalim's orders. Easy for her to say. Her goal was to free her people and take down their Maphra enemies. She wasn't betraying Scarlett. She wasn't leading an innocent woman to absolute hell. She wasn't lying to a mate.

Ransom forced his unruly mind and body back to business. He cleared his throat. "I'd do anything to protect my people."

Scarlett nodded and walked into the area they'd decided to camp for the blacklight. She shrugged off her pack and stretched her arms above her head. Ransom stared. His gaze zapped to her breasts, and his breathing stalled. Heat roared through him and concentrated in his groin. In the act of self-preservation, he removed his own pack.

"What do you want to eat? Mistress Aelene instructed me to keep up my energy levels. It's time to take one of her pills."

"What will the pill do to you?"

"It will make the prince assume he's using too much of my energy. We hope he'll back off and give my body time to recharge. My dragon does his best to repair me, but my healing abilities can't keep up with the prince."

Scarlett squatted by her pack and removed a foil blanket and several of the shrink-meals. "Eva gave me several cook blocks. I'll heat one, and that should be enough for the meals to cook. Sit. Rest. You're exhausted. I can do this without breaking a sweat."

Ransom sank onto a handy rock, his muscles heavy and weak now that they'd finished walking this whitelight.

As he watched, Scarlet spread out her foil blanket. She turned to him, concern evident on her face. "Use my blanket. I'll bring you food when it's ready."

"You don't have to wait on me."

"You have battles to fight. I have the easy part."

Ransom stared at her mouth, remembering their kiss and how her touch had stirred him, momentarily offering a diversion.

"Hey!" She clicked her fingers. "Focus."

He accepted the blanket, although he didn't need to use it to keep warm. It was better if he was cold since the prince hated lower temperatures. He situated the blanket and flopped down. His limbs twitched with the need for rest, and he stretched out, scarcely heeding the hard rock beneath his body.

Soon, Scarlett was shaking him awake with hot food. "We have soup followed by a pie. I'm not sure what's inside the pastry, but you can trust Eva's cooking. My sister-in-law is a magician with food. Where are the pills you need to take?"

"In the side pouch of my pack. One of the blue ones."

He sat up and sipped the soup. A rich, meaty flavor burst over his tongue. His next sip was more eager. Scarlett handed him a blue pill, and he swallowed it down with more soup.

Scarlett sat next to him. She didn't fuss about the poor campsite or the lack of amenities. Never once did she grumble about having to prepare their meal. Once again, he compared her with his sister, and Jacinta made a poor contrast. Sable, his youngest sibling, worked hard, and her presence had turned them into a family, the house where he and his siblings lived into a home. He wondered if Sable's work made her happy because, as Jacinta often pointed out, she was little more than an unpaid housekeeper. The thought gave him pause. Following in his father's dominant footsteps was the last thing he intended.

A pity it was too late to make the changes now.

He expected to lose his life in this endeavor.

"Oh, wow! This pie is amazing. It's like a traditional Cornish pasty with a savory and a sweet end. Hmm, peach and raspberry. How did Eva manage this? Taste this. Tell me what you think. Eva will want our feedback on the meals."

Ransom bit into one end and meat in a rich sauce exploded across his taste buds. He wasn't sure what the protein was, but it melted in his mouth. He wolfed it down. His next bite contained sweetness. Ransom slowed to savor the unusual flavors. As a dragon, he enjoyed his sweets, but this resembled nothing he'd tasted before. He finished it and turned to Scarlett. "Is there more?"

"Four more." Scarlett grinned. "Told you Eva is a talented cook and baker. She and my mother design the menus for our resort. We're always getting compliments and pride ourselves on ensuring our guests have access to suitable food."

Ransom ate three more pies and drank one more mug of soup—more than he'd eaten in ages.

A howl rippled through the mountains, and several more followed at different pitches.

"Daenys mentioned other tribes lived here, but she suspected most had died, thanks to the prince," Ransom said. "According to her, they were a peaceful tribe and worked with the Elevenoss people."

"At least they're not heading in our direction. Wherever they are, they're staying put. You should get some rest."

"Yeah." If he were lucky, he'd sleep for a while. "We'd better check the map first and decide which way to walk in the whitelight."

"Give me the map, and I'll plot an alternative route. I'll give you my reasoning for my suggestions before we start walking tomorrow."

"Thanks." He'd considered restraining her, but that hadn't worked last time. Frankly, he didn't care any longer. He'd brought Scarlett to Narenda. It was up to the prince to make sure she stayed.

Ransom settled again. He hated to close his eyes, to give in to his fatigue. With a sigh at the inevitable, he spent a few minutes corralling his dragon at the rear of his mind. His dragon hated Prince Kalim, and their animosity was mutual. With Ransom in the middle, things didn't go well for him.

"Ransom?" Scarlett whispered.

"Yes." He didn't open his eyes.

"Tell Prince Kalim you're coming to find him and make him understand this isn't a five-minute walk in the park. He must not feed on you if he wishes you to free them."

"That discussion won't go well."

"You have to make sure he understands the danger of overfeeding on you because if you don't discover the place where they're resting, they'll die."

"I'll try." Not a bad strategy. To date, he hadn't tried to gainsay the prince, not after Prince Kalim had demonstrated his powers. Just the thought of him taking over the minds of his brother and sisters and the other dragons who depended on him brought a shudder of horror. Scarlett was right. This time, he had to handle the prince differently and make the power-crazed man understand the dangers.

When he'd confided his worries to Daenys, she'd intimated the dragons were probably safe unless they attempted to travel in this region or flew too close to the mountain range that sang with resonance. But what if she was wrong? A curse slipped free. Sweat beaded on his forehead, despite the colder clime.

No, if Gryffnn sent anyone, it would be the *Indy* crew, and not one of them suffered resonance side effects. If Scarlett's brothers came, they should bear the same resistance as their sister.

Ransom drifted closer to slumber. His mind fought, but his body was exhausted. He was cold—so cold. He thought about wrapping the blanket around him but rejected the idea. It was better to maintain a low temperature.

A faint pressure pushed against his head, and a pop released the tension. Prince Kalim had arrived.

"Where have you been?" The imperious voice held seductive beauty, yet Ransom had discovered the prince's ugly underbelly.

"I had to travel to another planet to retrieve the woman."

"I've been able to contact you before. The resonance made you accessible at all times." Accusation and suspicion laced the arrogant words this time.

"I do not have answers." Ransom sought the right words. The faint pull at his temples indicated the prince drawing energy from him. *"I was merely following your instructions."*

The pull ceased abruptly.

"You do not taste right. Are you feeding your body?"

"Yes, my prince." The words almost choked him, but playing the game was important.

"I sense the woman, but our minds are not compatible. Describe her. Is she thankful for this opportunity I grant her?"

"I have not told Scar—the woman of her purpose. I thought you would prefer to tell her of the honor you do her."

"Yes, it would give me pleasure to speak with her and tell her of our future together."

The tug on Ransom's mind resumed.

"*May I request a boon, my prince?*"

The prince ceased his feeding. "*What?*"

"*The journey to your resting place is onerous. There are many mountains and valleys, lakes and much thermal activity between us and your haven. I can't fly, so I must walk. The woman is delicate, and I am not strong. I require all my strength to make the journey safely. If I fail en route, who will free you?*" A long speech for him. To his surprise, the prince let him speak.

"*I, too, require strength,*" the prince said after a pause that had Ransom's stomach roiling with nerves and fear. "*But you are correct. Each time our minds join, I weaken you. It is important for you to succeed. Now, tell me more about the woman. Is she worthy of a future king?*"

"*She is elegant and will make an admirable consort. Her beauty is without question, while her conversation is polite yet intelligent. She has kept up with me on this trek, so she has a strong body. I believe you will find her commendable.*"

Ransom didn't add that she bore a temper and could defend herself. Her tongue could be smart and sassy, and she'd dance rings around a weak male. Scarlett Mitchell was not a woman happy to stand in the background. She'd demand equality.

"*From the moment I glimpsed her face in your mind, I sensed she would be my savior. Her presence will help me awaken. I will be watching. Do not fail me.*"

There was a faint pressure as the prince pulled free then blessed silence and peace in his tortured mind. Ransom released his dragon from his barricade, welcoming his other half and his help in healing some of the damage the prince had inflicted. And luckily, the prince hadn't scooped up any stray thoughts or memories. Ransom hadn't allowed that to happen since his misstep with his dreams of Scarlett. Thankfully.

He frowned as he recalled the prince's last words. Scarlett was to be his savior. What did he mean by that?

7. Scarlett Insists on a Great Quest

Ransom woke with a curvy woman wrapped around him and a foil blanket covering them both. It was early still, with the blacklight lifting to give way to whitelight. The air was fresh, but he was relaxed and better rested than usual. The medicine Mistress Aelene had given him had worked. The prince considered him a feeble specimen.

Scarlett mumbled in her sleep and wriggled closer, her backside cozying up with his groin. Ransom tensed, his cock swelling at the feminine provocation. His dragon perked up with interest, and Ransom puffed out a lungful of air. *Wrap your arms around her. Kiss her. Make love. She's our mate. You might not get another chance.*

He couldn't.

He refused to take advantage of her trust.

Determined, he focused on the coming cycles. The prince required them to locate his resting place. If they failed, he'd have to find another stooge. Start over. Low on food, Prince Kalim didn't possess the luxury of time. Chances were he'd punish them for their incompetence.

Scarlett shifted against him again, ripping through his determined thoughts of the prince, their upcoming cycle. She sighed, and her black hair slid over his arm. Suspicion rose in him. One so fantastical, he...

"Scarlett, you're awake."

She released an unladylike *humph* and turned to face him. "And you're terrible at taking hints."

Ransom found himself speechless. He blinked, unable to hide his shock. Instead, he stumbled along the path his befuddled mind took him and hesitated at the conclusion he reached.

"It's obvious you're capable. Don't you want me?"

Ransom blinked again.

"This quest is dangerous. What if one of us or neither of us makes it out alive? Have you thought of that? Those howling creatures, whatever their species, are between us and our goal."

"Stop talking," he growled.

"Make me." She closed one eye in a wink.

Ransom grasped her shoulders to push her away, but instead, he drew her flush against his body. They fit perfectly. Her mocking smile goaded him, dared him, so he kissed her. At first, their teeth clashed, the fierceness of the contact a display of his dominance. But soon he gentled to a caress where he coaxed her to reciprocate. Her hands crept up to tangle in his hair, anchoring him, enticing him.

He tongued her lower lip, and she opened for him, inviting him to deepen the kiss. Ransom went slow, not because he was afraid of rejection, but because he wanted to savor Scarlett. Later, he'd haul back the memories of this moment to sweeten the pain that coursed through his body, especially after the prince fed from his energy.

Slow and deep kisses. Playful nips. Passionate caresses.

He tried them all and couldn't decide which he preferred. They were both breathing hard when he parted their lips and pressed his forehead to hers.

"Now that's what I'm talking about," Scarlett said.

"Has anyone told you you're a mouthy brat?" He punctuated this by kissing the tip of her nose.

"Sure, all the time. My brothers are bossy, alpha types. A bit like you. Big and strong and growly but marshmallow inside with women and those who are weaker and require protection."

"I am not a marshmallow," he stated, maintaining a direct gaze. "Whatever that is."

She grinned, and his pulse rate did a little blip. "That was a compliment."

"Your hair is beautiful. It's soft and smells of flowers."

Scarlett beamed. "Excellent. You understand the compliment process."

Ransom gaped, nonplussed by this woman.

"Greenlight," she whispered. "Every quest contains danger. Every great quest has an additional element."

"What?"

She winked. "Steamy hot sex."

"It's almost whitelight. We should—"

Scarlett slapped a hand over his mouth. "I want a great quest."

Her green eyes glowed with humor and determination, yet still, Ransom hesitated. Once she learned the full truth of why he'd abducted her, she'd hate him. She'd rain fiery curses on his head and threaten to gut him with one of the knives she carried, concealed in a sheath beneath the right leg of her trews.

"Before my brothers catch up with us. They'll accuse you of seducing me, anyway. I like you. I'm willing, so we should do the deed while we have peace." Her smile fell away. "Those howling creatures, whatever they are, stand between us and the prince's resting place. At least, where we presume he lies. Once we get closer, we won't have the luxury of letting down our guard. Come on. I've done a pros and cons list, and everything stacks up."

A list? Ransom dithered a few seconds longer before giving in and taking everything he wanted but didn't deserve.

He'd tell her. He'd confess soon. He would.

Grata, he was a bastard for snatching this slice of pleasure.

He stared at the lush lashes framing her green eyes. Determination hid in the swell of her firm lips and the stubborn tilt to her chin. Character traits he admired in a man, yet seldom found in a woman. Most females of his acquaintance eyed his home, listened to his family's reputation, and craved his status.

Not Scarlett Mitchell. While he waited for objections, she hadn't once complained during their arduous trek up and down mountains.

Yeah, he was a bastard for even considering her offer.

They'd both gone to sleep wearing their clothes. It made sense if they needed to hurry. Now, Ransom rolled away and stood. Without taking his gaze off her, he yanked his tunic over his head, then went to work on his trews. He tugged them down his legs, taking his foot linings with them.

"You need to eat more food."

Ransom laughed. Not something he usually heard from a prospective lover. Normally the minute scales on his cock fascinated females. "Why don't you disrobe too? Then I can decide how much food you need."

She gave a derisive snort but rose, anyway. "No man tells me what to do with my body," she said. "I enjoy food. I'll eat what I please."

As she spoke, she unfastened the black toggles that held her tunic together. The fabric whispered when it fell. Her trews were more form-fitting than his, and it was easy to come to a decision about her weight distribution before she stood before him naked.

She peeled the trews down her legs and straightened, meeting his gaze with a proud, almost arrogant tilt of her head.

He forced himself to remain still. "You appear to have mastered the correct food balance." Her curves were distinct and stunning, but she still wore her underwear. "Are you removing more?"

Scarlett laughed, her green eyes flashing. Beautiful green jewels. Had they changed color? He blinked. No, they remained the pretty green that had mesmerized him during their first meeting. She reached behind her back and released the closure of her chest binding. Slowly, she revealed her breasts. Pink-tipped, perfect handfuls. With a wiggle of hips, she worked her panties down long, golden legs. She'd already removed her foot coverings, and now she stood before him, proudly naked in the whitelight.

With a faint smile, she slanted her head. "Do you require hints on what to do next?"

"I have a few ideas." Ransom closed the distance between them. A sigh escaped him when her firm flesh pressed against his. This was a woman in her prime, and he found he enjoyed her bossiness and outrageous suggestions. In the future, when she learned the truth, she could never accuse him of using force.

This slice of paradise—entirely Scarlett Mitchell.

Their mouths met again in a tender kiss, a precursor for what would come.

Scarlett grasped his shoulders and drew him closer. A tiny swivel of her hips teased his cock and propelled a rush of excitement through him. With their mouths still caressing and tasting, Ransom lifted her and sat on their foil blanket.

Immediately, she pulled away and, with a hand to his sternum, pushed him flat on his back. She straddled his hips and offered him an impish grin. "I get to explore your tattoos. Those teeny-tiny scales on your cock. You can have a turn later."

Because he didn't want her to think she could get her way with everything, he dragged her down for another kiss and rolled them. "I'll go first."

She pursed her lips. "That was sly."

"I wouldn't want you to believe I'm a...what is the word? Ah! A pushover."

"Have you met people from Earth before?"

"I know one, and her quaint expressions have caught on with her mate and their friends. Sometimes, it is as if they speak a foreign language since my translator is of no help."

"A woman? Really? Which planet does she live on now? I'd love to meet her."

"Viros."

"Ah, the planet is ruled by feline shapeshifters. A triad. Have you met the rulers?"

"You want to chat about royalty? I thought you had something else in mind."

"Sex." She grinned. "I'm capable of multitasking."

"I prefer to concentrate on one thing at a time. Sex, it is then." He kissed her again, addicted to her taste and the enthusiasm she imbued in the action. This time, he allowed his hands to wander. Her skin was soft beneath his fingertips, his caress pulling a shiver from her. His calluses—a side effect of the jewelry design business and his hands-on approach to leadership. He explored her shoulders and biceps before he let his fingers wander to her breasts.

"Use your mouth," she ordered.

"My gel-bed at home is a huge, carved monstrosity, handed down through the generations. I've thought about donating it to someone who'd appreciate it and purchase something more to my taste."

"An interesting topic, but why are you telling me?"

"It has lots of rings and other attachments to help when discipline is required for an unruly partner."

Scarlett cupped his face with her hands, silently commanding his gaze. "Do you enjoy that type of thing?"

"I believe my father did, but not me. However," he added. "I see the benefit of a spanking to establish appropriate behavior."

"Hmm, we must try that sometime. Right now, a terrific old-fashioned bonking would hit the spot."

Bonking. He'd never heard the term before, although he got the point. The next time he met with Ry Coppersmith and his crew, he might drop that into the conversation and see what happened.

"We can do that," he agreed. "Both things."

He cupped her breasts, savoring the weight of the globes.

"Better." One green eye closed in a cheeky wink.

If they'd had more time, been in a different place, he'd have taken pleasure in going slowly and torturing them both. The thought brought the prince to mind.

Reality.

He started to pull away.

"Don't. You. Dare."

"We should move. Take advantage of the whitelight. We have no idea of what lies ahead and how long it will take to locate the prince."

"You abducted me. You forced me into this quest. You fix this or I'll make you suffer."

Ransom froze, met her anger with a scowl. She never faltered. Her fierce gaze made him want to scream his frustration. The prince didn't deserve this magnificent woman. He'd use her, suck her dry, and discard her when she was of no further benefit. After all these cycles at the mercy of the prince, he understood the royal's thought processes. His entitlement.

"Ransom. I'm here." Her eyes flashed. "You keep drifting off in your head. It's scary because I don't know whether the prince has connected with you or it's something else. Talk to me. Share stuff."

"I worry," he said simply because, bottom line—it was the truth.

"Can you do anything more than what you're already doing?"

"No." In his dragon world, he'd challenge the prince. He'd burn him to a crisp with his fire.

"You can't fight everything. All you can do is your best each day. My brother told me too much fear of what might happen can paralyze us. It's best to work with the things you can control and battle the other things as they come. Singly, they're not as scary. What-ifs are for fiction writers. Now, if you don't want sexual release, that's fine. Get me off, and we'll call this interlude a success."

Ransom stared in what was becoming a familiar reaction to Scarlett Mitchell. The woman's mouth. The words she uttered. She was fearless. Courageous. Magnificent.

Prince Kalim did not deserve her.

"Ransom!" She reached up and pinched his biceps, dragging his attention to her. "Must I tutor you on my pleasure points?" She sighed. "Things were going so well."

Nonplussed, he gaped at her. An insult loitered within her words. He could tell from the sly expression that had taken residence on her face.

"Oh, for great stars." She rolled her eyes and lifted a finger to point. "Lips. Neck and ear. Breasts. Inner thighs. Clitoris. That will do for a start."

Yet again, Ransom found himself gaping. Women from Earth were clearly a different breed.

She issued a put-upon sigh. "Very well. I'm perfectly capable of getting myself off. I thought you might enjoy helping. My bad."

As Ransom watched, she used her fingers to pinch a nipple while her other hand stroked down her body and slid along her cleft. Her eyes fluttered closed, and Ransom grinned. It started slow with a twitch of lips and lengthened into a gentle curve that dug deeper until his facial muscles strained with the broadness of it. This woman was a vixen. A minx. A challenge.

He leaned closer until his mouth was close to her ear. "Ah," he whispered. "So that's how you do it. This is new to me."

"Idiot." Her stroking, plucking fingers never slowed.

"Perhaps, I'll help."

"Jump in at any time."

Ransom identified the lightness inside as happiness. Something he hadn't experienced for a while. He traced his finger around the nipple she wasn't plucking.

"Mouth," she ordered without opening her eyes.

He obliged, enclosing the tight peak with his lips, but not doing anything else. Her scent wound into his lungs, his dragon pushing a sigh through Ransom's mind.

"More," she demanded.

Ransom used his tongue, circling her nipple before gently biting. Her moan of approval pleased him. Scarlett wouldn't be a silent lover. He sucked, giving her a pulling sensation while he cupped the weight of the breast Scarlett was busy tormenting.

"Yes," she whispered.

The scent of her excitement rose to him, and his own body tightened with need. Desire. Instead of acting on his wants, he caressed and teased Scarlett. He kissed and sucked. Licked and tasted. Pinched and tugged.

"Dragon-man," she whispered. "Your touch is magical."

Dragon-man? He grinned. He'd repeated the action so much, his face was aching, yet he felt lighter and more himself.

He eased away from her breasts and kissed a trail across her rib cage. She wriggled, and he stopped.

"Ticklish."

"Good to know."

"Don't even think about tormenting me with this discovery," she warned. "I will retaliate."

There went his sore facial muscles again. This was one ache he didn't mind. Ransom skirted the boundaries of tickling enough to amuse himself and not pull Scarlett-havoc down on his head. His tongue did a quick circle around her navel before he moved lower.

The entire time, Scarlett stroked her flesh at a languid pace, her caresses never faltering. Ransom inhaled her musky fragrance and desperately wanted to taste her pleasure, to drive it higher. He placed his hand on one muscled thigh and silently indicated she should part her legs farther. Now, he was able to see her wetness and her glistening folds. He glanced up and found Scarlett watching him, her eyes darker than usual and slumberous with passion.

"Let me," he said.

"Can I trust you to get it right? Your indecisive behavior is not inspiring me to believe you can follow through."

"You challenge me."

"Yes."

The stern note he'd forced into his voice never fazed her, and the woman attracted him even more. Nothing he did scared her when some women would've become quivering messes the instant he'd grabbed them.

Instead of arguing further, he lifted her hand away from her body. Her juices shone on her fingers, which gave him another idea. While she might believe she was torturing him, he had a trick or two in his seductive arsenal.

He raised her hand to his lips and carefully cleaned each of her fingers with his tongue. Her quick inhalation brought a thrill, although he kept this hidden. He sucked on each individual finger until her musky flavor filled his mouth. Job done, he placed her hand on her breast.

"Your role," he murmured before turning to his next task.

He ignored the pressure at his groin—his punishment for betraying her—and blew a slow stream of air along her seam.

"Please don't tease me."

"Don't tease me, she says, and yet you've made it into an art form. I bet you torment every man of your acquaintance."

"Huh! I don't get a chance with my brothers hovering like outraged chaperones. I have to use sneakiness to get anything past them."

He caressed with a gentle pressure and gloried in her moan. She elevated her hips into his stroke, impatient now for the gratification that awaited her. Aware of the ticking timepiece, Ransom settled in to please her. Her scent and taste filled his senses while his cock tightened even more. But he remained in place, sliding one finger inside her tight channel and stroking her internally while he caressed her swollen nub with his tongue.

Her thighs tightened around him, her hips lifting to increase contact.

"Ransom. More."

Her bossy demand pleased him, and he gave her what she wanted. Instead of glancing strokes of her nub, he gave her more direct contact while he added another finger to her sheath, filling her and testing where she enjoyed his touch most.

When he twisted her fingers to tease an upper wall, her body twitched. She gasped. Ransom repeated the move in conjunction with purposeful strokes of his tongue. The groan she produced had never sounded so sweet—a moan of pleasure and demand for more. He increased his efforts, and a moment later, her body tensed like a wire pulled too tight. Then, the spasms of her clit beneath his tongue and the rhythmic clenching of her channel around his fingers told him she'd snapped in the sweetest way.

He continued his stimulation but gradually eased off. When he rose to kiss her lips, her eyes were closed, her mouth curled in a smile.

"Ransom. I take it all back. You're a dragon-man who knows exactly how to play a woman's body. Thank you."

If anything, today's walk was more brutal than the previous day. Scarlett didn't mind admitting every muscle whimpered and cried surrender, although some throbbing might have been sex-related. A grin formed, and her gaze went straight to Ransom, who plodded up the mountain path ahead of her. The man had crazy good bedroom skills, and she hoped he might pick up where they left off tonight. She could always give the man a BJ. Blowjobs were always interesting.

What would her brothers make of Ransom?

A dragon in the family might make for a fascinating conversation, although Ransom still hadn't twigged to her shifter status. She'd bet the prince was screwing with quite a few of Ransom's dragon senses, which logically was why Ransom hadn't suspected her otherness.

She halted and rubbed her hands together. One thing—the temperature was dropping. The wicked breezes cutting through the valleys whistled straight from the snowy mountaintops while each breath carried a crisp, clean edge of frostiness.

Just as they were about the reach the peak of yet another summit, a howl rippled through the air. She froze, the terror in the cry raising goosebumps on her arms and legs. A shiver worked down her spine. The call held such anguish and pain. Her hackles rose, every sense warning of danger.

Scarlett hustled to catch up with Ransom, figuring they were stronger together.

A second mournful howl came from ahead. Scarlett pulled up her memories of Ransom's map.

"The howls are coming from the village," she said. A preternatural instinct sparked to life and fear blasted her again. *Danger.*

"Yes," Ransom agreed.

"Has someone attacked the village?"

"My best guess is the prince is using them as a food source, and he isn't careful about it."

"Prick," she muttered. "I'm lucky he hasn't tried to infiltrate my mind. Hopefully, I'll stay under the radar."

"Daenys suspected the Maphra were feeding on the Trolleris. She told me they were a peaceful race who kept to themselves but came to the Elevenoss tribe when they required the use of healers. I believe they trade with them too, but mostly live off the land."

"You two had quite the chat when I was elsewhere."

"Grata, Daenys is correct." Ransom stared into the valley below.

Thirty or more stone cottages perched on a slight rise above an open square where the residents might chat and negotiate over market goods while their kids played. Nearby sat a placid turquoise-blue lake. The water shimmered in the whitelight, and the waterfall that tumbled over the rock wall above the lake produced colorful rainbows. A peaceful place of breathtaking beauty, yet right now, a village full of pain-filled screams and horror.

"I count at least twenty bodies," Ransom said.

He what? Scarlett dragged her attention off the lake and waterfall to concentrate on the village and its residents. A Trolleris lifted his or her head and released a rippling howl. It echoed through the valley, full of sorrow and anger and terror.

"We will take this prince down," Scarlett stated in quiet fury. "No one should suffer this much."

"It's survival of the fittest," Ransom said.

"If the prince is an example of the fittest, why does he require us to journey here to unlock the cage his own people made? Why didn't they manufacture some way of ending their long sleep?"

"I don't know the answer to that, but you're right. We might learn more when we arrive at our destination."

Scarlett eyed the Trolleris people and watched several shamble across the open courtyard. "What will we do?"

"We have to walk through the village to continue our journey."

"Frying fungus," Scarlett muttered, shock knifing through her chest and stalling her breath. "They're feeding on each other."

A high-pitch scream resounded and bounced from rock wall to rock wall until the pain in it surrounded them and made her want to clap her hands over her ears.

"Did the prince cause the cannibalism, or is it something else?"

Ransom dragged in air and shrugged his pack off his shoulder. He grabbed his pills and swallowed one down with a few gulps of water. Then, he opened his backpack and removed a small blaster. "Have you used one of these before?"

"Take off the safety, point, and shoot."

"You keep this one. I have another." He belted a holster around his thigh and pulled out another blaster, checked it, and shoved it home again. "We might need to shoot our way through the village."

"I have a bad feeling," Scarlett confessed, anxiety making her stomach lurch and spin.

"You're not the only one." Ransom scanned the village common and straightened his shoulders. "Let's do this."

Scarlett trailed Ransom down the narrow track leading to the village. The entire time the danger prickling at her nape continued while the screams and cries increased in intensity. She pressed her hand against her churning belly, willing her trepidation to take a back seat.

They used a narrow swing bridge to cross the rushing stream. Not even the roar of the water concealed the anguished howls coming from the village. As they grew closer, the picture became clearer. Someone had infected the larger creatures with a disease or a virus, and they were attacking and eating the smaller, weaker Trolleris. Scarlett choked back a cry of protest when a big being grabbed another smaller one. As the captor chomped on its prize, the captive Trolleris wailed.

A child?

Anger surged through Scarlett. Helplessness.

Ransom signaled her to skirt the square. Scarlett saw the sense in this decision. They couldn't do much to help. Heck, they understood none of the circumstances and interfering might make the situation worse.

One of the larger Trolleris lifted his shaggy chestnut head. He bore a prominent nose, twice the size of a human's, and furry ears that jutted out like a pair of handles. His nose twitched, and he lumbered two steps, turning his bulky body in their direction.

His scarlet eyes glittered with malice.

The creature's big nostrils flared. His head cocked, and he shuffled toward them, his pace slow and onerous.

"They're zombies," Scarlett muttered. "Don't let them bite you."

Ransom shot her a searching glance. "You have seen this species before?"

"Only in the movies, and things seldom end well."

The creature froze. He threw back his head, his agonized scream rippling around them. The Trolleris clapped his hands to the sides of his head and cried out with such pain that tears formed in Scarlett's eyes.

She took half a step forward before Ransom grasped her upper arm and dragged her to a halt.

"It's best to keep our distance."

"But they need our help."

The creature clawed at his head, ripping out chunks of fur, his screeching distressed and ongoing. The other Trolleris retreated, both large and small. They cowered as if they understood what would happen next.

The screams broke off mid-shriek, and the large Trolleris expanded as if someone was filling him with air. His entire body—it grew bigger and bigger until his shell could no longer contain him. Finally, he exploded.

"D-did you see that?" Scarlett asked, her gaze on the spot where the Trolleris had been. "Exploding zombies. That's a new one."

"We should leave," Ransom murmured. "The prince has caused this. His feeding. We can help best if we stop the prince."

"Agreed," Scarlett said, although if the prince held these powers already while he was asleep, she hated to imagine his strength once he awoke. "Quick. They're coming to investigate. At least they don't move fast." She hastened after Ransom as he picked up the pace.

He came to a halt, and she thudded into his rear, slamming her forehead against his pack.

"Ow! Did you have to stop so abruptly? You couldn't have warned me?"

"Trolleris."

Scarlett peered around him. "Oh."

"Yeah," he said, his tone dry. "Any suggestions?"

"They look hungry."

"We'll shoot our way out," Ransom said.

"What if we tossed them food?"

"We're not sure how long our journey will take."

Scarlett agreed with his assessment and what he left unsaid. They had no idea what lay ahead. Besides, Ransom needed regular meals to keep up his weight. "What if you threw down flames to distract them?"

Ransom nodded and shrugged off his pack. "Keep them back with the blaster. Don't let them close enough to bite you. I don't want you to turn into a zombie."

"Me neither. I won't be able to manage both packs."

"Just keep watch while I'm shifting. Once I shift, I can carry it in my dragon form."

Ransom ripped off his clothes and boots, and Scarlett rolled them up and tied them to his pack while keeping watch. The Trolleris edged closer. Some foamed at the mouth, and their ponderous ambling *was* zombie-like. She fired the blaster once. Twice. Three times. The lead creatures—the larger amongst the group—stopped. Their heads bobbed. Not all of them had red eyes.

A Trolleris screamed, waved his arms, and clawed at his head. An instant later, he expanded and burst.

"Ransom, the ones with the red eyes are the ones that explode," Scarlett said.

Ransom never answered. Instead, his dragon surged from him. Black and gorgeous, his scales glittering in the whitelight. Seconds later, he spewed flames at the Trolleris, although Scarlett approved of the way he attempted to scare them rather than injure.

He paused and glanced at her with his slit-eyes. Intelligent and sexy. The inappropriate thought bloomed and tempted her. Scarlett wished they had time for her to touch his scales and study him at her leisure. Instead, she lifted his pack onto his outstretched claws and followed him as he edged around the courtyard to a path she hadn't noticed.

The Trolleris chattered amongst themselves, and again, the larger aliens took the lead. One of them glowered at Scarlett with flashing red eyes. It snarled in a display of jagged teeth and charged before pulling up so fast that it fell. Seconds later, the creature exploded.

Scarlett gritted her teeth and searched her peripheral vision. Sorrow filled her along with anger. If this prince had caused this pain and suffering, she'd gut his royal personage herself.

No one should have such power.

No one.

There had to be something they could do to stop the prince from waking and taking over this planet. Some way to halt this despot in his tracks.

Ransom let out another blast of flames. A younger Trolleris stepped forward instead of retreating. The flames licked his fur. He shrieked, and several others raced to him to pat out the fire on his shaggy coat.

"He's okay," Scarlett shouted when Ransom hesitated. "They've put out the fire. Keep moving."

In answer, Ransom sidled past the biggest group with Scarlett scurrying behind him. The Trolleris remained in position, although another one disintegrated, spitting chunks of chestnut fur and flesh everywhere.

Scarlett swallowed hard as the Trolleris fell upon the flesh. Horror filled her as she realized they were contagious. Each Trolleris that shoved tissue into its mouth shrieked, and their eyes shifted from nutmeg-brown to a glowing red.

A smaller creature made a break. It carried something in its arms and ran toward them. Desperation filled the Trolleris. It darted around a lumbering giant and burst between two other infected creatures before he or she tripped. The thing it had been carrying moved.

A baby?

Frying fungus.

Scarlett was running before she even issued the command to her brain. She didn't measure pros and cons. She didn't hesitate. The Trolleris child was in danger.

She sprinted for the youngster, determined to save it. Several creatures had already grabbed at the fallen Trolleris who'd been carrying the child. They snapped and snarled at each other, grasped her limbs, and...

Scarlett ripped her gaze away, not having the stomach to watch this barbarity. She reached the child just as another Trolleris grabbed it. Scarlett snarled, letting her feline sound in her voice. The Trolleris—a male, since he was so big— growled at her, froth splattering from his mouth.

Somehow, she had to get the child off him. His eyes were glowing traffic-light-red, and this did not bode well. Committed now, she grabbed the child and yanked. *Yes!* She glimpsed big brown eyes when she glanced at the child, yet he or she didn't make a sound. Scarlett retreated as Ransom breathed out some of his fire and stopped another group of foaming, snarling Trolleris creatures from cutting off her retreat.

In the instant she took her attention off the big, male Trolleris, he grabbed her and hauled her close.

The fetid stink of him churned her stomach. She swallowed convulsively, kicked, and snarled. Bloody hell, he was strong. For a moment, she thought she'd make it because she landed her boot in his groin. He let out a bellow. *Oh!* Seemed they didn't enjoy that. She kicked out again, but he grasped one arm, his sharp black claws snagging on her tunic. Scarlett almost dropped the child, but he or she clung like a vine, leaving her free to punch and strike the Trolleris.

In retaliation, the creature bit down on her biceps. Scarlett released a shriek of pain.

"I'm not your friggin' chew toy," she snarled, slapping and struggling.

Somehow, she kicked the Trolleris in the balls again. He fell to his shaggy knees with a pained groan, and several other creatures were on him instantly. Scarlett backpedaled, part of her amazed she still had the child.

"Run," Ransom shouted.

8. A Rescue and a Big Freakin' Disaster

S carlett sprinted to safety, barely flinching when a blaster went off to her right.

"Hurry." Ransom was naked, and he wore his pack on his back. He scooped up hers from where she'd dropped it. "Follow that trail. Don't worry about your pack. I've got it."

She followed his order without hesitation, adrenaline propelling her up the rise. Ransom ran up the path behind her, his exhalations emerging in bellowslike pants. Once the level flattened out, she slowed to catch her breath.

"They're not following," Ransom confirmed even as she scanned the area for pursuers. "I doubt they have the energy for the climb. It's not far to the top. We'll stop there for a breather, and I'll dress. Is the youngling well?"

Scarlett studied the clinging child and smoothed her hand over its head. Its eyes opened, and they stared at each other. "He or she seems to be fine. It's a youngster rather than a baby. The mother wanted us to take the child."

"Yes." That was all Ransom said.

Her brothers would've lectured her for hours and threatened to lock her up if she'd risked her life like that again. Although her brothers, cousins, and male friends would've done the same, endangering their safety to save someone who needed help.

Now that she'd stopped, the discomfort in her arm distracted her. The creature had broken her skin and drawn blood. She swallowed hard and ignored the throbbing injury. Once they reached the summit, she'd need to deal with this. Reveal a secret she'd hidden from Ransom.

The child patted her on the face but remained silent. How did the Trolleris communicate? She guessed she'd learn—if this wound didn't kill her.

Scarlett forced herself to tackle the sloping climb to the flat ridge at the top. Below in the valley, howls and screams continued to ripple and resound through the mountains. She wasn't certain whether bringing the child with them was an ideal solution. This quest became more problematic by the day. Her arm smarted, and each tortuous step reverberated through her body to her arm, where it kicked with a stinging twang.

The child turned into a heavy lump, a burden she could no longer bear. Numbness seeped through her shoulder, and all she could think was it was lucky Ransom had volunteered to carry her pack.

Somehow, she compelled her legs to function, taking one step after another. On reaching the hilltop, she dropped to her knees.

"Scarlett!" Ransom's shout held alarm.

"Look after the kid," Scarlett muttered. She set down the child.

"I smell blood," Ransom said, dumping the two packs next to the kid. "*Grata*! Scarlett, he bit you. Why didn't you say?"

"No time. Help me." Weakly, she loosened buckles, and the shrinkton leather her sister-in-law made them with gave, allowing her feet to slip with ease from her black boots. She wrestled with her tunic.

"Let me." Ransom whisked the tunic over her head.

Scarlett unfastened her bra and groaned as she wriggled free of her trews.

"Stop moving," Ransom said. "Let me see the bite."

"Help me." Scarlett panted. Tears burned her eyes as she struggled to push back her distress and center her mind to call her feline.

"Scarlett, let me check your wound."

Despite her lightheadedness from the pain, she managed a strangled laugh. "Immune. Your alpha crap doesn't work on me."

"You can't die." The anguish in his tone cut through her bluster.

"Need to shift," she muttered.

"What?"

Scarlett ignored the shock in Ransom to push off her panties. Then, she stood, her body wavering, and a shiver worked through her as the fresh mountain air frisked her skin.

She closed her eyes and pictured her feline—a sleek black leopard—holding the image tight as her parents had taught her. Her shift took longer than usual, but finally, her limbs acquired the contours of her other form, her bones cracking and reshaping at a lazy pace that worried her. Determinedly, she forged onward until her animal burst free.

The pain eased but didn't cease. Frying fungus, she hoped this worked. No way in hell did she want to suffer like the Trolleris. She sat, breathing hard, and waited. Ideally, it was best for her to stay in this form, but that wasn't practical now that they had the child to carry along with their packs.

Ransom sat back, eyeing her with concern, his eyes more dragon-like than usual while he was in his humanoid form. "Is the shift helping?"

He wasn't going to shout and rail at her for keeping secrets? Interesting.

At least her shift was dulling the pain. As for healing, she wasn't sure and couldn't communicate that to him.

The child cooed and pushed to his or her feet. Oh! *He* ambled toward her, and on reaching her side, he cuddled against her fur.

"It's a boy," Ransom announced the obvious.

A girlish giggle burst through her mind, and a purr erupted from her feline. That was interesting too. While she didn't want any man—and indeed not a bossy alpha—it seemed she'd found one. The sex had been a mistake. She'd known that, yet she'd forged ahead, anyway. Yes, he was dominant, but he also had a soft side. He'd understood her need to rescue the child. But still, should've made a list first. Ransom had become a bad influence, and she was reverting to her impulsive ways. She must halt this. Must fight or bad things might follow.

"Can you move?" Ransom asked and plucked the little Trolleris from her side.

The kid groaned in protest until Ransom hoisted him onto his shoulder. He pressed the child against his hair, and the Trolleris cooed and cuddled closer.

Scarlett teetered on unsteady legs, lurching from side to side as she tried to rise.

"Phrull," Ransom muttered. "You should move. We can't camp here, but we'll find a spot and stop early for this cycle. Can you carry the kid?" He lifted the child off his shoulder and approached Scarlett. "Let's see if he can cling to your back."

To Scarlett's surprise, the Trolleris child clung fast and didn't wriggle or slide off. Now, if only she could walk straight and keep herself upright.

Ransom dressed and picked up the two packs, his gaze on Scarlett and the child. Her gait wobbled at first, but she seemed to regain her strength. Not that his worry ceased. He could love this woman with her sassy tongue and energetic viewpoints. Grata, he was halfway in love with her already, although they had no future.

A feline shifter.

That answered a few of his questions.

Prince Kalim had sensed Scarlett's presence yet had failed to forge a mental connection. All of his feline shifter friends appeared immune to the resonance, which made sense since the prince's experts had designed their systems to enable them to feed on the planet's residents. The known ones. He wasn't sure how long the prince had slumbered, but the resonance had been present since before Ransom's birth.

Ransom watched Scarlett. She didn't look great. Somehow, he had to hide this from the prince and focus on the route ahead of them. And, given Scarlett's unsteadiness, they might require an extra cycle for her to recuperate.

"Keep going along this track," he said. "I'll consult the map and catch up to you." His heart ached at the slow, careful way she stepped, and guilt slid through him. He hadn't reacted fast enough. By the time he'd realized her intentions, she'd been too close to the Trolleris creatures for him to use his flames.

Ransom pulled the map from a side pocket of his pack. He spread it out and studied the surrounding terrain. They were closer to the volcano, although none of the landmarks matched the prince's descriptions. Ransom sighed and shoved the map away. He shrugged into his pack, then picked up Scarlett's and draped a strap over one shoulder.

He soon caught up with Scarlett. At least the next part of their journey was down then around the base of the volcano. From where they walked, Ransom caught glimpses of the valley below. There were a few gnarled trees and more greenery than in the valley where the Trolleris had built their village.

"Scarlett, can you make it under your own steam?"

She growled and kept trudging onward, so Ransom took that as a yes. Typically, by this time of the whitelight, he'd struggle and drag his feet. The Elevenoss potion and the prince backing off on feeding, plus his shift today, had left him stronger and more himself. This wouldn't last. The prince *would* feed on him again and drain his energy reserves.

Ransom passed Scarlett with his longer strides. "Keep coming down the trail. I'll find a campsite and return for you. You have to get better, Scarlett," he added. "We'll discuss lying and tricks played on innocent dragons. There might be spanking involved."

She released a testy growl, and his grin grew wider once she couldn't see his amusement.

The valley was green and peaceful, and even better, there was a hot pool, the water heated by the nearby volcano. He'd tested the temperature and found it safe for soaking tired, aching limbs. Ransom dropped the two packs in a sheltered clearing, set amongst trees. This blacklight, they'd have a fire since there was plentiful dried wood lying around.

Scarlett appeared just as he was about to go searching for her. That was one benefit of creatures who could shift. Their sense of smell was excellent, although his had failed him. He should've smelled Scarlett's feline—her otherness—yet he hadn't. A by-product of the prince's feeding? He wasn't certain, but it was an explanation.

"Let me take the kid. He's probably hungry." Ransom plucked the child off Scarlett. "It's best if you remain in your feline form. There is a hot pool through the trees in that direction. It's safe for you to bathe. Soak. I've heard the hot pools have healing powers."

Scarlett grunted an acknowledgment.

"I'll look at the bite once you shift. We have a basic first aid kit."

She grunted again.

"Now, let's find something for you to eat, little one," he said.

Scarlett prowled toward him, her gait steadier than earlier, but her demeanor suggested the bite still bothered her. She rubbed her head against his legs. Unable to resist, Ransom trailed his fingers along her spine, testing the softness of her black fur. Silky. It reminded him of the drift of her hair across his skin.

Scarlett grunted for the third time and pulled from his touch. Like an elder, she dragged her body toward the pool. Ransom frowned, concerned at the careful placement of her feet and the faint limp. It was as if she had to concentrate on the mechanics of operating four legs.

Still grimacing, he opened his pack and rummaged through the contents. He found a tube of dry biscuits, opened it, and gave the child one. What type of food did the Trolleris species eat? Judging from the lack of vegetation in their valley, his best guess was meat.

The kid gripped the biscuit, and when Ransom mimed putting it in his mouth, the child followed suit. Ransom got a glimpse of sharp white teeth before he chomped down. He kept eating, so Ransom figured the biscuit worked.

Ransom picked up the little fellow, placed him on his shoulder, and started collecting wood. With the fire ready to light, Ransom gave the Trolleris another biscuit, and they both went to check on Scarlett.

He found her lolling in the water, still in her feline form. The Trolleris cooed and reached out his arms in clear demand. Ransom let the kid down, and the child scuttled into the water to get to Scarlett.

"He looks comfortable in the water." Ransom sat on a rock and removed his footwear. He made quick work of his clothes, setting them in a neat pile by his boots. "We must give him a name. I've been calling him Kid."

Ransom waded into the warm water and sat beside the child. "Is the bite still painful?"

In answer, Scarlett rose from her sprawl and exited the water.

Her shift was a little faster this time, although sluggish.

"It's still sore, but the puncture has healed over." Scarlett reentered the water and reclaimed her spot.

"The color concerns me."

"Me too," Scarlett agreed with a frown at her right biceps. "If I froth at the mouth, shoot me with your blaster."

Ransom's throat choked up at the thought. He couldn't kill her. He refused.

"Promise me," Scarlett demanded. "I can tell you're humoring me."

"You're a woman. Why would I obey you?" Ransom said.

He grinned at her catlike growl.

"I mean it. Use your blaster and rid me of my misery. Tell my brothers what happened. T-tell them I love them."

Ransom scooped up the child and placed him on his shoulders. Then, he wrapped his arm around Scarlett's shoulders and dragged her close.

"Flynt and I need you, Scarlett." Nothing less than the truth.

She raised her chin but didn't move away from him. "Flynt?"

"Do you have a better name?" Ransom let his mind drift in a way he hadn't since his first Maphra encounter. Mostly, he locked away his private thoughts, trying to conceal them from Prince Kalim. Relaxation of this sort was rare.

The beginning prickles of intrusion at his temples warned of the prince's arrival. Ransom stiffened and slammed his thoughts and his dragon in a sturdy cage.

"What is it?" Scarlett asked, sounding more alert.

"The prince," Ransom said.

"I thought he only came when you were asleep."

"Me too," Ransom gritted out.

The Trolleris child—Flynt—climbed into his lap and cuddled against him while Scarlett reached for his hand.

"Why are you taking so long?" the prince demanded, his voice

pulsing through Ransom's mind. *"My people are dying. I need them alive."*

"The landscape differs from what you described. A volcano has erupted since you went into slumber. It is taking time."

"You are bringing the woman."

"Yes." Ransom's gut burned at this truth.

His head pounded, and he suffered a pull, a sharp tug indicating the prince drawing on his energy. The uneasy sensation continued for longer than usual, and when the prince released his mind, Ransom's thoughts were sluggish, his body trembling.

"Delicious." The prince made obscene smacking sounds that had Ransom twitching in distress. *"You taste different this cycle. Better."*

Ransom swallowed as nausea swirled through his belly.

"Find us," the prince ordered. *"Or I will feed on your people. My scientists are working on the way to do this. They are intelligent men. Do not fail me because you will not enjoy the consequences."*

The prince pulled from his mind with a harsh yank, sending reverberations through Ransom's skull. He lifted a hand to press against his temples, white noise filling his head. Grata, each time was worse. He couldn't endure much more of this.

Flynt crawled up Ransom's chest, scrabbling with his dark claws. Once he reached Ransom's shoulder, he pressed against Ransom's neck and cooed. His claws combed through Ransom's hair, each jerk sending more torture through his poor, abused brain. Flynt hummed, his breath warm against Ransom's skin. Ransom was about to lift him down, but the Trolleris child hummed again, and astonishingly, his brain picked up the sound. Ransom found himself humming in time with Flynt.

"What's going on?" Scarlett whispered.

Ransom didn't reply but kept humming. Weirdly, the sound helped his aching head, and the tension in his mind released. Ransom drifted, embracing the relaxation.

Flynt removed his clawed hands and ceased his chanting.

Ransom opened his eyes and blinked. Nut-brown eyes stared straight into his. He laughed and ran his hand over Flynt's head before kissing his prominent nose.

"Thank you, buddy," he said.

Ransom glanced to his left, searching for Scarlett. She no longer sat beside him.

"I'm here," Scarlett said. "I had to get out of the pool because I was turning into a prune. You and Flynt went into a trance. You've been out for ages. I was starting to worry because it's almost blacklight. My attempts to wake you failed."

"A trance? It feels like I've been sitting here for a short time."

"Ransom, I'm not doing well. I need help to get to our campsite."

Ransom stood and placed Flynt on the edge of the pool. In two giant strides, he reached Scarlett. Her face was pale while her arm where the Trolleris had bitten her was an angry purplish-red. She'd partially dressed, but hadn't donned her tunic.

Flynt scampered up to them, fast despite his size. He patted Scarlett's arm and made a new noise—a *tut-tut*.

"I'll carry you to camp," Ransom said.

Scarlett sighed. "Admit it. You're as sick as I am. We're in the middle of the mountains at the mercy of a despot prince. We're fucked."

Ransom ignored her burst of pity, although he didn't blame her. Depression often stalked at his side, and probably would again, given what lay ahead. He scooped her up and glanced at Flynt. The Trolleris child scampered in front of Ransom.

"Okay, buddy. You walk by yourself, but I can carry you when you need me to."

The kid appeared more self-sufficient than they'd realized since he led the way to the spot where they'd left their gear.

Ransom set Scarlett down and rifled through his pack for a foil blanket. He spread it out and lifted Scarlett to relocate her.

Flynt approached him and tapped Ransom on the leg. He cooed and patted his stomach. Ransom barked out a laugh.

"I'll get you a biscuit while I light the fire and heat the shrink-meals."

With Flynt eating his biscuit, Ransom started the fire. He heated a shrink-meal and discovered it was a meaty stew. He offered this to Flynt, and the kid seemed content. Some food ended up on his shaggy coat, but Ransom figured he'd wash.

Next, he heated water over the fire and added it to a meaty soup mix. He took this over to Scarlett. She was asleep, her face still much paler than usual. Worry slid through him. Should he wake her and get her to shift, or wait?

Ransom wavered about his course of action. He could use his com-circle and attempt to contact her brothers, or failing that, his brother. Gryffnn could get hold of Ry Coppersmith. Their friend would help without hesitation.

He tested Scarlett's temperature, then checked her arm. The swelling extended from her biceps and down her forearm, and a mass of purple, red, and black colored her skin. Still dithering, Ransom retreated to the fire and sat beside Flynt. The Trolleris patted his tummy again and cooed with enthusiasm when Ransom handed him the cup of soup.

As Ransom heated another shrink-meal, he reached a decision. He required help from either Scarlett's family or Ry Coppersmith.

Ransom gulped down his meal, not doing justice to the meaty goodness. Instead, he worried about Scarlett's brothers. What if they became upset? Phrull, who was he kidding? Of course, they'd be angry, which meant Ry was his best bet for help. He couldn't risk Scarlett's brothers saving their sister and placing his people in greater danger. Scarlett was their sister. He understood family and loyalty. He finished his meal, checked on Scarlett, and found her still sleeping.

Flynt's eyelids drooped with fatigue, so Ransom wiped his

chestnut fur, cleaning him as best as he could before placing him on the blanket with Scarlett.

That done, he retrieved his com-circle, powered it up, and attempted to make a call.

9. A Visit From Insects

Ransom woke in a hot sweat. No, it wasn't him, but the heat radiating from Scarlett. She was even worse this cycle, and he hadn't thought this possible. He rose and headed straight for his pack and his com-circle. He thumbed in the code for Gryffnn and hit send, straining to hear a response. Nothing but crackle. About to disconnect, he heard a distorted voice carry through the static and electronic noise. He spoke fast, not bothering with polite niceties.

"It's Ransom. I'm in trouble and need Ry's help. Call the crew of the *Indy* and get them—" Halfway through the connection dropped. Frustrated, he made another attempt, but the link was even worse. He'd try again, higher in the mountains.

He added wood to the still-burning embers and checked on their water. They were running short. He'd need to restock this cycle.

Ransom prepared food and smiled at the sleepy Trolleris

who scuttled over to join him by the fire. Flynt cooed when Ransom handed him hot food. At least his needs were easy to fix. Nourishment and protection, although the young fellow held hidden powers of his own because he'd cured Ransom's headache with his humming. Ransom suspected he was much older than they'd first thought, but he didn't seem to offer a threat. Yet.

Next, Ransom checked on Scarlett. Her arm had swelled, the skin now tight and shiny. Flynt pushed past him and placed his big nose next to the angry, puckered bite on Scarlett's arm. He cooed and glanced from Scarlett to Ransom. He climbed onto Ransom's knee and patted the hilt of Ransom's knife before getting down and going close to Scarlett to point.

"I should lance it, huh?" Ransom frowned and decided Flynt was right. It couldn't do any harm. Scarlett should shift to her feline again. A wave of guilt pummeled him. He should've woken her and insisted she transform instead of leaving her to sleep.

Ransom retreated to grab the medical supplies. He heated water and also his blade. When he approached this time, her eyes were open, but instead of her usual beautiful green, her irises were a milky white. He sucked in a sharp breath.

That wasn't good.

"What's wrong?" Scarlett whispered.

"Nothing," he lied. "How do you feel?"

"Like I've been in the middle of a cat-fight with all my brothers and cousins picking on me at once."

In other words, not her best.

Ransom wiped her sweaty face with a damp cloth. "Try shifting. You should've done that last blacklight."

"I woke up during the night and tried." She swallowed, and Ransom glimpsed her fear. "I couldn't sense my feline."

"Phrull," Ransom said without thinking.

She winced.

"Can you eat? We should keep up your fluids."

Flynt tapped his arm and smacked his clawed hand on Ransom's knife hilt.

"Uh, maybe later for food. Flynt is suggesting I lance your wound. His instincts have been right so far, and he's insistent. This is the second time he has proposed this action."

"Go ahead," Scarlett murmured. "I doubt I can hurt any worse."

Ransom dampened his cloth and wiped her arm. He stood and walked to the fire again to reheat his blade. When he returned, Flynt cuddled against Scarlett's head, doing his humming thing. As Flynt's humming continued, the tension released from Scarlett's limbs and torso.

Ransom sliced open Scarlett's arm along the healed seam of the wound before he could second-guess himself. She moaned, the anguished cry raising yet more guilt. It was his fault she'd been here. He should've ignored the prince's demands and traveled alone. Ransom tossed aside the knife and held her injured arm immobile to prevent the fluids from flying over any of them. The stench from the discharge forced him to breathe through his mouth. It held the same stink that the larger Trolleris males carried.

Flynt made a chattering noise and gestured at the gray pus that oozed from the cut Ransom had made. Flynt wrinkled his big nose, and Ransom took his meaning and agreed. Contact with the stuff coming from Scarlett's wound was a bad idea. With contamination in mind, Ransom cleaned what he could of Scarlett's arm before he doused it with an antiseptic spray. He considered bandaging the injury but left it uncovered. If it attracted bugs, he'd reassess.

Concern fought with regrets as he peered at her pale face. Grata, she appeared small and vulnerable, and more than anything, he wished she was lashing him with snarky attitude.

"Scarlett."

Her lashes flickered before she opened her eyes. Ransom frowned. Still that weird milky color. He didn't comment because he hated to scare her. "Can you manage some soup? Maybe water too."

"Yeah."

"How is the arm now?"

"It's not aching as badly. After I've eaten something, I might try to shift again."

"Can you feel your feline?"

"No."

Ransom hid his anxiety. Instead, he heated water and made Scarlett soup. He gave Flynt a mug too before he warmed a shrink-meal for himself.

With his meal in hand, Ransom sat on a rock near Scarlett and Flynt.

"I can't face a trek today," Scarlett said. "Sorry."

"Don't be silly. You need to rest. I figured we'd stay here for two cycles, although I must find a freshwater source. I'll do that once you're settled. Should I take Flynt with me, or are you okay monitoring him?"

"Leave him here," Scarlett said.

Ransom nodded.

"How is your head after your latest run-in with the prince?"

"Not too bad," Ransom said. "Surprisingly. I'm not sure what Flynt did with his humming, but my head isn't aching and I have an appetite."

After ensuring Scarlett and Flynt had everything they required, Ransom grabbed their empty water vessels and headed out of camp. He climbed a small hill and stopped to get his bearings. Still, nothing on the hand-drawn map matched, although Ransom was positive they were trekking in the right direction. The junction of the two mountain ranges sat near the horizon, and he'd used that as their guide all along.

The glint of a stream gave him a destination, and he figured he'd reconnoiter while he sought water. He scanned the horizon in all directions before turning to stare at the place where the two ranges met. The prince informed him that a valley ran between, and it was a beautiful spot with trees and a lake. None of that was visible. Instead, the ground steamed and mud pools bubbled. A metallic odor drifted to him as he searched for a pathway across the dangerous, unstable ground. He rocked on his heels, his hands fisting at the challenge. An obstacle he doubted anyone could cross on foot.

You could fly. The thought popped into his head. It was true, his strength had returned, and even if he couldn't fly again, a shift might help his mind and body heal.

Ransom set down the water vessels and stripped. Before he shifted, he tried his com-circle again. Nothing but more static.

He placed the com-circle in a pocket and stood back. Once he centered his mind, he let the shift flow through him. His transformation was quicker than it had been. More natural and hope rose in him. Perhaps the combination of potions and Flynt, and less contact with the prince, had helped. He flapped his arms and took a running jump.

To his horror, his mind was blank. Not one dragon instinct stepped up to propel his body off the ground. Instead, he crashed on the hard layer of stones and rolled down an incline for a distance before he found his feet and clawed to an abrupt halt. His heart thumped as he realized he'd stopped almost on the edge of a cliff.

Ransom picked himself up and stomped to his clothes. Thank the gods no one had witnessed that bit of foolery. *Grata!* What sort of dragon forgot how to fly?

Scarlett dozed after Ransom left. She woke abruptly, and panic roared through her when she recalled Flynt. She bolted upright, her gaze darting left and right scanning her surroundings.

"Flynt? Flynt! Where are you?"

"He is here," a masculine voice said.

Whoa! A dozen aliens stood behind the speaker, their bodies resembling insects rather than a humanoid species. Each bore skinny forest-green legs—at least six—and large leathery wings they kept tucked behind them. Tiny black scales covered their torso, knitting together to produce armor-type protection. They had one set of spindly forest-green arms. Two antennae swayed and tested the air above their heads, which were the most humanoid thing about them. While their upright stance made them more human, if Scarlett had spotted them flying in formation, her mind would've identified them as insects.

Scarlett pushed to her feet and slid her hand under the heap of clothes for her blade. Where was it? She always placed it close to hand.

"We intend you no harm." The man's huge, golden-brown eyes glowed with an inner light. They were captivating and obviously offered more peripheral vision than her own. "Talon recognized our presence and came to find us. He asks me to pass on a message."

"Talon?" Scarlett relaxed a fraction and stared while trying not to, but she suspected her gaping mouth still came across as rude. Best to confront the issue with honesty. "I apologize for staring," she said. "What is your race and planet of origin?"

"This planet is our home, although long ago, the Maphra race imprisoned us and used us as slaves. They let their scientists experiment on us, although their trials did not turn out the way they expected."

Flynt released rapid clicks and grunts. The insect-man lowered and raised his feelers.

"We are the Quito race. The experiments turned our youngsters into blood-eaters. They craved Maphra blood and passed on a disease that started killing the purple ones."

"Sounds as if they got what they deserved." Scarlett wavered on her feet. Her muscles ached and sang a song of pain. If she didn't sit soon, she'd fall. "Will you sit?"

"We cannot stay long. Talon wishes to travel with you to locate the prince. He will help you destroy the prince—a matter of revenge. You are sick."

"A poisonous bite." Scarlett indicated her inflamed arm. It didn't appear any better than yesterday, but it wasn't worse either. Unable to stand for a second longer, she plopped on a flat rock.

Flynt—no, Talon—jabbered away to the insect-man.

"He says you are strong and brave. Most beings succumb to the poison and do not survive this long. He apologizes for his tutor's attack and subsequent bite. His tutor…" He tapped his temple in the age-old signal for crazy. "Those of the Maphra race who remain are feeding on them, and it causes them so much distress, their minds snap. Talon is fortunate to survive. The youngsters provide little sustenance, and the Maphra ignore them to drain the adults."

A rumble ran through the valley, echoing for long moments. The ground shook beneath their feet.

"What was that?" Scarlett demanded.

"A tremor. The volcano grows in power and will explode again soon. We are leaving to join those of our people who escaped this region."

"This isn't the first time the volcano has erupted."

The insect-man flapped one of his arms in her direction, giving her a glimpse of the suction caps lining his hands. "It has always been active, but around two hundred rotations ago, the eruption was violent. The weather patterns changed after the volcano went to sleep, and we had much water from above. It was the warm, muggy weather that allowed our children to mutate and suck Maphra blood. Many of the Maphra became ill and died, and when it became apparent their scientists were fighting a losing battle, the king placed his precious son and some of those critical to the survival of their race in hibernation. This they did, building life support systems that were self-sufficient. Those Maphra who remained out of hibernation died from the bites we caused.

"I do not know how they intended to wake their people or how long they spent in stasis, but something has gone wrong. Their machines have failed, and the Maphra have resorted to feeding in the way of their ancestors."

"I heard they wiped out most of the Elevenoss race and destroyed many of Talon's people. They're threatening to feed on the dragons who also live on Narenda," Scarlett said. "The prince expects Ransom to find and release him."

"The volcano may bury them deeper below the surface." The insect-man's antenna flickered from side-to-side. "It may not kill them, but they'd be short of food unless they used the dragons as their supply."

"Great. So now we must find them and try to kill them before the volcano wakes," Scarlett said.

"Talon can help. He has many talents, including intelligence and cunning."

Huh! Interesting. "I'm too weak to travel yet, and Ransom isn't much fitter. The Elevenoss have given us help, but the prince controls Ransom," Scarlett said.

Talon jabbered, punctuating his clicks with several low growls. Scarlett focused on remaining upright. The ground beneath their feet vibrated, and she realized, the tremors had occurred frequently during the last day. She'd thought it was her shivering with fever.

Several of the silent insect people waded into the conversation, and it became animated. Finally, Talon growled wide enough to expose his teeth. The insect people's spokesman nodded, and the others fell silent.

"Talon suggested you let me draw the poison from your arm. My people fear you will give me a disease that might wipe out the last of our race. But, as Talon pointed out, if we allow Prince Kalim to continue unchecked, he'll destroy a third race while trying to free himself. We cannot allow that to happen."

Scarlett studied the insect-man before letting her gaze drift toward the other insect people who watched her with various expressions of distaste and rejection. To them, she was the alien—the strange outsider. She swallowed the surge of fear that struck deep. With the way her arm throbbed, she might die, anyway.

And if the Trolleris bite didn't kill her, Prince Kalim had her in his sights.

"What would this involve?"

"It will hurt," the man said with regret. "I'd drill into your wound and suck out the poison."

"But you'd become infected. No, absolutely not," Scarlett said.

Talon jabbered. The insect-man listened, his wings fluttering and resettling against his sides. Each of his now-silent followers relaxed at whatever Talon said.

"What did he say?" Scarlett asked.

"Talon believes you are our best chance of survival. This planet is special to our race. We have no chance of returning if Prince Kalim remains alive. The Trolleris bite will not worry me." His small mouth curved in what Scarlett thought was a smile. "The actual infection will taste like a treat, but I will also imbibe some of your blood, and it is that part that my soldiers fear."

Scarlett sucked in a deep breath and went with honesty. She could do nothing less. "I believe my blood carries a virus that killed many of my people. You mustn't. I'd hate to pass it on to you or risk others of your race. I... My brother's mate died because of me."

The insect-men burst into chatter, and there was much gesturing. Talon butted into the conversation, his tone harsh and discordant. The spokesman added his comments. Then, as one, they faced her.

"We thank you for your honesty. Most would've lied to save their skin."

"I-I couldn't do that. There is already enough death on this planet," Scarlett said.

The insect-man's antenna oscillated until they blurred. "Tell me of this disease you carry."

"We still do not understand what caused it, but it killed those who bore the feline shapeshifter gene."

"You are a dual being?"

A unique way of putting it. "Yes," Scarlett said.

More discussion ensued between Quito and Talon.

"Describe your symptoms," the insect leader ordered.

"My arm is painful and achy. I have no strength, and I'm getting headaches—blinding flashes of pain at my temples."

Talon communicated something, and she made a mental note to inquire about his age.

"The wound should not affect your mind." The insect-man nodded at several comments from his people. "We believe the prince is attempting to break through your mental shields to feed."

"He what?"

"He and his people must be starving. Let us do this. It will pain you. My people will restrain you to stop you from injuring me."

"Very well," Scarlett agreed.

Talon scampered over to her and climbed onto her knee. He placed his clawed hands on her upper chest and hummed. The insect-man barked an order to his people, and two stepped forward. They each grasped an arm, attaching their suction caps for extra strength. Suddenly, fear struck and she struggled to no avail.

"Shut your eyes," the insect-man said.

Following that instruction was easy. A second later, an agonized scream tore from her throat. A drill-like barb forced through the wound her feline genes had again healed. Tears leaked from her eyes, and she tried to move, but the two insect-men holding her in place were experts at their job. Scarlett bit her lip until she tasted blood. Her feline's snarl ripped through her mind as the pain increased. The edges of her brain went fuzzy, then the drilling ceased. Scarlett fought to full consciousness before discovering this wasn't over. A painful suction began, accompanied by slurping. Horror had a scream rippling around them. Her scream.

Darkness claimed her mind again, and this time, she didn't fight. She greeted the blacklight and the place where nothing hurt.

10. Scarlett Learns A Thing Or Two

When Ransom strode into their campsite, Flynt was eating berries. Where he'd discovered them was anyone's guess. Ransom prayed they didn't poison the Trolleris kid. Scarlett was asleep when he checked on her, her face a pale round amongst a tangle of black hair. Stealthily, so he didn't disturb her, he drew away the foil blanket to check her arm.

He drew a sharp breath, the air hissing through his teeth. The puncture marks from the Trolleris's teeth were still present, but now her arm bore two deep holes. On the plus side, they appeared to act as drainage holes. He could spray an antiseptic inside. He stood to collect his first aid kit.

Flynt's head jerked up. He raced over to Scarlett and hissed, baring his sharp teeth at Ransom when he attempted to approach. In another sign, Flynt placed his clawed hand over the wound.

Ransom frowned. "I shouldn't treat her arm?"

Flynt blinked at him. Three times.

"All right. We'll wait until Scarlett wakes and talk to her."

But Scarlett didn't wake. She remained unconscious for the next four cycles. Every time Ransom tried to check her arm, Flynt hissed and growled and bared his teeth.

On the fifth cycle, another one of those ground tremors woke him. Smoke puffed from the distant volcano—the direction Ransom had determined they needed to travel.

He checked on Scarlett. Still sleeping. Her fever had gone, and although Flynt hadn't allowed him to see her arm, her color seemed better. At first, he'd worried about Prince Kalim. Had he entered Scarlett's mind?

For once, he welcomed the prince's visit during the middle of the blacklight. The prince had railed and threatened and fed from him. He sensed the prince's ravenous hunger. Not for the first time, he wondered if he should turn away and leave the prince to his fate. Yes, he'd die, but the resonance in the mountain range between the prince and Ransom's people seemed to work in the dragons' favor. The Maphra hadn't determined how to break through the resonance they'd made. Instead, they had to rely on capturing the minds of dragons who blundered into the resonance zone.

Ransom sighed. He should rise, add wood to the fire, and make a meal to break their fast. Instead, he slid closer to Scarlett, forcing away worry. He had to assume the wound had healed because, despite not waking, Scarlett seemed better.

"Hmm."

It took long seconds for Ransom's beleaguered brain to process the sound hadn't come from him or from Flynt. "Scarlett?"

"Yeah."

"How do you feel?"

"I need to pee."

"Can you make it on your own?"

"Of course, I can," she retorted.

Her sharp response had him grinning. She was back.

He rolled away from her, smiling again as Flynt woke and chattered to her, patting his clawed hand against her hair.

Scarlett rose and wobbled. "Perhaps I do need help. My legs are as limp as spaghetti noodles."

Ransom stood and scooped her up. At least her eyes had changed from the weird milky white. They weren't her original green, but he could live with the golden-brown. He carried her to the outskirts of their camp and set her on her feet. "Can you see all right?"

"Yes, why?"

"Your eyes are brown."

"Really?" She wrinkled her nose. "That's weird. My vision is fine."

"That's all that matters," Ransom said. "They're still pretty. Call if you need me to come and get you. Maybe you should try to shift. You might feel stronger."

"No! I can't shift right now."

"Why?"

"Go." She flapped her hands at him. "I'll explain later. I could murder a hot drink."

Ransom turned to camp. "Very well. I'll make food."

When he arrived, he found Flynt had dragged pieces of wood, large and small, to the edge of their fire.

"Thanks," Ransom said. "We'll get some food underway. Scarlett needs to eat."

Another of those tremors vibrated the ground beneath their feet, and Ransom paused until they ended.

By the time Scarlett staggered back and pulled on her tunic and trews, he had water boiling, and Flynt was eating the first of the shrink-meals.

"We're running low on food," Ransom said.

"What? We packed plenty."

"We're feeding Flynt, and you've been sleeping for almost five cycles."

"Five? No wonder I'm thirsty." Scarlett gestured at the Trolleris. "His name is Talon."

"How do you know?"

Scarlett accepted the hot drink he handed her. "When you went for water, Talon and I had visitors. I could understand them, and they interpreted for me. I guess my translator needs an update. Yours too."

She told him about the visit and everything that had happened.

"You let him drill in your arm?" Horror filled him at the danger she'd put herself in by trusting a stranger.

"I wasn't getting better," Scarlett said. "Talon trusted them, so I did too."

"Can I check your arm? Talon has kept me away. The kid hissed and growled every time I tried to look at it."

Scarlett lifted her tunic sleeve. "It has healed, but I have a weird scar. They told me I shouldn't shift until after our showdown with the prince."

"Why?"

"I don't know. Whatever they did, it was Talon's idea."

They both glanced at Talon and found the Trolleris kid watching them with interest.

"If the volcano is about to blow, we need to hustle to find the prince," Ransom said. "Are you up to walking?"

"I'll have to be."

After they ate, they packed up everything and set off.

"Cease your hovering," Scarlett snapped several hours later. "If you wish to help, take my pack and go ahead. Find a suitable campsite for this evening, I mean blacklight, and I'll catch up with you."

Talon signaled he wanted to get down, and Ransom stooped to

set the Trolleris kid on a rock. Talon scrambled over to Scarlett and sat to chatter in Ransom's direction.

"All right." Ransom took her pack. "I'll come for you. Keep heading toward the volcano, and you won't get lost. If the path forks, I'll mark it for you."

"Go!"

Ransom went, hiding his delight until his back was to Scarlett. He'd missed her snappish retorts and quick mind. Grata, for a few cycles, he'd thought he'd have to return her body to her family. Facing her temper was nothing compared to the angst he'd suffered while she'd been unconscious.

Before he strode around a bend in the track, he glanced back. Talon was scampering beside her as she meandered up the incline to where he stood. The Trolleris didn't seem to be the child they'd assumed he was, and Ransom wasn't sure if this was a good thing or not. Scarlett had trusted his word during the visit with the alien insects. Still, she seemed to be on the road to recovery.

A tremor rocked him, and Ransom glanced toward the volcano. A black plume of smoke rose from the conical top, more prominent and blacker than the previous cycles. He upped his pace and pushed harder.

One decent thing had come from this journey. No, two. He'd regained a lot of his fitness, and he'd met Scarlett.

Blacklight was closing in again when Scarlett dragged herself into camp. Ransom had come back for her. He'd tried to hide his worry, but it was kind of cute. He fretted as much as her brothers. One huge difference. Ransom wasn't a sibling.

When he'd first seized her, he'd provoked her anger and fueled her determination to escape. He'd talked her around with his mention of precious stones. But since she'd learned the truth, her stance had shifted. She'd come to know Ransom, and the more she'd discovered, the more she liked and respected him. The prince—well, someone had to stop the tyrant. The way he preyed on other races to survive wasn't right. Daenys was right. Tiraq and its residents were close to Narenda. It could be her family, her friends, her people suffering next.

Dammit, she had to regain her strength to help Ransom rather than become a hindrance. Already, her illness had put them behind. They must locate the prince and soon.

"The good news is we're close," Ransom said. "The bad news—the volcano looks volatile and on the brink of erupting."

"Can we travel farther during blacklight?"

"It's best for us to rest. I recognize the two landmarks the prince mentioned. Give me your opinion when you check the map."

"I am tired," Scarlett admitted. Every instinct told her to shift, but the insect-men had been adamant that changing to her animal form would negate their fix to her arm. They'd indicated Talon would know when she could safely transform, which struck her as ominous. Scarlett heaved a sigh and tried not to dwell on the possible consequences of alien healing.

"Sit, and I'll sort out something to eat. Where's Flynt? I mean Talon."

Scarlett frowned. "He was here a moment ago." She turned to Ransom. "He's older and wiser than he seems."

"My thought too. You should've seen the way he protected your arm from me."

The ground shook yet again, and a rolling tremor tossed Scarlett off her rock seat. She rubbed her arse while noting the tremors were coming closer together.

"The chances of us leaving aren't stellar," Scarlett said.

"No." Ransom sighed. "Not me, at any rate. You could leave and save yourself and Talon. Prince Kalim will kill me."

Their gazes connected, and Scarlett's feline spat a snarl of protest even as she—her human side—accepted this truth. Once they released Prince Kalim, he had no need of Ransom. He'd feed on him to boost his own energy, sucking Ransom dry in the process.

"Well, we'll have to make the most of the days—cycles—before we locate the prince," Scarlett said. "We're having sex this blacklight."

"You're still recovering, although I appreciate the suggestion."

"We *will* enjoy ourselves," Scarlett stated. "If it makes you feel better, I'll let you do most of the work. Where is Talon? I'm not sure whether to worry about him or not."

"He'll turn up. There is a stream, just off to the right. It's cold water, but you can wash while I set up camp and sort out a meal."

"We'd better do half-rations instead of full. We don't know how many cycles we are from the prince."

Talon appeared then, dragging a furry creature with long ears. He pulled it over to Ransom, then pointed at the fire.

"Thank you," Ransom said.

Scarlett went to wash while the boys sorted out dinner. When she returned, the enticing scent of cooking meat drifted in the air.

As soon as she sat, Ransom handed her a leg of the roasted rabbitlike creature. It was charred in spots, but she didn't complain. Delicious.

With a full stomach, she found a soft spot and placed her foil blanket down.

"Hey, where are you going with my blanket?" Ransom demanded.

Scarlett turned, her mouth open to tell him it was hers, when she spied Talon dragging Ransom's blanket away. "Come over here and share mine. It's big enough for two."

"I need to wash first." Ransom stoked the fire and left in the direction of the stream.

Scarlett lay back and studied the night sky. So different from Earth with the extra moon and the other nearby planets.

She tallied how many days had passed since Ransom had abducted her from the resort. Not enough for her brothers to come yet. At least her brothers weren't heading into the path of the volcano. An eruption was imminent with the increased quakes and the sulfurous tang filling the air. The tremors never bothered Talon, but that didn't inspire her confidence.

"I thought you might've been asleep by now," Ransom said.

"Not a chance. I want your body and I intend to have it."

"I don't think—"

"No pondering required. Honestly, I don't normally have to work this hard to get a man."

Ransom sat on the blanket beside her and turned to look at her. His expression held worry, concern, and something—was that guilt?

"Something you want to tell me?"

He hesitated. "The prince forced me to find you. He wishes to mate with you, and I presume to start the next generation. At first, I refused, but he tortured me for cycles until I agreed out of self-preservation."

Anger at the prince burst through Scarlett before she forced herself to take several calming breaths. She was pissed at Ransom too. Might as well chuck in Daenys at the same time, although she *had* told Scarlett the truth. "I wondered when you were going to tell me everything. I knew. Daenys told me," she snapped.

"What? When?"

"During the trip through the meteor field. You slept."

"I'm sorry. Truly sorry. I didn't know what to do for the best, and I didn't... You were a stranger then."

Scarlett's muscles tensed, his economy with the truth bringing betrayal even though a part of her understood. "You could've told me the truth. I'm angry, dammit. Every part of me wants to cling to my rage, but I've seen the way he tortures you and how sick you'd become with him feeding off you so regularly. And your suffering makes me feel selfish, especially since Daenys says he could move on to Tiraq next." She sucked in another lungful of air. "I forgive you."

"I'm so sorry." Remorse carved into his features. "This isn't your fight. You're strong enough to reach the ship. Leave before it's too late."

Scarlett snorted. "So selfless of you. You dragged me here, and I'm staying to the end. The bastard prince is going down. He's caused too much suffering. To the Trolleris. The Elevenoss. The Quito. Your dragons. *You.* Someone must stop him. What happens if the volcano erupts before we find him? If lava buries his chamber even deeper, and it's impossible to release him. Or what if this eruption is so big it blasts down the mountain range that stands between here and your region? What then? What if that enables the Maphra to feast on your family, your friends? My family and friends?"

"But what will the prince do to you?" Ransom rubbed his hands over his face before he focused on her again. "I care for you. My dragon likes you. A lot."

Aw! Scarlett paused, his confession punching a hole in the last of her indignation and anger and sending her feline into a stupid happy dance. Her feline returned the sentiment. His courage. His tenacity. His protectiveness and caring nature. He bore many admirable traits. "If we die trying to stop the prince, we know we've done our best. All the more reason to enjoy each other now. Besides, isn't the prince trying to find a way inside my head? At least, that's my assumption. The Quito told me that was what was causing my headaches."

"How are you stopping him? I thought your feline blood might be the difference. My friend, Ryman Coppersmith, is a feline shifter, and the resonance doesn't bother him."

"Maybe the prince is stronger. I build a barricade in my mind before I go to sleep. Then I let my feline guard the barrier. She wakes me if the prince tries to force his way through."

"I should try that more," Ransom said. "When the prince first started visiting me in my comatose state, the resonance had fried my brain. The discordant music from the mountains damaged me, and it took time for my dragon to repair my mind enough for me to wake. It's not as if I have anything to lose."

"The fighting spirit. Excellent." She rubbed her hands together. "We have a plan! My life is on track. How much longer will it take to reach the prince?"

"One or two cycles. I'll show you the map again once whitelight arrives. Two of the landmarks are familiar."

"Excellent. Now we will celebrate the fact we're alive, and the volcano hasn't blown its top yet."

"I think—"

Scarlett rolled her eyes, although she doubted he caught her exasperation. Despite the whitelight's trek exhausting her, a bath and a hot meal had worked wonders. "I've forgiven you for lying. Everyone we've met during this journey needs us to finish this quest. We have to kick the baddie's butt and save Narenda. If I have to worry about this, I won't sleep. I won't be at my best when whitelight comes. We *both* need the stress-busting release of sex. You're a male. I've no idea why you're arguing. Kiss me, Ransom."

"One kiss?"

"Yes," she fibbed. It was kinda fun seducing this dragon-man instead of surrendering to a flirting male. She slid across the blanket before he could change his mind and plastered herself against his chest.

"You're naked," he spluttered.

"Give the dragon-man a prize." Before he could reply, she pressed her lips to his and settled down to working her feminine magic. She used her tongue, her body, her smarts, and smiled against his mouth when he groaned and drew her closer. He was way too easy. Now to get him out of his clothes.

She slipped her hands beneath his tunic and ran her fingers over his abs. The defined muscle she found thrilled her as did his rapid intake of breath. She parted their mouths.

"Remove your tunic so you can feel my breasts against your chest. You know you want to."

"You're a cheeky minx. A sly vixen."

"So my brothers inform me."

"I have a com-circle. I tried to contact my brother and also your resort. There is too much static. I heard voices, but they cut off. Not that I could tell what they were saying."

"You must stop this lying. I won't have it." She paused. "We'll try again tomorrow. Meantime, back to the subject at hand." Scarlett lowered one hand to stroke his swollen cock through his trews. She squeezed once and smiled at his heartfelt groan.

"What if Prince Kalim can sense what we're doing? What if he gets angry and flexes more of his muscle?"

Scarlett snorted. "Let him huff and puff. What's he going to do? Kill us and ruin his chances of escape?"

Ransom smiled without warning. "All right. You win. I can't fight both you and my dragon."

"I'll be gentle," Scarlett said, managing to keep a straight face.

"Huh! I'm past the point of gentle. The instant you mentioned sex, my brain stopped working. Most of my blood diverted to my cock."

Scarlett chortled, her eyes glowing. "Males are so predictable."

Ransom winked, a part of him wondering where this playfulness had come from. The corners of her eyes crinkled, and he stared, trapped in her gaze. Right now, the color hovered between green and brown. A bit like his own eyes.

He pulled away from her and stood to take off his clothing. Aware of her simmering impatience, he took his time, folding each garment as he removed and set them aside in a neat pile. Finally, he rejoined her.

"Are you finished?"

He grinned.

"You can start now."

His grin widened. "Some men might object to you bossing them around."

"If I don't state my needs, how do I get what I want?"

Her pithy reply resonated with him as images of previous lovers drifted through his mind. While he'd tried to give pleasure, he had no idea if his lovers had enjoyed the experience or if they'd wanted him because of his position. At the time of his death, his father had started negotiations to mate him to a female from another dragon tribe on a distant planet. Everything had stalled when his father died.

"Hey! You keep drifting off. It's not flattering."

"My apologies. The truth is now I'm staring death in the face, or at least coming close, I'm wondering about my life, and if I should've done things differently."

The impatience in her expression faded. "It must be difficult because you're responsible for your people. You remind me of my oldest brother. Saber has always held the weight of responsibility on his shoulders. I've watched him—the way he's given up things he's wanted for the benefit of our people. He's changed since he met Eva. My brother is more approachable, and now he shares the load. He's learned to delegate, and he takes time for himself."

"If we get out of this alive, I'll spend time with you."

"Ransom, we're partners in this quest, but I'm not the right person for you to hang out with. I have goals and aspirations, and marriage to an alpha male is not one of them. You're a leader and need a woman who can stand at your side. I'm not that woman."

Her gaze never faltered from his as she uttered these words. She meant them.

"So you're using me." Ransom swallowed, unaccountably injured by her words.

"Men do it all the time."

He started to refute her claim, then snapped his teeth together.

Now wasn't the time to argue. Now wasn't the time for hot and hasty words. Angry words. Any words. Now was for play, for life-balance. Maybe he just needed one of Scarlett's plans.

"Come closer," he whispered. "Let me feel your body against mine."

Now was the time for seduction.

Scarlett half expected an argument. Instead, she got Ransom in full seduction mode. He draped his arms around her while taking care not to jostle her arm. After a quick kiss on the tip of her nose, he settled in for a more intimate one. This kiss was thorough with the use of tongue and teeth and mouth, and it left her breathless. She clung and wallowed in the sensations—the nips, the caresses, the prickling in her breasts and lower.

He nibbled a quick path down her neck, his tongue stroking over the spot where her neck curved into the shoulder. Her feline sent a contented purr through her mind and pushed her canines into prominence. They slid through her gums, every instinct enticing her to use them on Ransom.

With difficulty, she forced back her cat, and she wriggled.

"Ticklish," she said in a patent untruth.

His attention to the mating site—the place where every male feline bit and marked his mate, and if she was a feline, she marked him in return—had her mind betraying her, conjuring a future she wanted no part of.

To her relief, he moved his attention to her breasts, and she relaxed to enjoy every tug, every pinch, every tender kiss.

About to protest because she neither wanted nor needed this slow build-up, he slipped a hand between her thighs. To highlight her preference for faster, she lifted her hips into his touch and groaned as his fingers grazed the perfect spot.

"Ransom." She imbued the word with every emotion that simmered through her. Lust. Enjoyment. Eagerness. Impatience.

She needed him inside her now.

"Are you protected against pregnancy?"

"Yes." *Oops.* Maybe. Her follow-up shot had been due when she returned to the resort. She counted the days and relaxed. It'd be fine.

His finger slid across her flesh and teased her clit.

"Ransom!"

"Shush."

He made sure she didn't repeat her protest by kissing her. And, to her relief, he rose over her and parted her legs farther apart to give himself access. The tip of his cock dragged across her clit, abrasive and unusual. Must be those teeny scales. So good. She shuddered at the starburst of pleasure. With an expertise that made her blink, he positioned his shaft and pushed inside her. Instead of driving deep, he teased her. He thrust a little deeper before withdrawing until he was just inside her. His lips nibbled down her neck again, and his tongue strummed over the mating site.

Ransom took his time to seat himself, and she was panting with need by the time he'd worked himself balls-deep.

"You're ready now," he whispered against her ear.

"You think?"

He laughed but stroked into her faster. He changed the angle a fraction, so the invade and retreat of his cock strummed her clit.

Ah, experience. This dragon-man knew what he was doing. Scarlet clung to him, arching her hips and encouraging him to drive deep. So perfect.

A prickly pleasure shimmered from where they joined, each stroke from Ransom driving her a little higher but not enough.

"More," she grumbled, trying to arch higher and rub the perfect spot. "More, dammit."

Ransom laughed but slid his hand between their bodies to give her what she demanded. From his first delicate stroke, every lady part stood to attention. His second stroke teased, but his third, in combination with the steady thrust of his cock, pushed her over the edge.

Scarlett cried out as pleasure streaked to her toes. Another ribbon pushed upward, and every particle of stress in her released, exploding and thrusting joy and delight through her nerve endings.

She clung to his shoulders, breathing hard as another series of ripples fired through her. She was vaguely aware of Ransom's hard breathing, the snapping of his hips as he increased the pace of his strokes. Then, he stilled deep inside her, igniting more tiny spasms. Lazily, she kissed his shoulder and breathed in his musky scent.

Ah, yes. There was something to be said for experience.

11. ARE WE THERE YET?

Ransom smiled as he listened to Scarlett chattering nonsense to the Trolleris and Talon grunting back at her. Neither understood the other, but the pair was enjoying their communication process. Scarlett seemed stronger today. He did too. Part of him had expected the prince to invade his sleep during the blacklight.

The prince remained silent.

A good thing, or not? Ransom hadn't decided.

Ransom hoisted his pack onto his shoulders. "Ready to leave?"

"Let's do this. Will we reach the right area this cycle?"

"I never got to show you the map, but yes. We're close."

"The smoke cloud is heavier today."

As she spoke, the ground shuddered beneath their feet.

Ransom's gaze went to the conical mountain top. "Tremors too. I guess we don't need to panic until it spits lava and heated rocks.

Should I carry your pack?"

"No, thanks. It's much lighter now we've consumed most of our food."

For most of the morning, they navigated a valley with little vegetation. Green moss covered the rocks, giving the dip between two ridges a splash of brilliant green. Slippery suckers though. Ransom breathed a relieved sigh when the terrain changed to scraggy trees. They stopped to fill their water bottles before they followed a path that dissected the valley and gradually climbed to another peak.

"Are we there yet?" Scarlett asked.

Ransom stopped. "Time to rest?"

"Please. I might as well check out the map."

Ransom nodded. "How about we stop at the top of this hill? That will give us a decent view of what lies beyond."

"Works for me. Hey, Talon. Do you want one of us to carry you?"

Scarlett was right. The Trolleris trudged, his breathing hoarse and wheezy, yet Talon hadn't complained about their pace.

"I'll carry you," Ransom said. "I'm taller, and you'll get a better view. We'll all check the map and decide if we can spot any more landmarks."

Ransom stooped to let Talon clamber on his shoulders before continuing his climb at a slower pace. It was cooler now, despite the fickle heat of the nearest star. Some higher mountains bore traces of ice.

Finally, they reached the ridge, and Scarlett halted beside him. He scanned the horizon.

"Ransom! Look!"

A fiery red rock shot overhead. As one, they turned to stare at the volcano. The smoke pouring from the top had blackened. Another glowing rock missile shot through the smoke and crashed to the ground.

"Well, dodging those will be fun," Scarlett said, understating the danger in a big way.

Ransom pulled out the map and unfolded the creased sheet. "Look at this. Do you recognize any of the landmarks? I thought I did, but now, I'm confused."

Talon tapped his shoulder with his black claws and pointed. Ransom followed the same line of sight.

"Scarlett, what do you think?"

Scarlett stepped close enough for Ransom to savor her scent. She smelled of him now, their personal fragrances combined, and that brought him great satisfaction.

"Talon's right." Scarlett compared the landscape with their rough map. "Only one mountain is there... No, wait. It looks as if that might be an old volcano. Look at the shape."

"I agree. We're getting closer. Can we make it that far before blacklight?"

"Let's try," Scarlett muttered as a lava-heated rock whizzed overhead. "We're right in the path of the rocks here."

By the time blacklight approached, exhaustion dragged their footsteps. They made camp but didn't bother with a fire. Instead, Scarlett added water to one of their remaining shrink-meals and they ate a cold meat stew.

Talon made his own bed on the other side of the clearing where they camped while Ransom and Scarlet set up their sleeping area together.

"Make love to me," Scarlett said, busily skimming out of her clothes.

"You're exhausted."

"I am, and so are you, but my gut tells me we'll find the place soon. I want to feel alive."

Ransom understood all she wasn't verbalizing. What would happen when they found the prince? He drew her closer and kissed her, then yanked off his footwear and clothes.

Naked, he lifted her and continued to kiss her before he kneeled and set her on the foil blanket. This time, their loving was slow and sweet, and when they finished, they curled their bodies together, neither of them wishing to lose contact with the other.

"Have you set your dragon on guard?"

Ransom yawned. "What?"

"I'm still telling my feline to guard the barrier I build in my mind before I sleep. My headaches haven't been as bad this cycle. I'm not sure if the prince has given up trying to access my mind or if he's too weak to try. Try it." She yawned. "Tell me if it works when we wake in the morning."

Ransom tossed and turned during the blacklight, but Scarlett wasn't certain if it was nightmares or the visiting prince. Although healed now, her arm ached and throbbed, and she could've sworn it vibrated, but that might have been her imagination.

Something crashed onto the ground near to them, and she sat up, casting out her feline senses. She stood and made her way to a point where she could see the volcano. Ah! That might make their quest to find the prince more difficult. Now, along with the tinges of smoke, lava poured in a river down the slopes. It glowed—a scarlet ribbon twirling downward, flickering enough to tempt a curious kitty to bat it with her paw. A snort escaped Scarlett, and she pushed her feline back.

"Not to touch," she said. "It's dangerous."

She stared at the problematic volcano and sighed before searching for Talon. The wee Trolleris kept to himself, especially at night. Her arm itched, and she scratched it.

Eek! Scarlett darted into a patch of better light to study the healed scar. The two holes left by the Quito man now bulged and vibrated. What the what?

She gingerly touched one bump, and it quivered beneath her fingertip. She swallowed, fear writhing through her at the unknown.

A sharp snarl had her stilling, and she whirled to find Talon watching her with bright eyes.

"I let the Quito tend my wound because you intimated it was a sound idea."

Talon gave a strangely reassuring squeak.

"If this kills me, I *will* come back to haunt you."

"Haw-haw-haw."

"You laugh," Scarlett muttered. "That is not a threat. It's a promise." She scowled at Talon for a beat longer. "Are you sure I shouldn't take to my arm with a pointy knife?"

Talon growled a toothy warning.

Scarlett bared her teeth and gave him attitude in return. "I'd make an excellent poltergeist."

"Haw-haw-haw."

"You laugh now." Scarlett lifted her gaze. "The volcano is spewing lava, and that's the direction we're traveling."

When she glanced at Talon, the wee monster had disappeared.

"Huh! Ungrateful wretch." Scarlett stomped to where Ransom slept and tried to get more rest.

When she awoke again, it was whitelight, and she was alone. A pity. She'd hoped to enjoy lazy morning lovemaking. Perhaps she'd suggest it once they—*if* they got out of this jam alive.

She rose and pulled on her clothes. Her arm—she yanked her gaze off the pulsing bumps, not wanting to think about what was going on beneath her skin. Hopefully, they'd come to a stream or lake soon because she wanted a bath.

Scarlett folded the foil blankets, shoved them in her pack, and stalked to where Ransom and Talon sat beside a small fire.

"The volcano is spewing lava," Ransom said.

"I know." She lifted her tunic sleeve. "Check out my arm."

As Ransom bounded to his feet, she studied him. His color was more natural, and the shadows under his eyes weren't as pronounced.

"They're moving."

"Yup. I informed Talon I was going to get a pointy knife and excavate. He snarled and showed his teeth."

"Haw-haw-haw."

Scarlett growled at the Trolleris. "Enough with the attitude, buddy."

"Is your arm painful?" Ransom asked.

"No, I'm hungry, and I want a bath, but apart from that, I'm fine. You?"

"The prince didn't visit me last blacklight."

"I woke up, and you were mumbling and tossing and turning."

"Yeah, I had weird dreams about my family dying."

"The prince having a tantrum?"

"I don't know. Before I drifted off to sleep, I built a fence with my dragon outside instead of behind it."

Scarlett drank the hot soup Ransom had heated before they hoisted their packs on their shoulders and started their trek for the day. Each step took them closer to the volcano. The route they followed twisted and wove through yet more valleys. Talon scampered ahead, moving at a fast clip.

The trail came to an incline, and Scarlett groaned. "I'm so tired of hills and mountains."

"Me too. I miss being able to fly."

"Have you tried?"

"Yeah, I hurt my nose on the bad landing."

"Ouch. I hate not being able to shift," Scarlett said. "And these throbbing things scare the bejeebers out of me. What do you suppose they are?"

A growl sounded. Talon.

"Where did you come from?" Scarlett muttered. "He's determined to protect whatever is in my arm."

She slogged up the incline and paused to catch her breath. "At least my fitness levels are improving. My recovery time is better."

"Scarlett. Look."

A substantial rocky mound, so perfect, it screamed artificial and man-made. Massive square blocks of rock sat in a stacked row, some two blocks high and others three. Gigantic stone heads sat at a distance, but it was simple to imagine the carved figures sitting atop the square blocks.

She sucked in a quick breath. "That must be the place."

"Creepy," Ransom said. "It reminds me of a burial mound."

A sharp pain stabbed at Scarlett's temple, and she held her head while she hastily strengthened her mental fences. "The prince knows we're here."

Ransom winced, the color bleeding from his cheeks. He inhaled and pushed out his breath with a strong puff. After repeating this breathing exercise, he sent her a weary grin. "The prince is not a happy man."

"You fought him off?"

"I did. Or at least he didn't persist."

"The exercise and food have helped. He entered your mind when you were weak from the resonance." A thought occurred. "Why didn't he use resonance on this side of the planet?"

Ransom shrugged. "According to the Elevenoss, he did. He killed most of them and only a few escaped. Perhaps their system failed? I don't know. It could be any number of reasons."

"Is there resonance here?"

"After I woke from my coma, the resonance didn't seem to affect me as much," Ransom said. "But no, it's not active in this region."

Scarlett frowned. "How do we cross the lava river?"

"We'll have to go around."

"Which way? Left or toward the volcano?"

"Left. If the lava started running during the blacklight, it might not have gone far. For all we know, another lava river is pouring out that side of the volcano."

"True," Scarlett said. "At least it looks like a lake in that direction. I might get my bath, after all."

They were skirting the lava hours later, although the stream was thinner. The lava gave off a constant heat, crackling and popping during its slow conveyor-belt journey down the valley.

Talon scampered toward them. He gave off excited shrieks and pointed.

"Ah!" Ransom said. "The end of the lava trail."

"And water," Scarlett said.

"It's not long until blacklight now. I suggest we ensure we're safe on the right side and find a place to camp. There's no point trying to work out how to release the prince when we can't see what we're doing."

"Makes sense. Do you know how to enter the chamber?"

Ransom sighed. "No idea. I might have to let the prince into my mind to learn more."

"Crap," Scarlett said in an understatement.

12. MOTHER NATURE HAS A TANTRUM

LATER THAT BLACKLIGHT

Ransom rose over Scarlett, his arms holding his weight. He kissed her before repeating the exchange with more force.

"Hard and fast," Scarlett demanded, her tone fierce. "I want to feel your touch tomorrow—on the whitelight. I need to remember this. You. Me. No matter the outcome."

"Yes."

He parted her legs and thrust home. He withdrew and slid back inside her, savoring the bite of Scarlett's fingernails, the glide of his cock into her clinging walls.

"Harder, Ransom. Make me feel good."

He laughed as she clung to him, meeting each of his plunges with a rise of her hips. A gasp. Her fingernails dug deeper, urging him on. Pleasure bubbled through him, growing bigger and better.

"Scarlett," he groaned.

"Yes. Yes. Right there."

The beginning of his orgasm prickled in his balls. It surged, digging deeper before his climax exploded upward, outward, taking him by storm.

Scarlett screamed encouragement, her pussy clutching at his shaft and prolonging his enjoyment. Then, her grip on him eased, and she sighed.

She reached up to draw his head closer and kissed him, slow and deep.

Grata loved this woman and wanted to keep her as his mate. The urge to declare this sentiment rushed through him, yet he withheld the words.

He had no right.

Scarlett groaned and held her head. Her features contorted in an agonized mask.

A long moment later, she breathed again.

Ransom hesitated, worried about speaking, apprehensive about the outcome.

"The prince is stronger," she muttered. "And angry. Or perhaps motivated is a better word. I don't know how you bear having him inside your mind. His mental prodding feels black and oily."

"The perfect description," Ransom said, accepting that he'd go to sleep this blacklight with no barrier to his mind. It sent his stomach roiling because he'd betray Scarlett the moment they opened the prince's chamber.

No, he had no right to express his love for Scarlett. Not when he'd captured her for the prince.

"Are you okay? Did your shield hold?"

Scarlett grimaced. "Yes, but it won't if he gets much stronger."

"We'd better not sleep so close together."

"Like hell," Scarlett said. "You might need me to wake you or help you pull away from him. Make sure he realizes if he kills you, he's screwing himself."

Ransom pulled a face and turned on his side. "I get the sense he's not willing to listen to reason any longer." Sleep was the last thing he wanted. If he could, he'd do without to have more strength to keep the prince at bay.

Scarlett pressed her naked breasts against his back, and he was fiercely glad she couldn't see his expression because he feared she'd glimpse his anguish.

Ransom hated this. If he had to die, he wanted his death to have a purpose. He'd skewer the prince through his rotten heart at the first opportunity.

Ransom closed his eyes after a hard swallow to remove the lump in his throat. He regulated his breaths, keeping them even as he willed his body to relax, his mind to drift. The last thing he did was to clear the protective barrier he'd built to make way for the prince's entry.

The prince exploded into his mind before Ransom had finished his conscious effort to open himself to the royal.

"Why are you traveling in the wrong direction? Who is the third being? I didn't give you permission to bring another. Why are you sabotaging my release?"

Ransom groaned at the pressure in his brain. Hurt. Hurt so bad.

"Answer me!" the prince thundered.

"The volcano is erupting. We had to find a way around the lava river pouring from it since it was too dangerous and wide to cross."

"The third being?"

"Scarlett has a pet."

"A pet?"

"A creature she keeps with her for companionship. It is a harmless animal."

"She will not require a pet when she is with me."

"How do we release you from your chamber?"

"Dig at the statue base. The one in the middle with the pointy hat."

"But the pointy hat—"

"Enough. You will release me on the next whitelight, or you will pay."

Arrogance. Ransom stilled at the rhythmic sucking on his mind that revealed the prince was feeding. His mind grew fuzzy, and he blacked out.

"Ransom. Ransom!"

The familiar voice drew him to the surface, to full wakefulness. His temples throbbed, and he stroked them, his mind full of fog. Unwillingly, he opened his eyes and winced at the bright light searing his eyeballs. His first vision was a slice of heaven—Scarlett's cleavage. The clothing item she called a bra cupped her breasts and lifted them. The red, sheer fabric set off her golden skin and pushed his mind to happier things.

"Frying fungus, Ransom. You've been asleep for ages. I feared the prince had sucked your mind dry."

"I feel as weak as a baby dragon," he muttered, psyching himself to stand.

"Did you learn where the entrance is to his chamber?"

Ransom frowned, searching through his foggy memories for the answers. "He told me the entrance was under the statues. The one with the pointy hat. From what he indicated, the statues are in a line."

"And they're not in a straight row now."

He recalled a bird's head with a cruel beak. He hadn't seen a pointy hat anywhere, but at least four other heads had been strewn around the area. Perhaps more. "No."

"Anything else?"

"He was angry because we backtracked, and he expects us to release him this whitelight without fail. His patience is at an end. And he demanded info about the third being with us. I told him

Talon was your pet."

"And?"

"He advised you wouldn't require a pet once he got his hands on you."

"*Eew!* I bet sex with him is some freaky mind thing, and his dick is the size of this pebble."

"*Haw-haw-haw!*"

Ransom stared at Talon and his display of razor-sharp teeth. The Trolleris's brown eyes shone with amusement. "You're lucky the prince hasn't entered your brain."

"Talon and I have food. Since you were taking a while to wake, Talon hunted. The rabbity-thing is ready to eat."

Ransom fingered her damp hair. "You had another swim."

"I did. Take some of your potion."

When she turned away to rummage through his pack for a potion vial, he spotted her arm. The lumps had increased, and her skin had stretched upward so it bulged outward—two purple-tinted growths. As he stared, they twitched.

"Is your arm sore?"

"It's uncomfortable rather than painful," Scarlett said.

Talon growled as she went to touch the nearest bump, and she jerked her hand away.

"Anyone would think this arm belonged to you," Scarlett snapped. "I'm not touching it, okay? I'm putting on my tunic."

She pulled her black tunic over her upper body, hiding her arm along with her bountiful curves.

"Drink your potion while I carve the rabbity."

Ransom swallowed down the potion and struggled to his feet. He had no idea how long the prince had fed, and that pushed a sliver of worry through him. He'd never faded to black before either. In his mind, he'd always known of the prince's presence.

Hopefully, they'd find the entrance. With most of his focus on the journey here and discovering the prince's whereabouts, he still had no clue how to defeat the prince.

He joined Scarlett and Talon by the fire, grateful for the heat from the flames. The temperature had dropped over blacklight.

"Are you cold?" Scarlett asked.

"Yes. The clouds fell to the mountaintops during the blacklight."

"We call that snow where I come from," Scarlett said. "Pretty at first but most inconvenient."

A shiver slipped through Ransom. He hated the cold.

Scarlett snapped her fingers in front of his face. "Plan?"

"I don't have one for once we get inside the chamber."

"We need a plan. I know. We'll lop off his head. You barricade your mind the best you can, and I'll do the same. We'll break open whatever life support system he's inside and decapitate him before he stands. I'll bet he won't be at full strength until he feeds, and since we're it, we should have a window."

"He has guards," Ransom said.

"Won't they be asleep too?"

"What if they wake when we break open the chamber? That would be the obvious way to protect the royal."

"Bah!" Scarlett slashed her hand through the air. "Stop poking holes in my idea."

"I'm just saying—"

"You're making excellent points," Scarlett said. "But we need a strategy. We can't leave him in his life support because what happens if he's lying, and he still feeds on your people?"

Ransom nibbled a piece of meat, groaned at the juicy, savory flavor, and shoved another piece into his mouth. He swallowed and licked his fingers. "We could toss him in the lava flow."

"Depends on what material his life support pod consists of."

Ransom nodded. "And there's that problem with the guards again."

"We're gonna make up things as we go along. That way lies

disaster."

Ransom grinned at Scarlett's disapproval, the tension at the pit of his stomach lifting a fraction.

"I like to have a plan," Scarlet grumbled. "Goals and charts and a business diagram. I measure the results. Crunch numbers. That is the way to get things done. It stops impulsiveness and unwise decisions." She wriggled, and Talon, who was sitting beside her, snarled. "All right. All right," she muttered, giving the Trolleris a side-eye. "I'm not touching the weird pulsing things in my arm."

"I'll try my com-circle again," Ransom said. "We need help." He pulled the comm from his inside tunic pocket and pushed several buttons before the com-circle crackled and whistled.

"Nothing," Scarlett said. "Who are you calling?"

"My brother."

She frowned. "There are mountains between here and your village. Can I try calling one of my brothers?"

Ransom tossed her the com-circle and ate more meat while she made her call.

"Saber?"

"Scarlett! Where are you?"

"Narenda."

"I know you're on Narenda," Saber said in his scariest voice. "Where on Narenda?"

"Near the volcano."

"Crap, it's erupting."

Scarlett blinked. "You're here?"

"Yes. We—"

"Who is with you? Listen, this is important. Are you getting headaches?"

"Yes, now you mention it. Casey is suffering the worst, though all of us are getting headaches of various degrees. Is the dragon with you?"

"Yes, Ransom, and one other. Before you sleep, make sure you build a barrier around your mind. It's an alien feeding on you. That's how he gets his energy, and he's starving. He's a Maphra. Let me talk to Casey."

Ransom leaned forward, listening intently. Talon appeared to be eavesdropping too.

"Casey, it's a Maphra prince feeding on you. Are you having nightmares too?"

"Crap, my unit and I ran into some of these guys on a different planet. Half of my men died before we worked out what was happening."

"What did you do?"

"Another race—the Elevenoss helped us make a potion. It helps, but doesn't stop the feeding. I grabbed my medical bag. I might be able to make up something to help."

"Feline shapeshifters seem to have an in-built defense. Get every feline with you to build a mental barrier before they go to sleep. I—"

The ground rippled beneath them, their feet riding the wave rippling beneath the surface. Rocks and the sparse plants buckled upward about a hundred meters from them.

"Frying fungus," Casey muttered. "That was a bad one."

"Scarlett, what's going on?" It was Saber again. "Are you okay?"

Scarlett checked for Ransom's reaction, and he nodded.

"Tell him," Ransom said.

"We're about to break a Maphra prince out of stasis and try to kill him before he slaughters us."

"Wait for our arrival."

"We can't. He knows we're here," Scarlett said.

"What's your plan?" Saber demanded.

"We're winging it."

Ransom heard a loud hoot and shocked disbelief coming through his com-circle.

Scarlett grimaced. "Not funny. He's demanding we release him.

He'll have guards, and our assumption is they'll wake when we enter the chamber where they're buried."

"Wait, the guy is underground?"

"Yup. Under a mound of rock with statues guarding the front. We have to find the entrance and dig our way in to release him. That's as far as we've got with our plan."

"We can see the volcano in the distance. We'll start pushing. You and the dragon should carry on, but take your time finding the entrance. Maybe we can overwhelm them with numbers."

"Who is with you?" Scarlett asked.

"Felix, Leo, Sly, and Joe. Sam came along with Casey. Some of Ransom's feline friends too."

Seven with Saber. "You all came," Scarlett whispered.

The comm started to crackle and hiss, the sound dropping in and out.

"Of course...did. We're...brothers."

Another quake shook the ground, the surface bursting closer to them this time. Talon released a snarl as rocks rained down way too close for comfort. She leaped to her feet, as did Ransom.

"What...that?" Saber demanded, his bossiness coming through despite the dropped words.

Ransom would've laughed, but the pressure at his temples darted tendrils of discomfort down the back of his neck.

"Talon, the third in our party," Scarlett said. "We're going now. The quakes are getting worse here."

Ransom groaned and fell to his knees, holding his head. Tendrils of pain speared from his temples, writhing deep—the prince exacting punishment for the delay.

"Frying fungus," Scarlett muttered. "Talk to you soon."

Ransom inhaled, exhaled, attempting to ride out the pain before the prince spoke. A groan squeezed from between his gritted teeth. This...agony. It had never been this bad.

Scarlett's hand settled on his shoulder. "Build your fence again.

Imagine a steel boot and try to kick him out. Tell him we can't help him if he's torturing you this way."

"*Where. Are. You?*" the prince shrieked.

The element of the crazy in the prince had never been so noticeable.

"*Coming. The volcano is creating problems.*"

"*You are not moving to my shelter. I caught the victory in your thoughts,*" the prince thundered. "*You delay so strangers can come to your aid.*"

"*The ground is shaking up here. You must get out of my head so I can function,*" Ransom said.

"*I will lose contact with you,*" the prince said, his voice still accusing but not as loud.

"*Your presence in my head makes me weak. If I'm exhausted, I cannot do the physical labor of digging you out of the rock mound.*"

"*You need not dig. Push the nose on the head statue and a door will open,*" the prince ordered.

"*Why didn't you tell me that earlier?*" Ransom asked, not bothering to hide his sarcasm.

"*I am telling you now. You must come.*" The prince pulled out of his mind with a force that had Ransom's gorge rising. At the last second, he angled his head away from Scarlett and vomited, barely missing Talon.

The Trolleris gave a surprised *eep*, and Scarlett laughed. Talon's eep changed to a toothy growl.

"Don't you snarl at me, you whippersnapper." Scarlett shook her finger at him.

"*Haw-haw-haw.*"

"I'm glad the pair of you think this is funny," Ransom said. "I feel like crap."

Both Scarlett and Talon yanked their shoulders upright, their humor fading.

Scarlett approached him. "Can you stand?"

"I need help."

"The prince is a moron," Scarlett snapped. "What is the point of weakening you so much that you can't stand on your own? At least it should give my brothers a chance to get here."

"The prince knows about your brothers."

"At least he'll have trouble feeding on them. I hope Casey finds a way to keep him out of her head. She's the vulnerable one." Scarlett slipped an arm around his waist.

As soon as she took his weight, he pounced. He dropped her over his arm while still holding her weight. Before her shriek of surprise echoed through their valley, he smothered it with his mouth and kissed her with everything he had.

"Ha! Not quite as weak as I thought," she said.

After an instant of struggle, she relaxed, letting him hold her and master her mouth. Her scent roared through him. He savored her spicy flavor, gloried in her touch. The contact centered him, leaving his panic behind.

With Scarlett in his arms, he felt whole—as if nothing could ever harm them.

Invincible.

Aware of the passing time, he pulled back and held Scarlett until she had her balance.

A smaller quake shook the ground.

"Did I rock your world?" Ransom asked with a sly wink at Talon.

"*Haw-haw-haw.*"

"Hilarious," Scarlett said, pulling a face. "I thought you needed my help. We have a plan—a partial one, at least. Why don't we get moving before the big, scary prince has another tantrum?"

Scarlett was right.

Ransom limped to their fire and doused it with water they'd collected from the nearby stream. With well-practiced speed, they packed away the last of their gear and trekked along the edge of the lava stream. They walked single-file, their pace slower than usual. Only determination got his body around the base of a hill and into the next valley. The view of the volcano and the prince's burial mound was better from here.

Scarlett halted beside him. "Frying fungus," she muttered. "That's bad."

At some stage during the blacklight, a quake had rippled through the area, resettling the heads in different positions. The line of enormous stone blocks they'd seen the previous cycle was no longer visible. The region looked like a playground for giants who hadn't tidied their toys once they'd finished. Added to that, a second stream of lava flowed from the volcano, and unless something else diverted it, the lava would flow through or around the mound of rock and strewn statue heads.

"We need a new plan," Ransom said.

"We could wait until the lava gets him."

"Another quake could easily make the flow change course."

"Yeah." Scarlett frowned at the rocky mound and the many heads lying at different angles.

As Ransom watched her, she lifted her hand to her arm and rubbed it. Talon spotted the infraction and snarled at her. He scampered toward Scarlett and used his sharp claws to clamber up her legs. An instant later, he perched on her shoulder, his nails digging into her arm, judging by the way Scarlett slapped at him.

"Quit digging in your claws, you wee monster," Scarlett snapped, confirming Ransom's supposition.

"Haw-haw-haw."

"Have I ever told you I used to play rugby? When we still lived on Earth." She started walking again as she spoke.

Ransom followed, wondering where this story might lead.

"I was an excellent rugby player. Fast and strong. The coach praised my passing skills, but it was my accuracy kicking the ball that impressed him." She stilled and angled her head to glance at the Trolleris. "You're about double the size of a rugby ball. How far could I kick you?"

Ransom choked back a chuckle as Scarlett and Talon squared off with glares.

"You claw me again, and I swear I'll kick you over that burial mound. A threat and a promise. Are we clear, wee monster?"

Talon lifted and lowered his head several times. A nod of acceptance.

Grudging respect in that nod.

"Let's do this." Ransom set off in determined strides.

They reached the first fallen head, that of a bird with a cruel beak and beady eyes. Up close, it was huge, towering over even Ransom's head.

Some heads were even more prominent.

"It would've taken a lot of effort and planning to position these statues. I got the impression the illness that drove them to take this step happened fast, and they didn't have time to find a cure," Scarlett said.

"That's what I thought. Unless this is a burial chamber where they bring their royal kings and queens."

Scarlett shrugged.

A quake rippled across the ground, and the statue behind Scarlett rocked.

"Watch out!" Ransom shouted.

He grabbed Scarlett and yanked her out of the way. In the nick of time because the head toppled, crashing down a short incline and kicking up a cloud of dust.

"Thanks," Scarlett said.

"Anytime." Ransom caught her close and kissed her hair while ignoring Talon's hiss of disapproval at the rough handling.

"The temperature is rising."

The heat didn't bother Ransom, but beads of sweat had formed on Scarlett's forehead. "Is your arm troubling you?"

"It's itchy."

"Take off your tunic, and I'll check it."

Talon snarled disapproval.

"No, Talon is right. We have to get inside the mound and find the prince. Where do we start?" Scarlett craned her neck. "The biggest stones and statue heads have moved since we first saw them."

"Let's work out a grid in the area where most of the biggest stones are and do a systematic search for the entrance."

"Ooh, goodie. A plan." She patted her chest. "Be still, my heart." *"Haw-haw-haw."*

Ransom laughed at Scarlett's roll of eyes. Wee Talon, as she called him, had a slow-blooming personality.

"Right. Let's spread out and move in this direction. Stay close enough so we can hear each other shout," Ransom suggested.

Talon clambered down Scarlett and scuttled to a position on Ransom's left. Okay, then. He'd thought it'd be a search zone of two but three would hasten the process. Ransom waited until Scarlett was in position and wondered about her arm as she shot Talon a glance and gave it a quick scratch. For some reason, Talon wanted her to treat her arm with care, and not for the first time, Ransom wished his universal translator worked for Talon's language. He'd make sure he and his people added the upgrade if he got out of this alive.

"Ready?" Ransom called with a glance at both Scarlett and Talon. "Keep walking until you come to a head or a base stone. Check each one and move on until you reach the far end of the mound."

The ground shook in another tremor. Small stones clattered and rolled while the larger statue heads vibrated. The rolling shake continued for long seconds, and Ransom fought to stay on his feet.

A rumble came from the volcano, and a loud crashing thump echoed around them. As Ransom turned to the volcano, an entire side of the conical top disintegrated. A wave of red and orange lava bubbled out and over, the force of it no match for the crater rim.

"We need to go faster," Scarlett shouted.

Ransom gave a curt nod and strode forward. He clambered up an incline, checked on and around the first plinth he came to, and moved on. *Phrull*, they'd never find the entrance with all this seismic activity.

Worry bled through him, the concern that no matter what they did, they'd die. If the prince didn't have a tantrum and kill them, the volcano or a quake would do them in. The low-level ache at his temples grew worse as the cycle progressed.

They each finished their grid and started on another one. The gnawing ache at Ransom's temples pushed and ground at his nerve endings until he thought he might vomit again from the pain. As he dragged his tortured body up an incline, his vision went in and out and sweat beaded his brow. With a groan, he heaved himself down the other side and stopped to search around the base of a head. He stared at the statue, finding it difficult to focus. He blinked several times to clear his vision. *Phrull*, even that hurt.

He doubled over, holding his weight on his knees. His legs trembled, and he fell hard on his knees.

"Ransom!"

He swallowed and turned his head toward her, a sense of dread pressing down on him.

Talon reached him first. The Trolleris let out a startled hiss.

"Have you found it?"

Ransom's head hurt so much that he was having trouble forming thoughts.

"Didn't the prince say there was a statue with a pointy hat on top of the entrance stone?" Scarlett pressed her fingers against her temple. "My head has started aching."

Talon growled and held a paw to his furry head. He hummed.

"You too?" Scarlett asked.

Ransom crawled away from where he'd fallen, and immediately, the pain reduced. He kept crawling on his hands and knees until he could form thoughts without his brain threatening to split into two.

Scarlett and Talon followed, although both wore bemused expressions once they caught up with him.

"That's the spot, but my headache got so bad I couldn't form thoughts. How do we enter the chamber with this pain? I don't... I can't function that way."

Scarlett sat beside him and shouldered off her pack. "Between the itching and the ache in my head, I'm finding the going difficult too. What have you got left in your first aid kit? Anything that might help?"

"I have blockers to aid in masking pain, although I don't know if they'll help. They haven't relieved my symptoms much in the past."

"What else?" Scarlett asked.

Talon wobbled closer, his balance challenged on the uneven ground. He sat beside Scarlett and growled when she swiped at her arm to relieve the discomfort.

"What would you have me do?" she snapped at Talon. "It's driving me crazy."

"I have a few medicine vials left that the Elevenoss gave me. Mistress Aelene told me it was stronger and not to use this unless the pain became unbearable." Ransom gasped, the end of the whoosh of air resembling a groan. He held his head and moaned, his thoughts scattered and in turmoil.

"Where are you? Why aren't you coming?"

The prince's whiny splatter-shot words rearranged themselves in Ransom's beleaguered brain.

"We're here but having trouble locating the entrance."

"It's under the statue with the pointy hat," Prince Kalim bellowed.

"The earthquake has made the statues topple. The ground keeps

shaking. Can you not feel the tremors?"

"Hurry, or you will be sorry." Prince Kalim yanked free of his mind, taking none of Ransom's energy.

"The prince?" Scarlett asked.

Ransom lifted his head, stiffening to prepare for more pain. This time, his head remained free from the darting aches. "Yes. I'd say he was panicking."

"He'll have noticed the earth tremors." Scarlett scanned their surroundings. "Where is he going to go? His people will be as hungry as him. There is no one here."

"The logical answer is he'll go to the nearest food source. My people," Ransom said grimly.

"Should we enter the shelter at all?" Scarlett asked.

"We don't know their powers or how long they can last in this state. Although he's determined to get out, we can't trust a word he utters."

Scarlett sighed. "So what you're saying is that we need to get in there and find some way of killing him and his remaining people before they kill us and every other living being on this planet."

13. THE PLOT GOES UNDERGROUND

Scarlett listened to her words and knew the answer before Ransom replied. Somehow, they had to disable the prince and make Narenda safe. If this same situation occurred on Tiraq, Saber and their allies would join forces to end the despot. No matter what the risk to their safety.

She and Ransom, Talon too, could do no less. They couldn't rely on the volcano to do their job for them.

"Where are your potions? How many did you say you have left?" she asked.

"Three," Ransom replied, his expression one big grimace.

"Take one now," Scarlett ordered. "Talon and I can't do this on our own. He's too short for one," she added in an attempt at light relief.

Ransom pulled a vial from his pack, his hand trembling so much

Scarlett feared he'd drop it.

"Let me." Scarlett uncorked the vial and handed it to Ransom. "Down the hatch."

"I don't enjoy taking mystery potions," Ransom grumbled.

"They haven't killed you yet."

Ransom wrinkled his nose and lifted the vial to his mouth. He swallowed the contents with a grimace. "It tastes as disgusting as it smells."

Talon tapped her on the leg and pointed at Ransom's pack. Then he pointed to him and to her. He growled and repeated the action, then mimed drinking.

"You want us to take one too?" Scarlett asked.

Talon nodded, enforcing this with a grunt.

"What do you think?" she asked Ransom.

"It has muted the pain in my head. It's there still, but I'll be able to function. Before...it was difficult to make my limbs work."

"All right," Scarlett said, rapidly deciding. "I'll do it, but mark this, Talon. If I die, you will live in fear."

"Haw-haw-haw."

Scarlett took one vial. She removed the stopper and handed it to Talon. He downed it without hesitation.

Scarlett opened the third vial, sniffed it, and grimaced. It stunk. No getting around that truth.

Talon growled.

"All right. All right. Ugh. It tastes disgusting."

"But it has dulled my headache. The pain struck hard up there. That must be the entrance," Ransom said.

Ransom's voice sounded as if it came through a tunnel, but he was right. Her head was no longer aching as severely.

"Let's do this." And kick Prince Kalim's royal butt, she added silently. Despite Ransom's promises, she'd yet to find any suitable precious stones. "You promised me gemstones," she grumbled as she approached a pointy hat statue.

"There are plenty of stones. Look in any direction, and you'll find them," Ransom said.

"Haw-haw-haw."

"Enough from the cheap seats. This must be the statue the prince mentioned, but which is the base stone?"

"It's close," Ransom muttered. "The pressure at my temples has increased."

Talon growled and pointed at a massive rock on its own.

"Why that one?" Scarlett asked.

Ransom gingerly approached the flat rock. Although it resembled others and smaller rock chunks buried half of it, the area attracted his closer attention. "My head hurts more when I'm near it."

"How do we get into the chamber? Do we dig, or is there a handy lever?" Scarlett asked, studying the oblong rock. Heck, Ransom was right. The pressure on her head—it was like being tortured in a vise. "They wouldn't make the chamber too easy to access. I mean, what if strangers opened it?"

"True."

Talon scampered around the rock and pointed, snaring their attention with one of his growls. He grabbed a smaller rock from the top of the oblong-shaped flat one and pushed it clear.

Ransom helped to shift the massive rock, and Scarlett offered her aid. Now, although her head ached, a barrier muted the pain.

Finally, they shoved the rock away and stared at a small hole.

"For an entrance, it's not big." Scarlett glanced at Ransom. "You and I would have trouble. We'd have to crawl, making us vulnerable to attack from the inside."

Talon growled and thumped his furry fist against his equally hairy chest. He prowled around the flat rock, pushing and poking. He pounced, his growl triumphant.

The rock slid with an ear-wincing grind, opening up a waist-high hole.

Scarlett went to dive through the opening, and Ransom grabbed her. At the same time, Talon bit her on the right calf.

"Slow down," Ransom ordered. "Plans, remember? We don't know if they added a booby-trap or a counter-measure against unwanted intruders."

Scarlett swallowed, a splash of embarrassment heating her cheeks. Ransom and Talon were correct. They needed to approach with caution.

"This must end so I can go home to the resort and have a hot shower and a decent meal," she muttered, keeping her gaze confined to her feet.

"I'd hoped you'd want to come home with me," Ransom said.

"Thanks, but I have plans. Things to do."

"Of course." Ransom's tone was stiff.

She'd hurt his dragon-man feelings. Too bad. They'd had sex. Great sex. No matter what her feline might want or crave, she refused to belong to any man.

"What's the plan now?" Scarlett asked. "I can't keep up. It's continuously changing."

Talon released a tiny growl and scuttled away from them toward the dark hole.

"No, wait," Ransom snapped.

Talon didn't listen. He darted into the entrance.

A silver arrow flew from the darkness. It sailed over Talon's head and barely missed Ransom.

"That would've hit me in the gut, or if I'd been bending down to get inside—"

"You'd be dead," Ransom interrupted. "Talon, take care."

A second and a third silver arrow fired from the dark depths of the chamber. Ransom jumped aside, the arrow lodging in his tunic sleeve. The third one missed.

Scarlett gasped. "Did it get you?"

"Just the fabric of my tunic," Ransom said.

"Do we have a torch? Talon, are you okay?"

A faint growl carried to them.

"I have a lamp. It's in the side pocket of my pack."

"No way are you toting a lamp in there," Scarlett eyed his pack.

"Back right pocket. The lamp is silver."

Scarlett fumbled in the pocket Ransom indicated and produced a silver square. "Where I come from, this isn't a lamp." She handed it over, and Ransom activated a switch.

The lamp illuminated a large area when Ransom directed it at the hole.

"Talon, wait there," Ransom ordered. "We're coming inside." He turned to face her, the hole going dark again because he'd redirected the light.

But before they could move, Talon shrieked and scuttled from the hole. He bounced up and down and slapped his claws at a long, hissing thing that had attached to his fur.

"Snake!" Scarlett backed up so fast, she tripped over a rock and fell on her arse.

Ransom yanked on the animal-creature—whatever it was—and threw it away from the entrance. "It's harmless, but its bite is nasty." Ransom kneeled beside Talon and checked his coat. "You're fine. Your fur is too thick."

"I wonder what other surprises they have in there," Scarlett said. "Did you see the prince?"

Talon shook his head.

"We need to get inside," Ransom said. "Ideas?"

"Well, we know a short-arse like Talon wasn't in danger. What if you and I crawl? We can leave our packs out here. From the glimpse I got, it looks as it only the entrance is low and we should be able to stand once we get as far as Talon did. Are there any more of those snake things?"

"They hide from the light," Ransom said. "As long as we have the lamp, they'll keep away."

173

Scarlett retreated. "I'm not so gung-ho about going in there. Indiana Jones keeps popping into my head."

"Who's Indiana Jones?" Ransom's eyes narrowed to dragon-slits while his body expanded.

Scarlet raised her right hand in a stop motion. "Whoa, dragon-man. You don't have to do the big, scary monster thing. It's a vid series. Entertainment. If you ever visit the resort, I'll treat you to dinner and a vid."

Ransom winced and cupped his aching skull.

"We need to hurry," Scarlett said. "We don't know how long it will take, and if the potion wears off, we're in trouble."

"Shush, someone might be listening."

"Good point. Let's do this." She scratched her arm, and Talon hissed a warning. She ignored him to keep scratching, and he leaped at her with bared teeth. Before she could shake him off, he nipped her. "Ow, you crazy wee demon. I am not the enemy."

"Cut it out. Both of you," Ransom snapped.

"Yes, Dad," Scarlett said, her tone syrupy sweet.

"Haw-haw-haw."

Scarlett stared at the Trolleris with irritation. "Bite me again and I *will* use you for a rugby ball."

"The pair of you are worse than dragon younglings going on their first flight. Not another word from either of you."

"Talon, you go first."

Talon shrank back in clear alarm.

"I'll shine the light to keep the worms at a distance. They won't come near as long as we have illumination," Ransom said.

"What happens if your lamp conks out?"

"It won't," Ransom promised.

Ransom gave Talon a tiny shunt toward the hole and turned on the lamp. Scarlett grinned as Talon peered in cautiously before he edged inside.

Scarlett crawled after Ransom, their progress slow and cautious.

It gave her plenty of time to appreciate the dragon-man's butt and strong legs. She liked him. She liked him a lot, and her feline approved. The problem—she craved independence. She wished to follow her dream. Yes, her brothers' mates all seemed deliriously happy, but each of them had moved to the resort. Each of them had changed their lives to be with their mates.

Scarlett refused to do that, to take a backward step and give up her freedom. Things she'd taken for granted on Earth.

Ahead of her, Ransom rose to his full height. Scarlett used her arms to propel forward and stood beside him.

The area inside the chamber was more substantial than she'd anticipated. Rows of casket-like boxes lined the walls and created aisles. Each was a bright purple color that reminded Scarlett of blueberries.

"Which way?" she asked. "How do we find the prince?"

"It would make sense for him to be toward the rear of the chamber in case someone entered," Ransom said. "Any ideas, Talon?"

Talon shrugged and scampered to the right. He took three or four steps and sank from sight.

Ransom darted closer and thrust his hand into the purple dust pile. He dragged out Talon, who now resembled a purple teddy bear with a big nose. Ransom set him on solid ground, and Talon shook himself.

Scarlett chortled at Talon's ruffled manner, and he turned a glare on her and bared his teeth with a hiss.

Now he reminded her of a pissed toy bear. Her grin widened. "Haw-haw-haw."

Talon marched closer, his glare evil.

Scarlett's smile faded. Talon's big nose twitched, and he sneezed, sending up a cloud of purple dust. He sneezed, again and again, each time raising a cloud of dust.

Finally, he gave a tiny sniff and bared his teeth at Scarlett. He lifted one of his clawed hands and pointed at her trews, which were now black and purple. *"Haw-haw-haw."*

"Look here, you wee growling ball of fluff." She took two steps, and Talon darted behind Ransom.

"Why me?" Ransom muttered. "Attention. Since I'm the only adult present, we're going this way."

"Watch out for traps," Scarlett warned, her head back in the game.

Talon, too, ceased his teasing and took on a serious air.

The three of them crept forward, taking a gap between two rows of purple boxes. Ransom shone the lamp in all directions, and a loud hiss began. Talon scuttled behind Ransom, and Scarlett didn't tease him. The hissing set her nerves jangling. She spotted hundreds of the creatures Ransom had called worms. These were various shades of purple, unlike the one that had attached itself to Talon.

"Why is everything purple in here?" she asked. "Purple used to be my favorite color, but those boxes are giving me the creeps."

Talon squeaked several times, his head bobbing, so she figured he agreed. *Agh!* Her arm. The itching was driving her crazy.

Talon growled at her. *Frying fungus!*

"You'll make an excellent parent," Scarlett commented. "You have eyes in the back of your head."

"Stop bickering," Ransom snapped. "Quiet! Can you hear that?"

Scarlett scratched her arm and didn't care if Talon snarled. She shouldn't have trusted those insect-men. The man who'd bitten her had left something behind, and Talon was in on the secret. It was frustration to the *nth* degree because she couldn't even interrogate the wee beastie.

She angled her head and discerned a faint bubbling.

"A gurgling sound." She plucked at her tunic, which was sticking to her torso. "It's getting hotter in here."

"Yes." Ransom wiped his hand across his sweaty brow.

"Is that lava we can hear?"

"I hope not." Ransom's tone suggested he thought otherwise. "Wait. I'll expire of this heat if I don't strip off my tunic."

"Ooh! Wonderful idea." Scarlett peeled off her tunic. She tied it around her waist for easy access. Her arm. Frying fungus, it itched. She turned to the light cast by the lamp and swore. "Talon, you wee beastie. What did that Quito man put in my arm?"

"Let me look," Ransom said.

His touch was gentle as he turned her a fraction to study the two bulging purple swellings. They pulsated and jiggled. *Creeeepy*. Her preternatural senses preached danger, and every foreign sound made her start. She loathed this underground prison and couldn't wait to flee.

"Is it painful?"

"No, but they're uncomfortable."

"Talon, come here," Ransom spoke in a no-nonsense tone, reminding Scarlett of her oldest brother.

Talon trotted over, his expression innocent. A pity his eyes betrayed him. Their shrewd intelligence indicated he had answers.

"Will these injure Scarlett?"

Talon waggled his head.

"Will they grow bigger?"

Talon again did a negative shake.

"Should I dig them out?"

Talon shook his head harder and swelled in size.

"Scarlett, can you bear the discomfort until we leave this chamber? I'll dig them out for you then."

Talon didn't make a protest at this decision, so she nodded. She glanced around and whispered, "What's our plan when we find the prince? If he's expecting a kiss from his true love to awaken him, one of you can do it."

"Haw-haw-haw."

Ransom chuckled. "What Talon said. You guys ready to move again?"

Scarlett gave her upper arm a sly itch. "Let's do this."

She trailed Ransom, and as they rounded a corner, the bubbling became louder, the heat higher.

"Not this way." Scarlett halted beside Ransom.

The entire wall of the chamber glowed orange and red. Trickles of lava ran down the wall.

"We'll backtrack." Ransom held his head as if it was aching.

Scarlett squeezed his arm. "Shore up your mental barriers. Make it difficult for him to get into your mind."

"It's hard to concentrate."

"You can do this. Don't let him win."

They retreated and hurried in the other direction, forging a path through the stacks of purple boxes. Something—maybe a quake—had toppled the top layer of boxes. One lay in the way, the lid open.

"It's a body," Scarlett said. "Or what remains of one. The box isn't big. A child?"

Ransom lifted it out of the way, and they moved onward, following a lit path through the warren of stacked boxes. In the distance, a faint light glowed.

"Where is the prince's security force?" Scarlett asked.

"Don't jinx us. They might spring at us from the next corner."

"Hmm, an excellent point."

They slowed their pace and trod with caution. Heat still radiated through the chamber but not as bad as it had been near the wall of lava. Scarlett's gaze traveled back and forth, each of her senses attuned to her surroundings. A faint hum sounded. Scarlett grasped Ransom's forearm and squeezed.

"I hear it," he murmured. "How is your head?"

"The pressure at my temples is increasing."

"Mine too," Ransom whispered.

The area between the stacks of boxes—coffins—widened, and she stepped up beside Ransom. Talon pushed between them, his clawed hands gripping both their legs.

One box sat on a raised dais. This one was clear, and she glimpsed something purple inside.

"What do we do?" Scarlett asked, studying the buttons on the box's side.

Before Ransom could answer or they'd discussed the situation, Talon darted forward and clambered up a set of steps she hadn't noticed.

"Talon, no!" Ransom shouted.

Ransom took half a step forward as did she, but it was too late. Talon's clawed hands slapped buttons, and the lid of the box lifted.

Scarlett shared a glance with Ransom, and he shrugged.

"Might as well see what's inside," he said.

Talon growled and jumped back. He sidled up to Scarlett and clung to her leg. Funny, the wee monster snapped and snarled and teased her, yet expected protection in return.

Before they could peer into the box, a purple form sat up. He was bald with a delicate nose and ears. Silvery whorls and a design of snaking curves covered half of his face. A wide yawn displayed a set of pointy teeth, much like the ones of the Elevenoss race. The man wore a purple cloak trimmed with what appeared white feathers. Apart from that, he was naked. He stretched and turned to glare at them.

"You took long enough!"

The imperious voice was one she'd heard before. The time he'd tried to force his way into her head and failed.

Skinny purple arms raised, stretched, and the prince stabbed another button. The side lowered, and shiny steps emerged with a whirr. He plopped a glittering crown on his head, then stood and wobbled a fraction before he gained his balance. He lifted his head and descended the stairs to stand before them.

"You brought the woman. Excellent." His gaze raked her, and he sniffed. "She will do to restart my population."

"I refuse to let that little dick near me." The purple prince didn't even come up to her hip.

"Scarlett," Ransom warned.

She sent him a side-eye. *No way!* She leaped at the prince and had a moment of satisfaction as the purple being's eyes widened. He raised his hands as if to hold her off, and in the next instant, she froze in position, unable to move her limbs. "Let me go, you purple moron."

"Ah, excellent. A feisty one. The crying females are no fun."

"Release her," Ransom thundered, taking a giant, intimidating step forward. "Grata!" The prince had frozen him too. "This is the way you treat those who've come to release you from your prison?"

Scarlett forced back her panic. At least Talon couldn't growl at her for scratching. A thought occurred. "Where are your people?"

"All gone," the prince said without a trace of concern.

"Where?" Scarlett blurted. Had each purple box contained a body rather than a man or woman ready to awaken?

The prince waved his hand as if it were of no consequence. "They made the ultimate sacrifice."

Ransom's facial muscles formed a frown. "The ultimate sacrifice?"

"They fed me when I required food." His tone was matter-of-fact as if it was no big deal that every single one of his people was dead. "Why did you bring him? I have no use for a youngling. I can't feed on him because his brain is underdeveloped."

Talon cowered, acting the ninny, and Scarlett narrowed her eyes at his odd behavior. She glanced at Ransom, relieved she could move her head at least. If they could figure out how to break free, they could take this little purple squirt without breaking a sweat.

Scarlett willed Ransom to glance her way so she could attempt to communicate her plan. The lava heated the chamber, and the temperature had risen since they'd entered. Somehow, they'd best His Royal Purpleness and get the hell out of here.

Meantime, they'd keep him talking. He gave off pompous vibes—a man who enjoyed hearing himself talk.

"What did you mean you don't like the crying ones?" Scarlett asked. What was Talon doing? The wee beastie had a plan. She could tell. So, she'd do her bit and distract the prince.

"His mother." Prince Kalim jerked his head in Ransom's direction.

Shock blasted over Ransom's features.

Damn. What had she blundered into with her nosy questions?

"What are you talking about?" Ransom demanded. "My mother died."

"Yes," the prince said. "Rotations ago, I captured your father's mind. I was initially cautious because my advisors couldn't predict how their trap would work on a dragon. We knew it killed the Elevenoss race, but dragons are stronger in mind."

Scarlett glanced at Ransom and understood the glassy shock in his eyes. He wasn't up to yanking answers from the purple moron but she could. He hadn't mentioned his mother, and she'd assumed she must've died when Ransom was a child.

"How did you capture Ransom's mother?" she asked.

"I wanted a breeding female. Our women are few, and our scientists failed to discover a method to make women in our labs." The prince stretched his arms and paced, seemingly enjoying an audience.

Scarlett bit back her urge to order him to get them out of this chamber, or it'd become their burial site. Did he not sense impending danger? Hear the pop of the rocks in the distance? Feel the rising temperature in the chamber? Instead, she forced herself to deliberate before voicing her questions. Nothing too confrontational. She needed to pull answers from him, and the second Talon did whatever he intended to do and freed them, she'd kick the prince's skinny purple butt.

No way, no way was he getting that little purple dick near her. Heck, perhaps it was a remnant of previous rotations, and the Maphra race didn't use them.

"How did you get Ransom's mother?" she asked.

"I did a deal. Baron Drake could continue to feed me or give me his wife. He didn't value her much." Prince Kalim tut-tutted. "I liked her fine until she started weeping. Cry. Cry. Cry. That's all she did. She made me lose my temper. Before I knew it, I'd sucked her dry to shut her up. Unfortunately, I'd kept my word and released your father's mind. A mistake I won't make again."

The prince ceased his pacing and turned to stare at Ransom. "I've learned much while my body has slept." He tapped his head. "The knowledge of generations of my people resides here. I have survived despite—in spite—of our enemies, and now with you, beautiful Scarlett, I shall repopulate this planet. We will build our empire on the dragon's backs. Their hard work shall be our gain."

Pompous, much! Scarlett glared at Ransom when he started to refute the prince's plans.

Talon climbed up her leg, his sharp claws digging into her flesh. She ripped her gaze off the prince to remonstrate, but he shook his shaggy head and made a shushing gesture with his clawed hand.

"How will you do that?" Scarlett asked. "They will fight you."

"They won't see me coming," the prince boasted. "You are under my control. We shall travel to the dragons. I can skim the brain energy to remain alive and contain my powers. Nothing will stop me."

"Me. I will stop you," Scarlett snapped. "You can't force me to breed your offspring."

"You have sentimental feelings for this dragon." Prince Kalim had resumed pacing, but he paused to point an accusing finger in Ransom's direction. "I'm not stupid. He thinks he loves you.

Mawkish, sentimental rubbish."

He loved her? Something inside her melted at the knowledge, and she closed her eyes to savor the warmth that filled her. She opened them to glance at Ransom. It was easy to tell his brain was busy. Her feline stirred beneath her skin. *Ah!* Could she shift and force her body out of this frozen spell?

"Bah!" The prince glowered at her in distaste. "I shall order the dragons to build a lab where I shall harvest your eggs."

"Well, that's a relief," Scarlett muttered, flexing her feline and relaxing her guard.

A sharp crack echoed in the distance, and a metallic lava scent drifted their way. It reminded her of the odor produced when she made her jewelry, and it was much closer now. Frying fungus, one of them had to do something. *Now.*

14. Yes, Your Majesty

No! The prince was lying. The shock had Ransom's mind blanking. *No.* His father had possessed integrity. He was sure of it. The same honor and valor Ransom tried to use in ruling their clan. Gryffnn ruled in his stead with the same boldness and fairness. His father wouldn't have acted that cowardly. Then he glanced at Scarlett, caught her sympathetic reaction. She believed the prince. His gaze went to Talon, and the Trolleris's brown eyes held the same sorrow and compassion.

Turmoil bubbled through Ransom's mind. Grata, could it be true? His mother? Had his father used her to save his own skin? Ransom thought back. He'd been a youngster still, but this explained so much. The mood swings in his father. The changes. His father's lack of patience and harshness. And his mother. One cycle, his mother had been there and the next...

As a child, he'd assumed she'd gone to her room since she'd never been strong, especially after the birth of his sister. Servants had whispered. He'd recalled that, but he'd never attended a funeral.

His father had changed after his mother's death. Later, as an adult, Ransom had told himself he'd mourned his lost wife. He also recalled the elders reiterating the unspoken laws about flying boundaries. None of them were to go into or near the mountains. While he and his friends had tested the limits, they'd never flown too close. The tolerance they'd obtained from working with the smaller stones to produce their jewelry had been enough to keep them safe. The prince hadn't gained control of his mind until he and Nanu had crashed in the mountains.

Was the prince telling the truth? One or two of the older warriors were still alive. They might know. His father's papers were the other option. He'd never gone through them—hadn't wanted to pry into his parents' private matters. Ransom swallowed. If he survived...

Grata! How could his father have traded his safety for that of his wife? He'd given her to the prince. Then, a truth struck him.

A horrifying one.

Who the hell was he to judge?

He'd followed in his father's footsteps, capturing Scarlett to offer in exchange for the safety of his people.

He'd done the same phrullin' thing.

While his parents' marriage had been one of convenience between clans, Ransom had lucked out and found a woman who completed him. One his dragon adored. Strong and mouthy and courageous. Scarlett would go down fighting at his side.

He glanced up again and met Scarlett's gaze. She winked at him. Winked! And despite, their lack of verbal communication, he could practically hear her probable words. *We'll kick his royal purple butt.*

Scarlett would fight to the end, and he could do nothing less. There was still time to fix this, to do the right thing and act with honor.

Think.

The loudest crack yet reverberated within the chamber. Talon hissed. Scarlett's eyes rounded. Ransom's best guess—the wall no longer contained the lava.

"The volcano is erupting again," Scarlett snapped. "If we don't get out of here, we'll all die."

"You speak falsehoods. I do not believe your trickery."

Ransom blinked. The prince might have magical powers, but he was an idiot.

"Go and look," Ransom said. "We can't go anywhere. That way. Walk toward the popping and cracking rocks."

"I can't hear anything," the prince said.

Scarlett shot him a side-eye while Talon's nose twitched several times.

"We will leave the chamber," the prince announced. "I would see this volcano that worries you so much. One at a time. You." He flicked his fingers at Ransom. He repeated the action, and illumination spilled into the chamber.

Ransom found himself able to move. Hesitating, he sought Scarlett's gaze, but she remained frozen in place.

"Go," she said. "Hurry."

Ransom nodded and strode from the center of the chamber. He glanced over his shoulder, saw the prince tottering after him, and increased his pace. Once they reached the intersection, Ransom glanced to his right. Grata! Scarlett was right. The lava had broken through and was crawling in their direction. Thankfully, the flow was a trickle, but that could change.

"This is the exit. Go back for Scarlett before she gets trapped. I promise not to leave. Where would I go? You control my mind. I can't escape."

The prince nodded. "Very well. Wait outside at a safe distance. We will be with you soon."

Ransom dived through the chamber entrance, furious at his helplessness. *Think!* His dragon roared, almost deafening him. *Of course!*

Ransom summoned his dragon, mentally stronger now that he had a strategy. The instant Scarlett crawled from the chamber, he'd let rip with his fire. He'd toast the phrullin' prince before the Maphra royal knew what had hit him.

"I hope you have a plan," Scarlett whispered to Talon who perched on her shoulder. "His purpleness is cray-cray."

"*Haw-haw-haw.*"

"Yup," Scarlett said. "Shifting might break through this spell."

Talon released an urgent growl and batted her head with his claws.

"I'll take that as a no. Someone's coming," she whispered.

Her pulse raced, each crack and groan of the walls shoving a new wave of fear through her. She didn't want to die this way.

The prince appeared, his breathing harsh. This exertion was taxing his physical body. He should reconsider if he expected them to carry him down the mountain. Given the opportunity, she'd kick his purple arse and cheer if he rolled.

"Quick." The prince waved his hand at her, and she could move her limbs again. "Don't try anything stupid."

Scarlett ran toward the prince while Talon clung to her shoulder.

"Leave your pet. He is slowing you," the prince ordered.

"Talon is coming with me." She raced past the prince, dodging the stacks of coffins to follow the same path Ransom had walked earlier. Even in her human form, she deciphered his scent trail. Sweat beaded on her brow, the heat from the lava flow more intense now. Tiny flames licked some coffins, the rancid scent catching at her throat. Smoke curled toward the roof of the chamber in black spirals.

Scarlett coughed and increased her speed, almost knocking

Talon off her shoulder. He growled and dug his claws into her shoulders. "Ouch."

Talon growled again.

"Leave the beast," the prince ordered from behind them.

"He is my pet," Scarlett snapped, slowing to allow Talon to regain his balance. "I refuse to leave him in danger."

Talon purred into her ear. Scarlett just bet he bore a toothy smirk. *Wee monster.*

The entrance lay ahead. Scarlett could see the brighter light. The cracks and creaks from the wall were constant now as the pressure of the lava increased. Once the chamber gave way, lava would engulf the space.

"Hold on, Talon," she whispered and increased her pace.

"Don't leave me behind," the prince complained.

Scarlett ran faster, darting around stacks of coffins and jumping over one that toppled. The wall of the chamber to their left exploded, and lava pushed through.

Talon snapped and snarled in her ear, but she didn't bother with a reply. The exit was ahead. She kept running and hurdled a fallen box. The metallic stench of lava was heavier in the air, the crackle and pop bringing an ominous warning. Something crashed behind them, and the prince shouted, but Scarlett paid no heed. She dived out of the entrance hole and crawled on her hands and knees until she was in the whitelight.

Talon released a warning growl, and she jumped to her feet.

A huge dragon sat waiting. Ransom. His gaze remained on the hole, and Scarlett translated the situation without the need for words. She darted to the side and out of the way.

The prince popped out of thin air, right in front of the hole. Ransom reacted with a stream of flames. The heat of them seared her cheeks.

Then the flames froze in mid-air. The second flick of his purple fingers immobilized Ransom in his dragon form.

"I should kill you for that," the prince shouted. He swaggered over to Ransom and kicked one of Ransom's legs.

It must've hurt because the prince limped as he railed at Ransom.

"Haw-haw-haw." Talon smothered his chuckle against Scarlett's ear.

Scarlett sneaked closer. If she could jump him from behind, she might escape those magical, flicking fingers of his.

At the last moment, the prince turned, sensing the rear attack. He froze her in position.

He turned to Ransom. "You, dragon. You will fly us to your home."

"He can't fly. Not since you put him in a coma and started feeding on him."

"You lie," the prince said.

"Release him. Let him show you. He can't fly any longer. You'll have to walk if you want to get off this mountain." Scarlett didn't hide her satisfaction at informing the prince of this.

A high-five for consequences.

"I don't believe you." The prince waggled his fingers at Ransom and Ransom's dragon fire spewed across the mouth of the chamber. "Fly."

Ransom shifted to his humanoid form. "I can no longer fly."

The prince stomped one purple foot. "Transform back. You are lying."

"Give him a demo," Scarlett suggested.

"All right. But stand clear. I have little control."

"Excellent advice. I do not wish my traitorous queen to get injured before she provides me with offspring. Stand beside me and behave. If you disobey me in this, I shall punish you." The prince was so matter-of-fact, she believed him.

"I will obey," she said, adding in her mind, *as long as it suits me.*

The prince surveyed the area and frowned. "I did not believe

189

the volcano would do this much damage. Come, stand clear of the entrance." He turned to Ransom. "Fly."

"I can't," Ransom said.

"Fly."

With a shrug, Ransom shifted to a dragon.

He moved to a flat area and started running and flapping his wings. He rose into the air to a height of perhaps her shoulders before crashing to the ground again, despite his wings flapping. The ground shook as Ransom struck hard.

"But how will we get off the mountain?" the prince asked again.

Scarlett wanted to punch him, but it was essential to keep her mobility and await her chance. "How long have you been in the chamber?"

"Over one hundred rotations," the prince said. "My scientists are—were brilliant. It was a pity they had to make the ultimate sacrifice.

Scarlett eyed the prince with distaste. How the devil did he expect to survive without his advisors? Or collect her eggs? Prince Kalim had not made wise decisions, yet he didn't understand the danger his selfishness had caused. The man was an idiot.

The prince turned to Ransom. "Perhaps you can carry me. Yes, that should work well."

The itching on her upper arm was driving her crazy. Talon growled in warning, once again against her ear to keep the prince from hearing.

The prince sauntered closer to Scarlett, and she flinched at the masculine appreciation in his dark eyes. She bit back a snarl and wished she'd taken the time to don her tunic instead of giving him skin to ogle.

Talon ceased hugging her head and moved down her shoulder and arm. The claws on his feet scrabbled across the two itchy spots, and she almost groaned at the relief.

The purple prince leered at her breasts, which were showcased in her favorite sexy bra. Frying fungus, she would've packed sports bras if she'd known she'd need to run around mountains and face an ogling prince.

The prince walked a slow circle around her, ignoring the ominous rumble of the volcano. Something was off with his hearing.

Scarlett shared a quick glance with Ransom, who remained in his dragon form. The ground rumbled beneath their feet.

Prince Kalim halted when he faced her again and planted his hands on his skinny hips, his legs asunder. "With you as the mother of my children, we will conquer this planet, although—" He peered at her arm, the scrapes and bruises on her torso and screwed up his face in distaste. "You will require cleansing and delousing before we begin. Medical treatment and the like."

The things on her arm were wriggling and vibrating worse. She wanted to dig in her fingernails and itch, itch, *itch*. Scarlett glanced at her arm, her eyes rounding. They were—

Talon sliced his claws along the base of the raised areas. Two black missiles shot straight from her arm and dived into Prince Kalim's chest.

Scarlett gaped, shock rooting her to the spot. The prince screamed and clawed at his pectoral muscles, but whatever those things had been in her arm, they'd drilled inside him.

Talon growled a warning, and Scarlett backed over to Ransom. Seconds later, the prince exploded, his shrill scream of fear and pain echoing loud enough to rival the grumbling volcano.

Scarlett squeezed against Ransom's dragon chest, staring in amazement as bits of purple goop rained down from the sky. The insect things had disappeared—or died, perhaps.

"Is that it? Did the prince... Is he gone?" Scarlett whispered and stared at the bloody wounds where the itchy protuberances had been. A slow trickle of blood ran down her arm, but her feline was already healing the site. "I'm not itchy anymore."

"Haw, haw, haw," Talon said.

The ground rumbled under their feet again, a long, rolling, ominous tremor.

"We should leave," Scarlett said. "I don't like the look of that volcano."

Talon let out a low growl and scampered over to her, holding out his furry arms in a demand for her to pick him up. As she situated him on her shoulder, her gaze settled on the volcano in time to see the entire side give way.

"Ransom," she shouted.

A river of lava swept over the side, much bigger and faster than the flows they'd already seen.

"Run!" Scarlett shouted. Frying fungus, they weren't going to make it.

Ransom bellowed and hunched down. *"Quick, get on my back."*

The words formed in her mind, and she never hesitated, forgetting about dignity and scrambling up on Ransom.

Already, radiant heat emanated from the fast-approaching lava river. Flames danced across the surface, and the rocks sizzled and popped.

Talon issued an alarmed squeak when he fell, but he saved himself by digging his claws into her calf. Then, he climbed up her torso, monkey-fashion.

Ransom ran, and she and Talon thumped against his scaled side. His wings flapped, but he didn't lift off, just kept fleeing.

Scarlett glanced over her shoulder. The lava had already reached the chamber and engulfed several fallen statue heads. She checked the terrain, and her heartbeat stuttered. They were approaching a cliff. Her gaze returned to the lava.

They were gonna die.

15. FLY, DAMMIT. FLY!

T he heat radiating from the lava increased. Ransom sprinted toward the cliff. He flapped his wings, but nothing happened. *Grata, death beckoned from every angle.*

Knifing pain writhed through his temples. Instinctively, he blocked, closing down his dragon side. He stumbled, heard Scarlett's cry as she slipped. At the last minute, she righted herself. Behind the mental barricade he'd erected, his dragon snarled and aimed fire at his cage.

Ransom ran. He hurtled toward death as the fiery lava heat burned his back.

His dragon burned through his mental fence, and the burst of unrelenting pain had him running blind. When his vision cleared, he was two strides short of the cliff.

Then, it was too late.

Gravity hurled his big body over the edge.

Scarlett's scream rippled with fear, with panic. It prodded him. *Do something.* He was better than his father.

Fly. Fly, dammit.

He flapped his wings, attempting to slow their plunge. His dragon side hollered at him.

Fly!

The ground grew closer. Grata, he didn't want to die. He wanted to claim Scarlett and live a peaceful life. He lifted his wings and forced them back down. While his brain understood the process, it refused to fire and communicate with his body.

"Fly, Ransom. Fly," Scarlett screamed.

He repeated the up-and-down flap of his wings. Had he slowed? He got a rhythm going. Up. Down. Up. Down.

Yes! Their drop was slowing.

He forced his wings to move faster, and their steep descent flattened out.

"That's what I'm talking about!" Scarlett shouted. "You've got this."

Ransom wasn't so sure. The ground seemed to be approaching at a dizzying speed, and he forced himself to focus, to soar like a bird. To fly.

His dragon shoved at his mind, grasping for complete control. A dominant roar filled his mind, blasting him with a show of temper.

Suddenly, Ransom understood. He blanked his mind and yielded.

Their crazy free-fall became a controlled dive.

His dragon leveled out their screaming speed and angled upward. They slowed and whizzed over the heads of a leap of black leopards. Onward, they flew, their descent down the valley controlled and more leisurely, until in the distance, Ransom spotted their spaceship and another larger one parked beside it.

The *Indy*.

His friends had come.

Ransom allowed his dragon to land them before saying a silent thank you. *"We can join again now,"* his dragon said. *"We will be strong again. Better together. So tired."*

"I understand. I didn't before."

"Need rest."

"And food," Ransom said.

Scarlett slid down his side and landed with Talon perched on her shoulder. She bent and kissed a red rock.

"Haw-haw-haw."

"You thought we'd die. Admit it, you wee monster."

While they argued back and forth, Ransom shifted. This transformation was sluggish and slower than average, but long moments later, he reformed into a humanoid.

"Are you all right?" he asked Scarlett.

"That was a rush," she said, her eyes bright and golden. "Terrifying. A journey of many days in several panicked minutes."

"Yes." An understatement.

Scarlett turned to stare in the direction they'd come from. "Waves of lava are pouring over the cliff. Did I see my brothers, or did I imagine them? I was so busy clinging, I didn't take in much scenery."

"It looked as if your brothers had joined forces with my friends," Ransom said. "It will take them perhaps two cycles to return, even if they push their speed."

"Excellent. Time to recover and perhaps fossick for precious stones. I didn't see a single gemstone on that mountaintop, and you promised."

"I lied," Ransom admitted.

Scarlett sniffed. "I know, but I understand. Promise me you'll never lie again, and we're good. It can't have been easy learning about your father and how he handed over your mother to save himself."

"After having that purple monster inside my head, I can

sympathize, but he could've found another way. He would've wanted to save as many of the tribe as he could. At least, I hope that figured into his assessment of the danger."

"I hope they have food on their ship because our remaining supplies are still up there on the mountain," Scarlett said.

"We can leave a note and fly to my clan."

"If it's all the same to you, I'd prefer to leave my next bout of flying for a while." A shudder raced through her. "I thought we would die."

"Haw, haw, haw."

"Silence, you wee beastie. Your claws have left marks on my shoulders, and they're throbbing. Your terror marked me. Don't deny it."

"How is your arm?"

Scarlett frowned at it. "Still weeping. Once we find something to eat, I'm going to shift. Then, sleep. We can both sleep knowing our dreams will be pleasant, and any nightmares will be of our own making."

Ransom nodded. "I left a few cans of stew in my ship because the shrink-food you purchased was lighter. We can eat that now."

Soon, they were feasting on mystery meat with gravy. While the stew didn't come close to rivaling the shrink-food, it was hot and filling. All three of them ate a hearty meal.

"Could we use the ship radio to contact my brother?" Scarlett asked. "To tell them we're back at the ship?"

"Excellent idea. My com-circle is under the lava."

"I'm just glad it's not us," Scarlett said, following him to the ship's bridge.

He pushed several buttons and scanned his hand. The controls came alive with lights.

Scarlett put through the call.

"Scarlett?" a male voice demanded.

"Yes, Saber. It's me. We're at the ship."

"You couldn't have flown down before we started this long trek?" No mistaking his tone for anything except testy.

"No, it's a long story, and we'll give you the details on your return."

"It will take us at least two days to reach your position," Saber said.

"That's okay. We're exhausted. Bruised and battered. We could do with a rest."

"Scarlett?" Ransom called from the doorway.

"Gotta go," Scarlett said. "Thank you for coming. We'll see you soon."

"We have visitors," Ransom said once Scarlett ended her call.

"Who?"

"The Elevenoss. Talon has gone to greet them."

"I wonder what they want."

Ransom reached for her hand and twined their fingers together, every particle of him wanting to show ownership in case one of those handsome Elevenoss males thought to flirt with her.

"Steady," she murmured. "No need to growl."

Ransom blinked and closed down the possessive growls coming from his dragon side.

When they reached the Elevenoss delegation, Daenys stepped forward and bowed. "You are alive. Excellent news."

Talon spoke in a series of clicks and screeches, and Daenys grinned.

"He tells me you are heroes."

Talon uttered something else and laughed. *"Haw, haw, haw."*

Daenys spluttered, her grin widening while the rest of her group chuckled.

"What's so funny?" Scarlett asked.

"You cannot communicate with Talon?"

"No," Ransom said. "Our translators do not compute his language."

"Ah, I will fix that for you." Daenys murmured a chant, then clicked her fingers. "He says your insults to the prince were funny. You told him he had a small purple dick."

"I might have done that," Scarlett said. "He had a wee-man complex."

Daenys chortled. "Thanks to you and the dragon, plus Talon and the Quito race, we are rid of him and his greed. We can once again live in peace in our original homelands."

Ransom thought about asking them how they traveled through time before deciding he didn't wish to know. "What about the volcano?"

"Talon says it is not near our lands. Now that the prince is dead, I believe the resonance in the mountains will fade if it hasn't already. Both of our races should be safer now." Daenys turned to one of her men, and he presented her with two bags. "I understand you are both gifted jewelers. We wished to give you a small token of our thanks."

Ransom accepted one bag and Scarlett the other.

"If you wish to visit or to trade or exchange services, you are welcome to visit," Ransom said.

"Likewise," Daenys said. "We will contact you once our people settle in our homelands again."

Talon interrupted with clicks, and this time Ransom understood his meaning.

"Talon wishes to go with us," Daenys said. "But he would visit with your people at a later time. He says you amuse him."

"Haw, haw, haw," Scarlett said with bared teeth.

Talon beamed and scampered over to her. He indicated he wished her to crouch and signaled the same to Ransom. They kneeled beside each other and leaned down a fraction. Talon rubbed his giant nose against Ransom's, then stood back and did the same to Scarlett.

"Haw-haw-haw." Talon chortled and lifted one clawed hand in

farewell. "I like them. They have great courage," he told one of Daenys's party.

"We will see you again." Daenys bowed before following her people to their ship.

"I will miss Talon," Scarlett said. "Although his sly humor irked me. I wonder what is in these bags? Oh! Ransom, look." She held up a raw stone that glinted blue. "These are beautiful. There is a mixture of stones. I haven't seen anything of the like during my fossicking."

The pale blue stones reminded him of the lakes they'd passed deep in the mountains.

"Customers will pay high prices for pieces made of these," Scarlett murmured.

She was right. Ransom yawned. "I don't know about you, but I intend to hit the sanitizer room and get some sleep."

"Oh, yes," Scarlett agreed. "You go first. I'd do a quick shift. Hopefully, it will help my aches and pains."

A short time later, Ransom stretched out on his gel-bed, his mind light and ache-free. The weighty worry about the prince—the wondering if he might or might not appear, had gone, leaving his mind to wander.

"Shift over," Scarlett said.

Ransom squeezed closer to the wall to make room for Scarlett.

"What will you do now?" she asked as she squeezed her naked body close to his.

"I was hoping you'd come with me," Ransom said.

Scarlett lifted on her elbow and offered him a gentle smile. "I thought you understood. This was a temporary fling. A vacation before I start my business. I have a plan and a set of steps to reach my goals. I'm so close to gaining independence. Staying with you would be a backward step."

Ransom opened his mouth, but only a croak emerged. They were mates, but she didn't feel the same way as him. He swallowed to lubricate his dry throat. "Talon is right about your courage. You will succeed at whatever you attempt."

"Thanks." Scarlett grinned at him. "Now, all I need to do is to persuade my family to give me the freedom to follow my dreams. We should celebrate. Are you too fatigued for sex?"

"Not too tired." Ransom swallowed again. Scarlett was right. A celebration to reconfirm they were alive. And if he couldn't have Scarlett, at least he'd have this short time and his memories. It wasn't as if he deserved to win her love and loyalty.

Scarlett leaned over him and licked his lips, unlocking his beast. Ransom rolled her beneath him in one fast move. He plundered her mouth, cajoling her groans and passion to the surface. He savored the rub of her breasts against his chest and set about teasing her into desperation. A nip at the base of her neck did the trick. She pressed closer. Her legs curled around his hips.

"Now," she demanded.

"Not yet."

He skimmed her breasts with his hands, tantalizing but not giving the pressure he'd learned she enjoyed. A nip at her hip. A lick along the fold of her thigh and torso. Ransom parted her legs and traced her slit with one finger. Her delicate scent filled his nostrils while her folds glistened in the faint light. He allowed himself a quick taste, a swirl of his tongue across her clit.

Scarlett tugged on his hair, stirring restlessly under his ministrations.

"Now," she ordered in a bossy demand, then did some nipping of her own.

Her sharp bite at his pectoral muscle reverberated right through him and acted as a prod to his cock. He groaned when she repeated her nip.

"Scarlett," he whispered, urgency raging and pushing his pulse rate to a frantic race. He guided his shaft to her.

"Yes," she whispered, lifting her hips in an invitation.

He thrust, driving into her heat while releasing a hiss of pleasure. "You feel amazing."

"Of course." She laughed. "Now, make me come."

"You're a bossy woman. I prefer to follow my inclinations." Ransom pulled back and slid home in one smooth motion.

"If I tell a man what I want, and he follows some of my directions, I get to enjoy myself," Scarlett whispered. "If I leave it up to my sexual partner, I'm often disappointed."

"You haven't met the right man," Ransom said. "I don't require direction."

Scarlett rocked her lower body, taking him deeper. "Perfect. Do that again."

Ransom laughed. "Let's do this my way. I'm the one on top."

A snort escaped Scarlett. "So if I'm on top, I get to set the rules?"

"Does it matter if we both receive pleasure?"

"I've yet to have the proof."

Ransom laughed. Spending time with Scarlett and sharing this intimacy with her pushed away his lingering fears. "We've done this successfully before."

"Never with so much chatter and comment," she said with a wink.

His dragon released a growl that echoed through his mind. Without Prince Kalim's presence, he felt surprisingly lightheaded. Or was that Scarlett? Ransom thrust and retreated, holding her close, breathing in her scent. He cupped one breast and savored her smooth skin, the weight of her filling his palm.

Memories.

Her warm flesh massaged his length, gripping him sweetly. Her fingernails dug into his shoulders, no doubt leaving her mark. He withdrew and slid into her heat again, aiming for slow, but his balls tightened in exquisite pain. His next thrust had him gritting his teeth, and when Scarlett climaxed around his shaft, he could hold on no longer. His seed bubbled up, and he released with a grunt, the pleasure seeping into every muscle.

Ransom kissed her, an unhurried kiss but one full of passion. With this kiss, he tried to communicate the depth of his feelings, his wish to walk into the future with her at his side. For an instant, he thought she understood because she cupped his cheek in clear affection.

"Scarlett, I'm sorry I abducted you and placed you in danger. I didn't want to, but the prince insisted. He threatened my people. I could see no other way. I was ready to betray you and—"

"Stop," she whispered, placing her hand over his mouth. "I admit I was angry at first, but the truth is, if I'd stood in your boots, I would've made the same decision. We worked as a team—you, me, and Talon. All of us were required to take down the purple prince. He's gone now, and we're all safe."

"I don't deserve your forgiveness."

"Too bad. You have it." She moved her hand and kissed him.

Moments later, he separated their bodies and drew her close, wanting to say so much, wanting to demand Scarlett give them a chance. Instead, he held her and pulled every memory close—something to sustain him while he devised Plan B.

16. SAD PARTING

"**S**carlett!"

A man's voice rippled over the clearing and echoed around the surrounding hills—decisive and, if Ransom read the tone right, worried and angry.

"Ah!" Scarlett said. "Our rescue party has arrived. Come and meet my brothers. I'm sure you'll like them."

"What aren't you telling me?" Ransom asked, suspicious of her wide grin. "That look is sassy and full of secrets."

"All of my brothers captured their mates and stole away with them. I'm the only one who is escaping and following *my* plan."

"Saber, we're here," Scarlett shouted.

Huh! That was what she thought. At present, he was making a strategic retreat to learn and formulate a strategy worthy of this woman. Scarlett Mitchell would not escape—not when they were mates. She might not experience the same pull as him, but that didn't negate the bond's existence. They had much in common. Their love of jewelry design. Their strong family ties. Their desire for a different path.

He'd never confessed to anyone how much he resented the leadership thrust on him after his father's unexpected death. His father had trained him to lead since he was the oldest child. Everyone expected it of him, yet he'd dreamed of forging a different way.

He sighed and followed Scarlett.

Gryffnn, even though he didn't see the strengths in himself, was an excellent leader, and with Kaya at his side, the clan was in safe hands.

Five naked men who bore a resemblance to Scarlett stood together, each with a serious expression. A lone woman stood with them.

Ry Coppersmith, the captain of the *Indy*, peeled off with three other black leopards. No doubt to get clothing.

Scarlett ran up to the men and threw herself at one.

The man wrapped his arms around his sister while he glared over her shoulder at Ransom. "What happened to your arm? Why do you have a bandage? And what's up with your eyes?"

"My eyes? What's wrong with them?"

"They're golden-brown," Saber said.

"Oh! They work okay. I haven't looked in a mirror since I left the resort. It's a long story." Scarlett stepped from her brother's embrace. She gave Casey a quick hug. "I'm fine. In one piece. You'll want to get home. Why don't I tell you everything on the way? Ransom, my brothers. This is Saber, Felix, Leo, Sly, and Joe. And this is Casey, Felix's mate."

"Pleased to meet you." Ransom offered his hand. "Scarlett speaks highly of you all."

Not one brother moved to accept his friendly overtures.

"You abducted her," Saber said in accusation.

"He had a noble reason," Scarlett said.

"Let him speak," Saber snapped.

"Scarlett is right. I had a reason for my actions, although from what Scarlett has told me, each of you seized your mates."

One stepped forward, his face twisting. "Not I."

"That's true, Sly," Scarlett said. "Although there was abduction involved."

"Hey!" Ry shouted. "Are you ready to leave?"

"Where are we going?"

"To the dragon compound," Saber said.

Scarlett nodded. "I'll travel with Ransom."

"No, go with the others," Saber said. "Grab my clothes, Felix. I'll travel with the dragon."

The *Indy* took off first, and Ransom strapped in, waiting for them to clear before taking off too.

Saber clicked his harness into position and turned to him. "Tell me everything."

So Ransom did. He started his story from the moment of the trip into the mountains, where he and Nanu had crashed. He spoke of the hell he'd found himself in, and how the inexplicable—at the time—dream of Scarlett had set him on this road. Ransom was still talking when they landed at their spaceport.

"That's one hell of an adventure," Saber said when he finished.

"One I never want to repeat."

"You love my sister."

"I do, although Scarlett seems oblivious. Like your sister, I have a scheme. I intend to become her mate."

"You say Scarlett has a plan?"

"She seeks independence."

"Scarlett has been pushing against family constraints for some time, but she hasn't mentioned anything. I thought she enjoyed her work."

"Her first love is jewelry design," Ransom said. "She wants to set

205

up her own business."

Saber nodded. "What will you do?"

"Support her dreams. Keep popping up in her life until she realizes I love her and will encourage her in her goals. I have contacts in the jewelry business. She hasn't realized how helpful I could be." He shot a glance at Saber. "How we complement each other."

"She's not a kid any longer. I keep forgetting that," Saber admitted. "To me, she's always my baby sister."

"I have two sisters. I understand."

"Come and visit if your clan can spare you," Saber said. "You can meet my mother and the rest of the family."

"I have your support even though I abducted your sister?"

"You tell an entertaining story." Saber winked at him. "When you visit, I'll divulge how I met my mate, Eva."

Ransom stood with a sigh. "My brother is waiting for me. My friends. I guess... This doesn't feel like home any longer. For the last half a rotation, the Maphra prince controlled me, and now I'm at a loss."

Saber unfastened his harness and rose. He squeezed Ransom's shoulder in silent sympathy.

Ransom followed Saber Mitchell from the ship to the large spaceport to join his friends and family. He forced his lips to curve as he hugged his brother, two sisters, and other clan members. While he was pleased to see them and relieved that this ordeal was over, he felt flat. Disorientated. Perhaps all he needed was to slip into his routine again.

His gaze strayed to Scarlett, who was speaking with Camryn Coppersmith. Camryn was also from Earth. A growl echoed through his mind, and Ransom wanted to howl in concert. Letting Scarlett leave would test him.

Scarlett hugged Ransom goodbye with a tightness in her chest. If it weren't for her family and his family, she would've given him a proper kiss and squeezed his muscular arse. Now, she forced her hands to release their grip on his broad shoulders and stepped back.

"Bye," she said, the pressure on her chest rising to constrict her throat, her power of speech.

With a general farewell wave, she followed her brothers and Casey to their ship and strapped in for the journey to Tiraq.

For once, she'd participated in a full-out adventure. Now she understood the dizzying fear and crazy peaks of celebration, she hated to return to dreary days researching prospective guests and checking them in on arrival.

"Did he hurt you?" Felix asked. "If he did, we can return and break him."

She laughed, but even to her, it sounded forced. "We worked together. No one kicked anyone's butt apart from that purple prince. The man was delusional. He wanted to repopulate the planet with children, and I was to be his broodmare."

"Poor man," Sly said. "He had no idea what he was getting into with you."

"Is that arm sore?" Leo asked. "Shouldn't it have healed by now? And what is up with your eyes?"

"The eyes—no clue. I guess I'll consult with you, Casey, but my vision is perfect." Scarlett frowned at her bandage. "The itchiness in my arm drove me crazy before the insect things burst out and killed the prince. It's a relief to have them gone. Believe me, a scar is a small price to pay. Talon knew the truth, but I'm glad I didn't understand I was playing host to creepy-crawlies. Well, not at first, anyway."

"I hear you," Leo said with feeling.

Scarlett reached over and squeezed Leo's arm because he'd had experience with a Spiderus alien. He'd understand her turmoil at the idea of being a host for an insect.

"I can't wait to get home."

A lie. It was time to inform her family of her wishes, to get her plan on track. Yes, the first quiet moment she had, she'd consult her lists and add a new bullet point—*tell Saber and Mum about my plan to open a jewelry shop on Dalcon.*

Twelve cycles later

Today. Scarlett could not bear this tedium for one second longer. Mungo, Joe's mate, could deal with the guests. With visits to the resort in high demand, two of her cousins had joined the research team, and they were naturals. They didn't require her help.

She'd updated her business plan, and her to-do list, and the premises on Dalcon were hers if she wanted to forge ahead. All she needed to do was pay the first half-rotation of rent in advance, and the biggest hurdle—inform Saber of her plans. Yet, she hesitated, waiting for a sign, one of her premonitions, and they weren't forthcoming.

"Scarlett."

Scarlett blinked and focused on her mother.

"You haven't been to see me this morning," Anna Mitchell chided. "I wanted to check on your arm." She shook her head. "It's difficult getting used to your brown eyes."

"My arm is fine." Scarlett rolled up her tunic sleeve to prove it.

Her mother tutted as she prodded the two red marks. "You will have a scar."

"Honestly earned, Ma. Those are fine badges to wear on a body." She supposed she should inform her mother about her upset tummy, but the last thing she wanted was one of her mother's nasty potions.

"I thought a girl would be easier after having five boys," her mother said with a rueful smile. "That's what I told your father. I bet he's cackling away in heaven after watching your adventure. You're as impossible as your brothers."

"Ma, look. There's Hew Grantlach. He's heading this way." Her mouth twisted at the thought of her father. Hopefully, he hadn't seen *everything* because she'd misbehaved, and it had been fun. She missed Ransom—talking to him, sleeping next to him, touching and kissing him.

Faint color crowded into her mother's cheeks. "Is my hair all right?"

Scarlett returned to the present. "You're beautiful, Ma. Why don't you take Hew for a walk on the private beach? Take a picnic lunch?" She and her brothers approved of the Grantlach.

Her mother nodded. "I might do that." She hurried to intercept Hew and embraced him. They hadn't seen each other for a while, although the pair spoke via com-circle.

"Hey, Scarlett," Mungo said in her adorable Scothage accent, reminiscent of a Scottish drawl. She set down her aromatic soup drink. Her brow furrowed. "What's wrong? Ye've gone pale."

"Ever since I arrived home, I've suffered from a queasy stomach. I didn't say anything to Ma because I didn't want her to foist a potion on me."

"She'll be busy with Hew for the cycle. Casey might help ye. Take the cycle to rest."

"I need to speak with Saber, anyway," Scarlett said. "Are you sure?"

Mungo flicked a lock of red hair away from her cheek. "Aye! I enjoy working on reception and meeting the lasses, ye ken."

"Have at it." Scarlett pressed a hand to her roiling stomach. The incoming guests today were hurting her head.

Once she departed from reception, and the aroma of Mungo's drink faded, her stomach settled. Saber wasn't in his office. Her stomach rolled as she passed the main dining room, and a horrid suspicion occurred after she calculated a personal statistic. She backtracked, deciding that speaking with Casey was imperative. Felix's wife was an ex-soldier and possessed medical experience.

While she now pursued her interest in design and fabric and made garments to sell in the high-end resort store, she was the perfect one to help Scarlett with this *situation*.

She found Casey alone in her workroom. "Do you have a minute?"

"Sure." Casey glanced up from the fabric she was draping around a chubby tailor's form with an extra set of arms.

"I haven't felt well since I arrived home. My stomach is queasy."

"Did you tell your mother?" Casey asked, a frown on her brow as she stared at her dressmaker form.

"I didn't want to answer her questions."

Casey's head lifted, her focus laser-sharp. "What questions?"

"It's possible I might be pregnant," Scarlett murmured.

"Oh. Oh!" Casey said. "I can do a scan for you. It's 99.9 percent reliable. I thought you were on birth control."

"My shot was due around the time Ransom abducted me. I thought it would be okay." Scarlett sighed and rubbed her face. "No scrub that. I didn't care. We were too busy trying to stay alive."

"Let me get my medical kit. It's in our bungalow."

"I'll come with you," Scarlett said. "I'm hoping to bump into Saber. He's not in his office, and I want to talk to him."

"Problem? I mean, more than one problem?"

"No." Scarlett straightened. She'd have to amend her plan, perhaps stay at the resort.

Casey grasped Scarlett's arm and shook her back to the present. "Don't panic. Not yet until we take a reading."

"Ma will be disappointed in me."

"Maybe initially, but she keeps hinting at more grandchildren. According to her, one is not enough."

"Yeah, but I'm the only one without a mate."

Casey took Scarlett's arm and dragged her from the workshop. They strode along a path lined by plants with bright pink leaves and pale pink flowers. To the right, soft music and women's laughter came from the pool. They passed one of Scarlett's cousin's ambling toward the guest beach with a female guest.

Casey led her down a side path and used her palm print to open the lock on the gate, which led to their family and employee area. They speed-walked past several bungalows before turning off to Casey's.

The interior was beautiful, with Casey's tasteful use of color in the casual furnishings. According to Felix, she went for a minimalistic look, the product of Casey's military upbringing.

"Do you want anything to eat or drink?" Casey asked over her shoulder.

"No, please put me out of my misery."

Casey disappeared and returned with a scuffed leather bag. "Is the dragon-man the father?"

"If I'm pregnant. Yes," Scarlett said in a sharp tone. "There was no coercion or anything of that nature."

"Do you miss him?" Curiosity sounded in Casey.

"Yes," she said without hesitation. Funny, Saber had asked Scarlett the same thing yesterday. "We were alone for the entire journey and only had each other to rely on. I keep turning around to tell Ransom things, and he's not there."

"Do you like him?"

"From the first time I met him," Scarlett admitted.

Casey opened her bag and removed a small square box, no bigger than her palm. "You've met before? Before he grabbed you from the resort, I mean."

"Yes, he caught me pilfering precious stones on Narenda." Scarlett grinned at the memory. She would've loved to see his face when he'd found her gone.

Casey powered up the box, pushed several buttons, then tapped in a series of commands. "I've set the machine to read for pregnancy. Just lie down for me. I'll place it on your belly."

"Should I strip?"

"No, it will read through your garments," Casey said.

Scarlett toed off her boots and stretched out on the couch for Casey. Her breath caught as Casey held the black box above her abdomen. She wasn't sure what she wanted. She'd have an excuse to see Ransom again if she were pregnant, but that was a double-edged sword. Trapping a man—no, that wasn't her style.

"Do you know if a feline shifter can have offspring with a dragon?" she asked.

"Hmm." Casey still peered at the readings on the machine. "What?"

"Yes, they can have offspring," Casey murmured. She raised her gaze to meet Scarlett's.

"*What?*"

"You're pregnant with twins."

Scarlett gaped at Casey.

"Did you hear me? Scarlett?" Casey asked.

"Two babies?"

"Yes."

"Are you sure?"

"The reading is 99.9 percent reliable," Casey reminded her.

"Don't tell anyone." Scarlett sat up and thrust her feet into her boots. "Not even Felix. Promise me."

"I promise."

"I want to break the news myself." Scarlett knew Casey would keep her word.

"What are you going to do? Scarlett? You have a weird expression on your face."

"Make a plan," Scarlett said. "Thanks, I'll see you later."

She found Saber in his office with Felix and Leo. Saber was busy talking and broke off mid-sentence when she tapped on the door and entered. "Saber, I wondered if I could have a word." She glanced at her brothers and sighed. "I might as well speak to you all."

"We can talk," Saber said. "What's the problem?"

Scarlett dropped onto an empty seat beside Leo and swallowed hard to settle the arrival of nerves as she stared across the compudesk at her oldest brother. *Get it out, Scarlett.* She clasped her hands to stop them shaking.

"Scarlett?" Saber prompted.

"I don't want to work here. I'm bored with doing the same thing day in day out." Scarlett paused. Saber wasn't shouting. Neither were Felix and Leo, and that encouraged her to continue. "My dream is to focus on my jewelry designs and open a shop on Dalcon. I have a business plan and everything," she said. "I've saved enough currency for a financial cushion if my sales aren't as robust as my projections. There's just one problem." Scarlett swallowed again. An audible gulp.

Saber's expression didn't shift. "What sort of problem?"

Scarlett hesitated, then decided to spit it out. "I'm pregnant. With twins, according to Casey."

Saber stiffened, but she still had trouble reading his expression.

"Who is the father?" Leo demanded.

"We'll gut him," Felix added.

"You will not touch a hair on his head," Scarlett snapped. "Last time I heard it takes two to make a child. That's if you're doing it the natural way."

"Is it the dragon?" Felix asked.

"None of your business," Scarlett snapped again. She turned to Saber, and he bore a weird expression.

"Are you happy about this pregnancy?" Saber asked.

Scarlett considered. "I've only learned about it." It meant she had the best excuse to see Ransom again. She hadn't realized she'd miss him so much. "I think I'm pleased, although I'll need to rejig my master plan."

Leo snorted.

"You and your plans," Felix said. "Your baby—excuse me,

babies—aren't on the plan."

"Neither was a quest to find a purple prince," Scarlett said sweetly. "Maybe I've decided I enjoy going off-piste occasionally. Changes are cleansing and not always a mistake."

Saber understood her reference and glowered at her. "Lori catching the virus wasn't your fault. I've told you that. All of us have told you."

"It doesn't lessen the guilt," Scarlett retorted.

"I feel guilty whenever I recall how I gained ownership of the resort," Saber countered. "We both have to admit we've made mistakes. Own them and don't repeat them. We must step forward into the future and do our best to compensate for our past."

"Scarlett," Leo said. "You harbored a virus of sorts a second time. It enabled you to stop the suffering of the Narenda inhabitants."

"The residents of Tiraq too," Saber said. "Ransom cares for you."

"I know." Although they hadn't spoken to each other since parting on Narenda. Why hadn't he called? "Works both ways. I could've called him," she muttered to herself. "I like him a lot."

"Is he your mate?" Felix asked, his eyes narrowing until he resembled Saber at his most fierce.

Scarlett shrugged. "How do you tell?"

"You think about the other person even if you don't want to. Parting from them makes you feel like crap, and you'll do anything to keep them safe," Leo said. "They might irritate you at first, but the idea of ripping off their clothes and fucking them makes you come alive."

"Oh," Scarlett whispered.

"He's your mate," Saber said.

"I've been unhappy with life since we left Narenda." Scarlett counted the points off with her fingers. "I can't get him out of my head. He's the last person I think about before I fall asleep and the first one when I awake. Every time I have a thought, I wonder about Ransom's opinion. I'm not as upset about these babies as I should be. He has messed up my entire plan, and I'm not stressing about it when normally, I'd be a real grouch. And once he comes to mind, my next thought is sex. Oh!"

"They're mates," Felix and Leo said at the same time.

"I talk to Ransom every morning," Saber said. "We talk about you. The dragon is crazy about you. He told me he'd never have escaped the prince if it wasn't for your help. He loves you, Scarlett."

Hope dawned in Scarlett until her mind constructed a roadblock. "But two babies. I don't want to trap him. And the other thing—I want to pursue my jewelry enterprise. Ransom must take care of his people. They're the reason he fought so hard. Did you know he intended to exchange me for their freedom?"

"He told me," Saber said. "He feels bad about it. Scarlett, if anyone threatened our family, what would you do? I know what my decision would be. The prince placed him in an untenable position, and Ransom did the best he could under the circumstances. He never surrendered but kept fighting, unlike his parent."

"You admire him," Scarlett said in surprise.

"You like him," Saber pointed out. "Why shouldn't I?"

"I'm confused," Felix said. "Are we beating up the dragon or welcoming him to the family?"

Scarlett frowned, then a solution presented itself. "An abduction," she whispered. "I'll abduct him."

17. A Capture After All

Drake clan home, Narenda

Ransom stood outside in the garden, watching the whitelight take over from the black. Every muscle and tendon ached with fatigue and cried out for sleep, yet his mind was too busy. Slipping back into a routine was surprisingly tricky.

Gryffnn and Kaya had everything under control, even though they'd left to visit Viros. They'd also had time to go on a romantic outing while completing their daily responsibilities. The soldiers were training under Torg, the flight captain. The young apprentices were busy designing jewelry for the clan to sell at the new markets his brother and sister-in-law had arranged. There were plenty of raw stones in the storage bunker. Niran Vasilakis, the leader of the Incorporeal people who lived in the village, was busy rebuilding homes after an arsonist had torched their properties.

Nobody needed him.

"You're an old fool," Ransom muttered.

He was safe. His people were safe, and early reports were that the resonance had faded to a level most of the dragons could handle.

"Don't make a move," a harsh voice said.

Instinctively, Ransom tried to turn, but a weapon—a blaster by the size of it—dug into his ribs. Someone slapped a cloth, smelly and impregnated with a type of drug, over his nose. Before he could object, he crumpled, hands catching him before he struck the ground and lost consciousness.

"How long will the drug take to wear off? Are you sure it won't hurt him?" Scarlett asked. She turned to her brothers, all five of them having helped her with this abduction.

"I checked with Gryffnn. He indicated the drug is fine for dragons. I consulted him about the dosage," Saber said.

Scarlett nodded, nerves simmering at the pit of her stomach. What if Ransom wasn't interested in her? "What if this goes badly wrong?"

"You have your com-circle. Call us. We can be here in a few hours. I've given you Gryffnn's and Kaya's contact numbers. They're back tomorrow." Saber wrapped his arm around her shoulders and hugged her to his side. "Instead of stressing about what ifs, act with decisiveness. Do you want to recall your past and have regrets?"

"No, but what if he rejects me or thinks I got pregnant on purpose? What if he thinks I'm trying to trap him?"

"Then we'll be there to pick you up and help you move on," Joe said.

"The dragon is a fool if he walks," Sly said. "He didn't strike me as dumb."

Leo stalked closer and grabbed her into a quick hug. "Did the purple guy hit your head or something? Where is our feisty sister?"

"Yeah," Felix said. "You want this dragon guy, you go out there fighting. Don't act defeated before you speak with him."

Scarlett nodded. "You're right, but things have become real since I discovered I'm pregnant. The stakes are larger. I have more to lose."

"I understand," Saber said. "Once I met Eva, everything changed. You've got this." He kissed the top of her head and stepped back. "Bring your dragon to visit once you're done here."

"Thanks." Her brothers' confidence had her shoulders straightening and her courage climbing to normal levels.

"Call if you need us," Saber reminded her, and with a wave, her brothers boarded their ship and headed back to Tiraq.

Gryffnn had suggested a spot for their campsite, and it was perfect. A clearing set near a pond and a waterfall. Gryffnn had arranged for a tent and supplies while Eva had prepared food and drink, perfect for a romantic tryst. She had the ingredients for seduction, now it was time to apply them.

Scarlett went to check on Ransom. He was still asleep in the tent where her brothers had left him. She squatted beside him and checked his temperature. Normal.

While she waited for Ransom to regain consciousness, she pulled out her jewelry-making supplies. She'd use this time to put the finishing gloss to the ring she'd made for Ransom. Although she wasn't sure if he'd wear a ring, she wanted to offer it to symbolize her regard. Weird, but until they'd parted, she hadn't realized how he'd crept into her heart. The separation had underlined the depth of her feelings for the dragon.

Her dragon.

If anyone had told her she'd be pregnant and happy with the situation, she would've scoffed and perhaps bloodied their nose. As Casey and Eva had pointed out, pregnancy didn't need to halt her jewelry production. Waiting for the babies to arrive allowed her to increase her stock while she could still generate income through sales at the resort store.

With that in mind, she'd spoken to the agent on Dalcon and told him she was no longer interested in the premises he'd found for her. Even if everything went pear-shaped, she'd forge ahead with a revised plan. Flexibility didn't equate with failure. Saber said it meant she'd grown up and was adulting. Not a word she'd ever expected her brother to quote. She smiled, aware she was lucky to have the support of family.

She removed the ring from the protective pocket of her bag and took to it with a special polishing cloth. A golden-colored band studded with pale blue stones. She'd sorted the gems and chosen the ones that, in a different light, appeared almost green. To her, they symbolized Ransom's dual nature and their pairing.

A faint groan emerged from the tent, and Scarlett tucked the ring away and went to investigate. Yes, he was waking. His eyelids flickered, and she turned away to pour a glass of water. Gryffnn had told them the sole side effect of the drug was thirstiness.

Finally, his eyes remained open, although tension rippled through his frame. Too late, she recalled that this abduction might bring bad memories for him.

"Ransom, are you thirsty?" Scarlett leaned forward so that he could see her.

"Scarlett? Where are we?" His face creased into a frown. "Is this a dream?"

A chortle burst from her. "Here, drink some water."

Obediently, he accepted the beaker and drank every drop.

"Want another one?"

"Please." He drank the second beaker of water. "Is this real?"

Scarlett grinned, reached over, and pinched his arm. "I've abducted you."

"What?"

Scarlett edged closer. "Ransom, you've filled my thoughts from the moment we parted. I missed our conversations, our kisses, our lovemaking."

"You said it was sex." Accusation shaded his tone, but his expression told her nothing.

"I was wrong. It took me time to understand my feelings for you. For so long, my grand life plan has driven and stopped me from bad impulses. I was slow to realize you are the best thing that has ever happened to me." Scarlett grasped his hand in hers. "If you don't want a future with me, I'll understand, but I didn't wish to wonder any longer. Instead, my brothers helped me, so I had a chance to speak with you."

"You abducted me."

"Yes." Scarlett lifted her chin. He wasn't reacting in the way she'd predicted. "You kidnapped me first. I thought this was the perfect solution."

Ransom hauled her into his arms, and a blink later, she lay beneath his hard body. "You haven't left my thoughts," he admitted. "My dragon wanted you from the instant we saw you stealing our property."

"To be fair, I didn't realize I was taking raw stones from your property."

"I wanted you," he said, his eyes glittering.

"Why didn't you come to the resort?"

"I was working up to it," he said. "How long have we got together?"

"A few cycles before my brothers expect my call."

"Excellent." Ransom kissed her.

Although she had more to tell him, it could wait. She curled her arms around his neck and held him closer, savoring his scent and leashed power. During their separation, he'd gained weight. She smiled against his lips. So had she.

A long time later, he parted their mouths. "What of your future?"

"I planned to start my business, selling and designing jewelry. I still want to do that, but I want you in my life, at my side."

Ransom helped her to sit up and stripped off her tunic and bra. He divested her of her footwear and clothing before he scrambled from his garments. "Where are we?"

"Narenda. Gryffnn set up the camp for me. We're camped in a clearing in the forest. It's near a pond and a waterfall."

"Ah." Ransom smiled, his eyes glowing and his dragon half peeking through. He cupped her face. "Your eyes are still brown."

"It's startling seeing my reflection in the mirror. Feline shapeshifters always have green eyes. Now I stand out as different."

Ransom pressed a gentle kiss to her lips and pulled back. "You were born to stand out, Scarlett Mitchell."

She wrinkled her nose. "It appears I have a dragon mate."

Ransom stilled. "Mate?"

"My feline knew all along, but I ignored her to blindly focus on my life plan instead."

"Mate." This time his tone held reverence. "*Mine.*"

"Yes, as you are mine. Felines mark their mates with a bite here." She fingered the fleshy patch where the base of his neck met his shoulder.

"Dragons bond with dragon mates. An invisible bond clicks into place, and both experience the tie. It doesn't occur with every dragon. Only a special few experience this oneness."

"What about between different species?"

"I've never asked Gryffnn and Kaya because I thought it was too personal, but I do not doubt the strength of my brother's relationship," Ransom said.

"Would you let me mark you?"

"Yes." He never hesitated.

"Along with stealing me, it appears you pilfered my heart, Ransom Drake." A sense of rightness and celebration settled in her. The certainty that this curveball *should* be part of her life plan. "Make love to me."

"My pleasure."

Their lips met, and hands caressed and stroked. Pleasure and delight—happiness—soared through Scarlett. There was no hurry this time, but still, the passion between them built and flew. He entered her with one smooth stroke, filling her body as he filled her heart.

"I love you, Ransom," she whispered before her lips teased the pad of flesh at the base of his neck. He groaned, his hips flexing and driving his cock deeper.

Scarlett finally understood the possibilities and the freedom in loving another being this much. As the beginning prickles of her climax started, she bit down until she tasted Ransom's blood. With the stroke of her tongue, she lapped away the coppery lifeforce and felt the wound stitch together.

Ransom cried out, stroked into her twice. She shattered, and something clicked inside her mind. *Togetherness.* Seconds later, Ransom climaxed, his big body shaking with the force of his passion. Both of them were breathless as Ransom rolled onto his back and draped her over his chest.

"That was amazing," he whispered. "The moment you bit down. It both hurt and shoved pleasure through me."

"Let me see." She parted their upper bodies to study the mark she'd given him. "Oh. I wasn't sure if it would stay. You have a tiny black cat tattoo now."

"The dragon bond locked into place," Ransom whispered. *"We belong to each other."*

"We mind-speak!"

"We did before." Satisfaction filled his words as they popped into her mind. *"You're a better conversationalist than the prince."*

Scarlett shuddered. *"Please don't say that, even in jest. Fancy a swim, or are you hungry?"*

"A swim then food."

Scarlett nodded and rolled off him. Once they were both

standing, she stroked the tiny black cat tattoo.

Ransom shuddered and released a moan. "If you keep doing that, we won't reach the pond."

Laughing, Scarlett wove her fingers with his, and they ambled toward the pool.

"The water looks refreshing."

"Refreshingly cold," Ransom said.

"Is it deep enough to jump?"

"It is."

"Together?"

"I love the sound of that," he whispered.

So they jumped.

"Oh!" Scarlett shrieked, popping up. "That is freezing."

"The water comes directly from the mountains."

"Luckily, I have hot food and cold. We can warm up in the whitelight's heat." Scarlett swam the length of the pond and back. "I've had my swim."

Ransom laughed, and she loved the glimpses of his dragon and his natural humor.

"I have something to tell you," she blurted. Her pulse raced because even though they were mates, she wasn't sure of how he'd take this news. "And something for you."

"A gift?"

She nodded. Weren't children a gift?

"All right. Let's dry off and warm up," he said. "Then you can tell me."

Scarlett produced the robes Kaya had suggested, and once dry, she slipped into the warmth with gratitude. She'd liked Gryffnn and his mate. Soon her hands cupped a mug of warm soup, and she could no longer dither.

"I made you something." She set aside her cup to open her jewelry equipment bag and pulled out the ring she'd made for him. "On Earth, it is a tradition to exchange rings. It is a physical sign to non-shifters that one has a mate. Hold out your left hand." Scarlett slid the band onto his ring finger.

"It's stunning," Ransom said, and his sincerity shone through. "I have a necklace I created for you. It's in my chamber. But meantime, I give you dragon words of joining. I promise to love you and our children. I will honor you and care for you in sickness and in health. You are the mate of my heart, and with you at my side, I am the luckiest dragon on Narenda."

Tears stung her eyes as emotion squeezed her heart. "Have you thought about children?"

"When you're ready. When we're both ready. I might visit Viros to see if there is a market for our jewelry."

"Viros," she whispered.

"I would take my mate with me. The royal family has invited me to stay at the castle. What do you say?"

"I'd enjoy that very much." Scarlett nibbled her bottom lip, nervous about telling Ransom of her pregnancy, her belly swirling with her anxiety. Or it could be the dreaded morning sickness thing. She grabbed a dry biscuit and nibbled on it. When she glanced up, Ransom was studying her in concern.

"What's wrong?"

"I must tell you something, and your possible reaction worries me."

"We are mates." He tapped the mark she'd given him. "I wear your mark, and the goddess has seen fit to bestow us with a mating bond. Whatever it is, we will deal with the problem together."

"I'm pregnant," Scarlett blurted.

Ransom blinked. He stared at her.

"Did you hear me?"

"Pregnant, but how?"

She wrinkled her nose. "The normal way. We made love, and during the fun process, a reaction started."

"I know how to make babies," Ransom said.

Surely, he didn't think she'd slept with another! "It's yours."

"I never doubted that." A slow grin curled across his lips. "We're having a baby."

"Two."

His brows shot upward toward his hairline. "Two?"

"Twins," she confirmed. "They run in our family." A thought occurred, and tears burned the back of her eyes. Aghast at her wayward emotions, she sucked in a deep breath and struggled for control. She had to tell him, make him understand. "Ransom, the last thing I want is for you to feel trapped with me and these babies. Stars, I should've said this before I marked you. I kept telling you all I wanted was a fling. Now, you'll think I abducted you to get you to support me and the babies. That isn't my truth. I-I missed you. Life felt flat without you, and my plans didn't seem as important." A tear spilled free and ran down her cheek. "I came because I wanted you. *You*. Not the material things you can give me. My family—if this meeting had gone pear-shaped, my family would've helped me. My heart would be dented, but I would've had support."

"Sweetheart, stop worrying. If there is one thing I learned about you during our quest, it is that you say what you mean. You're honest and have integrity. I understand what you're saying because my life was black and white without you in it. Your presence brings color. I want you. I want our children. Full stop." He grinned. "Two children." Ransom reached for her and plucked her off the rock she sat on. He set her on his knee, and seconds later, his mouth covered hers. "You fulfill me, my mate. I will cherish our children as much as I love you. No matter which of us they take after, I will shower them with affection."

"My plan didn't include children."

"Are you upset?"

"Surprisingly, no. As Saber pointed out, I can still follow my dream and design beautiful jewelry. I've come to realize I am happier when I'm with you. We make an excellent team, and I'm not afraid to step into the future with you. Somewhere along the line, you sneaked into my heart and never left."

"Same for me, sweetheart."

He sealed their love with a decadent kiss, then they crawled into their tent to rest and didn't emerge for a long time.

Best abduction ever.

Thank you so much for reading Star-Crossed with Scarlett. I'd love to learn what you thought of Scarlett's and Ransom's adventures, so please consider leaving a review at your favorite online bookstore, Goodreads, or Bookbub. A review would make my day!

And, a bonus offer. Talon was a fun character, so I decided to write a story from his point of view. If you'd like your FREE copy of *Talon the Trolleris*, please check out my newsletter (https://www.subscribepage.com/p7k2j7). You'll also score a FREE copy of *My Scottish Lass*, the prequel in my Middlemarch Shifters series, as well as learn about upcoming releases, sales, and other promotions.

Please turn the page for an excerpt from Black Moon Dragon, from the Dragon Investigator series.

EXCERPT – BLACK MOON DRAGON

Restless, Manu tossed and turned on his narrow bed. After his long flight the previous night and the test flight for a newer version of his stealth gadget today, he should've fallen asleep. He stood and walked to the tiny kitchenette where he had the basics. Hot food, courtesy of an old microwave, a kettle, a fridge to keep milk and beer cold, and a sink. A window above the sink allowed him to look over the rear of his property at the totara trees and the unkempt grass. The grass and weeds out front were just as bad, but he'd found the neglected appearance kept away visitors.

He poured himself a glass of water and scanned the trees, wondering if he'd spot the ruru again. About to turn away, he glimpsed a spark of light in the long grass. As he stared at it, confused as to what it was, the bright spot grew larger.

Fire!

Manu raced outside via a side door, heedless of his nudity. With the lack of rain, he might lose his warehouse if that fire spread. Damn. He could hardly beat out the flames with his hands. He sprinted back inside and grabbed a fire extinguisher. By the time he returned with the extinguisher in hand, the flames had doubled.

He skidded to a halt as he noticed a woman, cursing and swearing as she thumped the flames with... Was that a T-shirt?

"Get out of my way," Manu snarled and pulled the pin on the extinguisher. He aimed at the base of the fire, terror racing through him. If this didn't work, he might lose everything.

The foam doused the flames and for a while, he thought he'd win, but the breeze picked up, breathing new life into the blaze.

Once the contents of the extinguisher finished, he cast it aside and raced for the hose.

"Make yourself useful," he ordered. "There are old sacks inside the door. Grab a pile and help me put out this fire."

Probably wasting his breath. He didn't bother waiting to see if the woman obeyed but turned on the water and ran out the hose. It was too short, but he aimed the flow at the surrounding grass. To his relief, the water doused some of the flames, and he relaxed once he realized he'd halted the spread.

The woman appeared, her black hair blowing around her face and obscuring her features. A stranger. What the hell did she think she was doing trespassing on his property? Hadn't the padlock told her he didn't welcome visitors?

She attacked the flames with the sacking while he continued to flood the area with water. Finally, the fire vanished, and only charred grass and the delicate green fragrance coming from the woman remained.

Manu shook himself. What the hell? He stomped back to his warehouse, dragging the hose with him. After turning off the water, he coiled the hose, leaving it tidy for next time, and switched on the outer lights. He wanted illumination while he interrogated his intruder.

From the corner of his eye, he spotted the woman's stealthy retreat. "Where the hell are you going?"

For an instant, she froze then she bolted, darting toward a hole in his fence. Obviously, the spot where she'd entered his property. Manu sprinted after her and grabbed one kicking leg before she squeezed free. Fear and desperation gave her strength, but he was even more determined. He hauled her back and dragged her closer to his warehouse. She kicked but didn't shout or screech in the usual feminine manner. She didn't speak at all, just renewed her struggle.

Manu grasped both of her arms and shook her a little. "Stop fighting."

"You're naked." Her gaze darted down his torso, lingered on his groin, and skittered away with the speed of a frightened rabbit. Beneath her dark brows, her brown eyes were rounds while her brown skin hinted at a combination of European and Maori ancestry. She stood tall, perhaps six inches less than his six-four height, and she was solid. Muscular rather than fat. The baggy jeans and burned T-shirt she'd donned didn't do her justice. Through the burn holes in the cotton, he glimpsed a flat stomach and her breasts pushed against the fabric, hinting at their fullness.

Startled by the burst of heat in him, he sucked in a deep inhalation. A huge mistake. Her fresh green scent filled his lungs and stirred his taniwha from his usual sulk.

"Why are you on my property?"

"I wanted somewhere to sleep."

Truth.

"Why did you set the fire?"

"I didn't!"

This time her words held a crisp edge. *Lie.*

"Give me one reason why I shouldn't call the cops."

Her brown eyes widened. "No. Please don't do that. I—"

"Stop. If you're going to tell me you'll do anything in exchange for me turning a blind eye to this, don't go any further." He froze as her gaze slid to his groin again and cursed inwardly as his cock filled and lengthened.

He shoved her away but pinned her with a glower when she gathered herself to run in another escape attempt.

"Don't," he warned in a harsh growl.

"I-I'm not running. I'm gonna be sick." She made a hoarse sound from deep in her throat and lurched to the right.

Manu glanced away, wanting to give her the illusion of privacy while every one of his senses focused on her. Instead of a vomit and stomach acid stench, ash, charcoal, and smoke filled his nostrils. His gaze whipped back to her, and he cursed. He grabbed one of the unused sacks he hadn't returned to his warehouse and beat at the flames that licked over the flattened grass. The woman made a croaking sound and spat another line of sparks. At least this one was on a patch damp from his firefighting efforts, and the dry stalks sizzled but didn't catch.

Now, he watched her closely, and despite the soot and burned grass, he kept catching whiffs of her personal scent. It reminded him of standing in a patch of native bush, and he dragged her perfume deeper into his lungs. Underlying the fresh green was a hint of flowers and honey.

Nectar, his taniwha, supplied helpfully. *I like it.*

Every muscle in Manu's body locked, his mind snapping and popping, so great was his shock. Beneath his tenseness, his beast quivered like an unruly puppy ready to break his master's order to stay. Manu swallowed hard and cautiously sniffed. This time, he groaned faintly as he dragged in her scent. *Crap on a stick.* He closed his eyes as she barked out another croak. Once she stopped, he beat out the new fire.

"What is your name?" Manu understood his taniwha's stupid giddiness and excitement while he—the man—trembled as if he balanced on the edge of a cliff. One wrong move and he'd free-fall.

"Name."

She wiped her mouth and met his gaze with trepidation. "I don't know what is wrong with me."

"Name."

"Jessalyn McKenzie."

"Finished?"

She hesitated before releasing the tension in her shoulders.

Manu held out his hand, and caution slipped over her face before she grasped his fingers. He hauled her to her feet, so rattled by her scent and appearance, he forgot to temper his strength. She bounced against his chest. Jessalyn grunted at the impact, and he steadied her with his hands at her hips. A mistake because now her enticing scent flowed through his lungs. His mind groped to understand while his taniwha thumped out a victory haka.

This stranger... Jessalyn McKenzie was his mate. This woman was the one nature had determined to be his perfect match. He eased his grip on her hips and ignored her gasp and his swelling dick.

"How long have you been breathing fire?"

She blinked once, her dark lashes screening her brown eyes. Her swallow was audible, and anxiety shrouded her like the traditional feather cloak handed down through the generations in his family.

"Tell me." He snapped out the words, and she jumped.

His taniwha stirred beneath Manu's skin, and it was easy to discern his displeasure. He was scaring their mate.

"S-six weeks."

"The fires in the Domain?"

She gulped, her gaze darting to the battered runners on her feet. "Yes."

"Do you enjoy lighting fires?"

"No!" Her gaze snapped to him, and she tried to yank free. "Enjoy this? I have no control, and that's scary. There's something wrong with me, and it's not the kind of thing I can consult about with a doctor. They'd lock me up."

Manu frowned. He'd watched her poor control but assumed he'd scared her or made her nervous. But her lack of finesse was a problem. It was a matter of time before the cops caught her. He'd seen and listened to the media coverage—the speculation of a firebug lighting fires in the Domain. The press had interviewed several homeless people who slept rough in the nearby bush. He'd witnessed the glow of fires during his flight the previous evening.

An insidious thought crept through his brain, and his hands tightened at her hips. It had become obvious to him, she didn't know why she was breathing fire. And her control. She had none. She was a danger—to property, to herself, to the taniwha people.

Jessalyn McKenzie might be the woman destined as his mate, but if she didn't exert control on her taniwha, his people would fear for their safety and bay for her blood. He'd have no option but to execute her.

What is up with Jessalyn and her fire-making skills? Learn more at my website.
https://shelleymunro.com/books/black-moon-dragon/

ALSO BY SHELLEY

Middlemarch Shifters
My Scarlet Woman
My Younger Lover
My Peeping Tom
My Assassin
My Estranged Lover
My Feline Protector
My Determined Suitor
My Cat Burglar
My Stray Cat
My Second Chance
My Plan B
My Cat Nap
My Romantic Tangle
My Blue Lady
My Twin Trouble
My Precious Gift
My Grumpy Wolf

Middlemarch Gathering
My Highland Mate
My Highland Fling
My Elusive Mate
My Valiant Princess
My Highland Wedding
My Highland Billionaire

Middlemarch Capture
Snared by Saber
Favored by Felix
Lost with Leo
Spellbound with Sly
Journey with Joe
Star-Crossed with Scarlett

House of the Cat
Captured & Seduced
Claimed & Seduced
Merry & Seduced
Stranded & Seduced
Seized & Seduced
Hunted & Seduced
Festive & Seduced
Betrayed & Seduced
Enticed & Seduced

Dragon Investigators
Blue Moon Dragon
Blood Moon Dragon
Black Moon Dragon
Snow Moon Dragon

ABOUT AUTHOR

USA Today bestselling author Shelley Munro lives in Auckland, the City of Sails, with her husband and a cheeky Jack Russell/mystery breed dog.

Typical New Zealanders, Shelley and her husband left home for their big OE soon after they married (translation of New Zealand speak - big overseas experience). A twelve-month-long adventure lengthened to six years of roaming the world. Enduring memories include being almost sat on by a mountain gorilla in Rwanda, lazing on white sandy beaches in India, whale watching in Alaska, searching for leprechauns in Ireland, and dealing with ghosts in an English pub.

While travel is still a big attraction, these days Shelley is most likely found in front of her computer following another love - that of writing stories of contemporary and paranormal romance and adventure. Other interests include watching rugby (strictly for research purposes), cycling, playing croquet and the ukelele, and curling up with an enjoyable book.

Visit Shelley at her website.
https://shelleymunro.com/

Sign Up for Shelley's Newsletter
https://shelleymunro.com/newsletter/